WICKED SURRENDER

BAY RIDGE ROYALS
BOOK FOUR

HEATHER LONG

For you.
Yes, you.
Don't argue with me.
When I said it was for you, I meant it.
Now lace this bitch up and wear it with pride.
For you.
Always.

SERIES SO FAR

FOREWORD

Dear Reader,

Welcome to Wicked Surrender, this is officially book 4 of the Bay Ridge Royals. If you have not read Shamelessly Loyal, Battle Lines, or Deceptive Truce, please set this aside and go grab them. This series is best read in order.

All of that said, what do you *need* to know? Let's talk, previously, for the Bay Ridge Royals...

Dude...

Right, and as much as I'd like to leave it at that, let's go with the TL:DR: Ezra was a drunk dick, and an asshole. Bodhi was on point and looked after Lainey in his own way. Adam was fighting for Lainey, trying to get his best friend to talk to him and still mad that Ezra boned Lainey. Ezra did kiss him rather spontaneously in the middle of a fight which just floored him. And Milo? Well, he sacrificed himself to King's whims in order to protect Andrea meaning that he and Ezra have to learn to work together.

Needless to say nothing really went to plan.

For those who would like more details, we picked up in Deceptive Truce where Battle Lines left off. Lainey is missing Milo fiercely. In particular, she is feeling the ache of his loss. Life, however, does not allow her to linger too long in her feelings.

With Ezra's bodyguard accompanying her, she resumes the business of living—including charity, Benedict business, her grandfather, and her sister. She also plays a harsh game of push and pull with Ezra.

When he shows up at her place, they end up having sex again. She admits she told Milo about them and why. Ezra struggles with it, but she asks him to stop just taking off on her. To stay and he promises he will—then Adam shows up.

These boys, I swear, just let themselves in. It does not go well when Adam discovers Ezra there and a fight erupts. The fight ends rather abruptly when Ezra lashes out that Adam never sees him. Then he kisses Adam. Horrified at not only putting his feelings out there, Ezra takes off.

Ezra spends the next several days avoiding Lainey and Adam both. Milo and Ezra are forced to spend time together courtesy of King and when King plans a few days away, he sticks Ezra with Milo.

In a peace offering, Ezra drops Milo off at Lainey's and tells him to stay out of sight with her for the weekend. Then he also leaves but he doesn't tell anyone where he's going.

The reunion between Milo and Lainey is sweet, they also declare how much they love each other (finally!). Milo also tells her he doesn't want his sister to know about his work with King.

Adam continues to work on how to take King down while also dealing with his family. Margareta Waldemar changes his assignment from killing King to befriending Milo and he has no idea why.

Bodhi's hunt continues, but his reacquaintance with Lainey prompts him to invite her to go with him when she needs to get out and away. He trusts her with some of his secrets, but not all. Still, he's there the night of the Fire and Ice Ball on New Year's Eve when everything collides and the Grahams announce the engagement of Ezra to another woman and he is swift to whisk Lainey out of the ballroom.

This brings us to Wicked Surrender. Wow. It doesn't seem like it's a lot until you're typing it all up. While there are ties back to the 82nd Street Vandals (both familial and friendship), you do not have to read that series.

That said, *this* series contains some spoilers for 82nd Street Vandals, there's no way to get around that. If you do decide to check out 82nd Street Vandals, be sure to start with *Savage Vandal*.

For a little housekeeping. Bay Ridge Royals is a why choose romance with characters exploring and coming to terms with their evolving sexuality including a possible bi-awakening, identities, and relationships.

TWs: Mentions of SA. Kidnapping. Intimidation. Car accidents. Threats of violence. Discussion of trafficking. Smuggling. Be kind to yourself, this is a dark romance series.

Thanks for checking out Wicked Surrender, I can't wait for you to get to know them.

Happy reading.

xoxo

Heather

P.S. Human voices only. All the work involved in this and all my novels from the stories themselves to the covers, to editing, to the audio are human-produced materials and voices only.

BAY RIDGE ROYALS

The Families
Benedict

Reed

Graham

Adley

Clifton

Marlowe

Cavendish

Main Characters
Elaine "Lainey" Benedict

Milo Hardigan

Adam Reed

Ezra Graham

Bohdi Cavendish

PROLOGUE

ADAM

YEARS EARLIER...

"Get your left up," Liam O'Connell warned with a smirk on his face as he delivered a one-two combination that had damn near broken my jaw the first time we sparred like this. I wasn't a fan of facial bruises. They were too hard to disguise for formal events, and they pissed my father off.

The latter was fine, but the former could cost me. Still, I got my left up and not only blocked both hits but pivoted, rolling along his arm the way he'd done to me so many damn times. I got one punch toward his kidneys, but he was too fast for the second.

Laughter exploded out of him as he half-danced, half-bounced away from me, gloved hands in the air. "It's about fucking time!"

Panting, I glared at him and the open grin on his face.

We were both sweating. But where I felt like I was constantly on the run, Liam didn't chase me. It was like he knew I'd have to come at him.

"Nice move," he said, the ease of that compliment seemed to cost him nothing. Then why should it? The wealth and affluence of his adopted parents aside, Liam seemed far more comfortable in the streets. He loved the fights. He didn't even seem to care about the *whys* behind the fights.

Frankly, I was more likely to let him have them. When the king contacted us about assignments or warnings to be meted out, it was the one area where Liam rarely asked any questions. Then again, most of his opponents were grown men and capable of wading into the fight even if he left them hopelessly outclassed.

"Thanks," I said, still panting, then spit out my mouth guard.

We wore them more to keep from cutting the inside of our mouths or maybe losing a tooth. The bruise on my jaw promised me that it had only helped *some*.

"I'm never going to win one of these, am I?"

That cost me some to admit. We were roughly the same age. He didn't outweigh me anymore, even if there were times I was convinced he'd been working out by bench pressing a car. Still, it didn't seem to change the results. I'd worked with any number of trainers over the years, but I learned more from him in our random spars than I ever did in those rings.

"Depends on how much you want it," Liam told me, after spitting out his mouthguard. He moved over to the side of the ring where we'd left our water bottles.

I followed, stripping off one glove so I could crack the

bottle open. I gave him a moment to drink then drained a good third of my bottle before I focused on him.

"How much I want it?" I'd challenge that assertion. "I sure as shit don't want you to kick my ass so easily."

"It's not that easy," he said, ducking under the ropes to sit on the edge. The interior of the gym was warm and humid, even if most of the lights were off. The ancient air conditioning couldn't keep up. We rented the space and shut it down so we could work out here when we wanted. Not that he was around as often. Instead of coming back east for university, he'd stuck closer to Braxton Harbor.

Made sense, I supposed, and the king hadn't protested.

Yet.

I had a feeling that was coming. We'd all been summoned to the city between semesters. New orders, I had a feeling.

"My ego appreciates the attempt," I told him as I dropped to sit next to him. "But you don't have to humor me."

"I'm not," Liam said. "You don't care about the best. You don't care about winning."

That was bullshit.

"When it comes to fighting me."

I scowled.

"Look, you and me, we connect in a few areas. But you don't see me as competition."

I wasn't sure how to feel about being read so clearly. Liam O'Connell was not my friend, but he was my ally. "Good to know."

"Now, if I go after something you want or try to keep you from something you want?" The corners of his mouth tilted. "You'll hit like a tank, but you won't let me see you coming."

Yeah, I wasn't so sure about that. Before I could respond, the door to the gym slammed open and the third member of our little "sparring" club arrived, late. He looked like shit too, hair askew, eyes bruised, and clearly...

"Drink water," Liam said as he studied Ezra, just like I did.

"I'm fine," Ezra said, jerking his shirt off with one arm and letting it land on the duffel bag he'd dropped. There were fresh red marks on his back, visible when he turned away, and I curled my fingers into a fist. Those weren't just fresh bruises but distinct signs of welts.

He toed off his shoes before shucking his sweatpants until he was wearing only his shorts. Just like us.

"Drink water," Liam repeated. "You're hungover." It was more a statement of fact than a criticism. But the raw fury on Ezra's face as he stalked forward had me bouncing off the edge to intercept.

Liam rarely threw the first punch, but Ezra could bait a saint and none of us were that. "Don't," I ordered him, one hand on his chest and that yanked Ezra's fury from Liam to me. "I mean it. You want to burn off some rage, you spar with me first."

Although easy going with a sarcastic edge, Liam didn't pull his punches. Ever. He could fucking kill Ezra if Ezra decided to take his mood out on him.

"Whatever," Ezra said, rolling his head around. The crackle of tension writhing over him seemed to leave the illusion of a wave of heat rolling off the pavement. "You said get here to fight, I'm here to fight."

"Mouthguard," Liam ordered. "Then come here, I'll wrap your hands."

"Don't need them," Ezra argued before he shoved past Liam.

I didn't sigh; the cheerful idiot was in a mood. He craved pain, but I didn't have to say a word because Liam hauled him backward. He had a hold of his wrist and locked his arm in a grip that could easily break it.

"Mouthguard," Liam repeated. "Hand wraps, and gloves. Or I'll knock your ass out right here and go back to sparring with him myself."

The air buzzed with his wild energy, and it tickled over my flesh like the static gathering just before the electrical storm hit.

"Cooperate," I suggested, catching Ezra's gaze. He might want the beating. Maybe he even thought he deserved it. Neither of us wanted to be the ones who had to deal it out.

All at once, the fight seemed to go out of him. "Fine," he said, and it was the closest to admitting surrender he ever got. "I'll wear them."

Liam caught my eye from behind Ezra and raised his brows. Did I want him to interfere more? No. Whatever this was, I'd literally need to beat it out of Ezra because *something* had happened.

Ten minutes later, Liam eyed us both then lifted his phone. "I have to make some calls. Try not to spill too much blood while I'm gone."

"We'll be sure to save it for you," Ezra said around his guard, and I rolled my eyes. I appreciated the time though, because even after he was geared up, Ezra rolled into the ring just ready for a fight.

He swung hard and wide. His movements were jerky. He wasn't *thinking* just flailing, striking out, reacting to some attack only he could see. So I played defense, keeping him on his toes and having to chase me. It hit me that was also why Liam stepped out. Giving me time with Ezra to chill him out.

"Want to tell me what happened?" I blocked his next two swings.

"No." Succinct.

I switched directions on him abruptly, stepping into his strikes, then turning him and sending him flying. He tumbled, his shoulder hitting hard before he was back on his feet. Real pain flashed across his face. Not my favorite method of getting through to him, but sometimes, Ezra had to get out of his own head.

Alcohol.

Pain.

Those were his preferred methods.

Pissing him off was mine.

Liam's prowess in the ring paid off here. He'd taught me to move and keep moving. Never repeat the same maneuver—especially if it was successful, 'cause it was easier to anticipate—and to keep my opponent on his toes. The chase lasted several minutes as Ezra's temper began to fray.

When he spit out the mouthguard and charged at me, I took him down in a tackle, twisting his leg up and then shoving his shoulders against the mat with my legs locking him down. He had one arm free.

"You asshole," he spit, but I didn't let him go.

"Odd way to say you're tapping out," I told him, aware of the strength in his leg where I had it bound and the pressure I had to keep on his other thigh to keep him from closing the scissors the way I had. We were both sweating and slick. One slip and he could turn this on me.

"Just fucking hit me," he muttered.

"No," I told him. "Not until you tell me what's wrong."

Because the bruises and welts might be fresh, but they

weren't new. His father had some twisted fucking idea that beating Ezra's habits out of him would work. Ezra never talked about it, not even when I'd had to put him back together after a particularly brutal bout.

Ezra groaned, the denial in his eyes. Whatever it was, he didn't want to talk about it. I didn't care. He needed to tell me.

"I can't help you if you don't tell me," I reminded him. The fight left him and he sagged, then tapped my leg. I loosened my hold and let him go, but I didn't move away. For his part, Ezra lay there on the mat, panting.

"They found me a wife."

"I'm sorry," I said, eyeing him. "What?"

"Dad—business partner in Russia and Eastern Europe. His daughter. She's fourteen and away at school. But she will be spending the holidays with us so I can get to know her."

I frowned as I studied him then pulled out the mouth guard. He was serious. "Fourteen is too young to get married."

"Not in New Hampshire or Massachusetts. Though you and I both know it has nothing to do with age." He covered his eyes with his forearm. "They are negotiating the contracts."

"For what?" Arranged marriage was a really old school concept.

Really old school.

"For terms. Stock. Money. Investments. Her family is powerful, it will give us what we need to make the expansions. Eventually, we'll absorb their businesses into our own. Lots to inherit for future progeny."

He made it sound like a fait accompli.

"How long?"

"I'm assuming eighteen, though her father wants me to be a little older. A little more settled. So—that's something. That's part of the negotiations, particularly if I have to *wait* for my bride to perform her so-called duties."

I snorted and Ezra shot me a weak smile.

"We'll get you out of it. We have time."

"Sure," he said, but he didn't believe me. "Who knows, maybe he'll find someone else in the meanwhile..."

Or Ezra could. We were twenty-one this year. Three years would make him twenty-four. "How old?"

"What?"

"How old does her father want you to be?" How long did we have? There had to be a way out of this. Granted, money and inheritances were all tied up in family business. But we could find something.

"At least twenty-five. Though I suggested she might want to go to college, you know. So maybe we can push it until she's at least twenty-two."

"That's at least seven, eight years..."

A lot could happen in that time.

A lot.

CHAPTER
ONE

EZRA

I'd been present for drinks before guests arrived. My suit had been waiting in my room along with the pale blue waistcoat, tie, pocket square, and cufflinks. The icy blue was not my first choice. Hell, it wasn't my second. I'd ordered a red and gold set, particularly after I'd gotten a brief look at Lainey's dress. Matching her was step one of the night.

Step two—I was working on that.

Even a check of the closet didn't turn up the correct suit. Calling the valet provided even less assistance. There were no red waistcoats available. The ice blue had been selected by my mother. So it was either just wear it and not rock the boat or go pick a fight in the ninety minutes we had before guests began arriving.

"I adore you."

The whisper of those words was a caress to ward off the agitation in my mind.

"I can't—I adore you for wanting to protect me. But I can't abandon any of them—including you."

The suit didn't matter. I'd deal with my parents after the party. Deal with all of it. The Fire and Ice Ball was the crown of the year for them. While I didn't give a damn about their business or social credits accrued via the annual event—they *did*. They couldn't stop me from doing what I wanted, but they could make it a great deal more difficult.

Better to grease the wheels.

Once dressed, I headed to the solarium for pre-party drinks, but the butler intercepted me. "Mr. Graham would like to speak to you in his office."

Of course he would. I checked my watch. "Has my mother come down yet?" Starting the night off on a bad foot with my father was fine. Normal almost. Mother tended to sulk, and her mood would continue to decline until it infuriated my father. That just made it unpleasant for everyone.

"Not yet, I'm afraid. There was an issue with her dress, so she will be another thirty minutes."

An issue with her dress. Right. Not my circus... "Then I'll go see my father." Leaving him, I headed down the stairs. Harrows Park had been fashioned after a renovated Tudor palace in England, right down to the landscaping. While the original had been built during Norman times and was ugly as fuck, the Tudor renovation had given it a hint of Italian elegance courtesy of the Renaissance. Harrows Park softened more of the lines with white stucco and marble, creating a gleaming effect, particularly in summer. The interior courtyard included Roman frescos and Greek columns.

In a word, it was ostentatious as hell. Wealth on display in a somewhat crude and vulgar fashion as my grandmother used to say. But she was a descendant of Russian royalty. While the Romanovs had been deposed and most of them executed because their lavish lifestyles were so far remote from the common person, she believed we should never forget our aristocratic roots.

Frankly, I didn't care about the roots or the history. All of it was soaked in blood and tragedy. What we needed was a clean break, an amputation of the diseased limbs and cauterization so it didn't repeat itself.

Maybe *I* needed that.

At his office door, I knocked once and waited. There were two guards stationed in the hall already. They were dressed up for the event, and they didn't pay any more attention to me than I did to them. Security would be everywhere tonight. Just because this event brought everyone to us didn't mean my father wanted to give them free run of the house.

"Enter," he called, and I let myself in.

The door closed out the sound from the rest of the house. Even if it was quiet out there, it seemed almost silent in here without even a suggestion of ambient noises. Seated on the far side of an old oak desk that had been hand-carved at least two centuries earlier, my father glanced up from his computer.

"Get yourself a drink," he ordered, then motioned to his glass. "And refill mine."

I hadn't planned to start this early. With Adam planning to be here this evening along with Lainey, I wanted my wits about me. No way Adam would let me get away with putting him off again. Lainey was on my side. Thank *fuck* she was on my side.

Confessing my feelings had taken everything I possessed. A part of me firmly believed she would reject me.

Why wouldn't she? I was damaged fucking goods, and she deserved so much better than us

"I could never hate you..." she'd whispered. *"Even when I wanted to kick you in the balls, I didn't hate you."*

The reminder steadied me as I retrieved my father's glass then moved over to the bar. Mixing up the martinis took no time, and I filled his glass then my own before returning to this desk. I flicked a look at the old clock on the table behind him. I didn't want to lose track of time.

"Have a seat," he said without glancing up from his computer. No sooner did I take the seat than my phone vibrated in the inner pocket of my jacket. I pulled it out of my pocket and frowned at the message from a number I didn't recognize,

Tapping it open, I went cold. Pictures had begun to download. A series of them. The woman in them was barely recognizable. In fact, I wouldn't have even been able to place her until I saw a birthmark on her right breast. It was the shape of a paw print. She used to joke it meant she was a real animal.

But...

Across the desk, my father closed the laptop and leaned back in his seat. He stared at me and I met his cold gaze.

"What the fuck is this?" I had zero intentions of pretending he hadn't been behind the photographs.

"Poor girl," he said, picking up his drink and swirling it around. "Genevieve was her name? Whitten? Maybe. Just got word a few hours ago."

"What happened to her?" Arresting my reactions took serious focus.

"Well, from what I've pieced together," Father continued, pausing to take a drink of his martini and nodding approvingly. "Well made, son. Well made. As for the girl, she was apparently kidnapped from her bed a few nights ago."

I hadn't heard anything.

"Her parents were quite beside themselves, but they were hoping for a ransom offer so they kept it quiet." Father shook his head. "True pity. She was raped, repeatedly, both with physical objects and by people. There were at least four semen samples, or so I was informed."

Ice began to drill into my heart.

"Apparently, she experienced numerous wounds, including a beating—most likely with a cane. She had several broken bones, and her fingernails were removed along with three teeth."

I was going to vomit.

"Cause of death is most likely shock due to severe trauma, but the coroner indicated the damage was far too severe to narrow it to just one cause." He took another drink. "It's a real pity, she seemed like an intelligent girl. You were acquainted?"

"If we weren't, this would be a pointless exercise." Because he was merely laying out the groundwork.

"Possibly." He gave me the smallest of smirks, a humorless smile. "Wealthy young woman, only daughter of her family, and their primary heir. Now she's going to be buried in a closed casket ceremony. The true tragedy—the family has no idea why this happened. No ransom was demanded, no terms offered, just—relentless, ceaseless, pain. A real agony."

I knocked back the whole of my martini and swiped the pictures closed. "Why?"

"You're not a fool, son, not a fool in the slightest. Tonight, your mother and I will be announcing your engagement to Oksana. You've played the delaying game for years, but it's time for you to step up and take your place."

"I—"

"Will listen and not speak unless I demand an answer." Ice crashed down on me at the implied threat. "You are not so old or big enough that I can't still put you down. Tonight is important to your mother. You will not disappoint her."

"I don't want to marry, Oksana."

"I don't care," he retorted. "You have played fast and loose for the last few years, and I allowed you to sow your wild oats. Your dalliances with that boy three years ago—I covered that up and dealt with it. The same with the one you discovered in high school."

I didn't move.

"Normally, I would applaud your discretion, but your choice in partners..." He made a scoff. "As for the Benedict girl..."

"Don't you dare threaten her..."

"Threaten her?" My father chuckled. "I don't have to threaten her. You already have. You think Oksana's family is pleased to know you're courting another heiress or that you've snuck away with her to our island? I covered it up for you, but I won't any longer. Understand me and understand me very clearly: you will cooperate. You will celebrate this marriage to Oksana, and you will honor that engagement, or what happened to that girl will look like the warning it is meant to be when Benedict disappears. If you think I can't get to her..." His look was pure malice. "You forget who you're dealing with. I don't want a war with Leopold Benedict, but Oksana's parents will be present tonight and he expects the announcement."

My stomach went sour.

"I won't have any more of my business or interests

delayed for your prurient desires. The wedding is in six months. You will have her pregnant by then, or shortly thereafter. I want my first grandchild to arrive before my sixty-first birthday. If it's not a son, then you will continue to get her pregnant until the next heir arrives."

Words failed me.

"She's not a broodmare," I snapped. "And I'm not some stallion you put out to stud."

He snorted. "You forget who you're speaking to," Father said, and a knock on the door interrupted us. "It's time. We'll be announcing the engagement tonight, make your peace with it, and make sure everyone believes it. Your mother. Oksana's father. Me." With that, he circled the desk. "Enter..."

My mother appeared in a cloud of perfume and smiles. "Oh, don't you both look dashing."

I stood and pasted a smile on more out of automatic habit than anything else. The photos of Genevieve burned into my brain. Father hadn't even been subtle about his threats. He would murder Lainey.

It wasn't just about killing her, it was about making her suffer.

Suffer like Genevieve had. Acid burned along my esophagus as I faced my mother. She was dressed in a stunning Dior, a personal design, and looking like a perfect empress in ice blue. Belatedly, it hit me that father and I wore matching waistcoats and ties. It was all suffocating me.

"Did you give Ezra the good news?" Mother beamed at me.

"I did," Father said, pressing a kiss to her cheek before he clapped me on the shoulder. Pain rippled through me as he gripped me tight enough to force imprints down to the bone. "He's a little dazzled by it all, but he's excited. Aren't you?"

"Definitely," I said and couldn't even muster up a fake lie. I was too busy looking for the way out that didn't cost Lainey or Adam. Avoiding Adam the past few weeks had been the right call. Father wasn't threatening him—if he knew...

No, he didn't know. Couldn't know. Only one other person knew, and she wouldn't say anything. She'd protect my secret, and I had to protect her.

"Oksana is so excited," Mother told me. "I might have let it slip a little because I didn't want her to be too stunned. It never looks good, you know."

"Of course," Father said. "Let's have our drink, darling, before the guests arrive." And we spent the next twenty, hellish minutes, making the smallest of small talk. It was excruciating, and the whole time, I couldn't get the pictures of Genevieve out of my head.

As soon as they were greeting guests, I made three calls. I had to confirm Genevieve was dead. Then I checked on the two other lovers he'd mentioned. They were also dead.

When he said cleaned up, he meant removed and swept away. No matter how I tried to examine it, I couldn't find a way to get us out of this. When Lainey appeared at the party, I couldn't take my eyes off of her. She was—perfection. Asking her to dance was a mistake, but I needed to talk to her.

To warn her.

The whole time we moved on the dance floor, I could feel my father watching us. Feel the way his gaze bore into me. Warning her could get her killed, and I didn't see Karagiani anywhere. Then it was too late, and he was making the announcement.

I had to sell it.

Sell everything.

Then I dipped Oksana and kissed her. The whole time, my heart died and ceased to beat. When I straightened, my father beamed, and my mother looked near tears but with happiness and my kotyonok was walking out with another man.

"Good choice," my father said as he shook my hand and Mother hugged Oksana before she hugged me. I wanted to slug him, but I played my part to perfection. When the music resumed and the applause and congratulations fell off, I turned to find Milo and Adam both glaring at me.

This night was far from over.

But it didn't matter. I was already dead.

TWO

LAINEY

"...**H**is engagement..."
"...bride-to-be..."
"...Oksana..."

The words all replayed in my head, backed by an enormous amount of static. When Ezra and I had danced, the whole time there was something bothering him. The agitation had rolled off him in waves, and it was more than just the normal upset. Whatever it was, he couldn't seem to get the words out, then...

Then his father called him up there.

If not for Bodhi standing there, with his hand resting at my lower back, I might have given in to the staggering sensation threatening to overwhelm me. His *engagement*? Throughout the entire announcement, I'd kept my gaze narrowed on Ezra. His eyes had gone blank as had his expression. As vibrant and passionate as Ezra could be, neutrality was not his strong suit.

Spontaneous applause broke out when Oksana's name had been announced, and the woman flushed as she went toward them. Unlike Ezra, she didn't seem used to the attention, and Ezra went to meet her, taking her hand—her left hand. The pear-shaped diamond gleamed under the lights.

For a split-second Ezra's gaze crashed into mine, and the suffocating emptiness in it broke my heart. Then he dipped her into a kiss, and the chip he'd carved off my heart smashed to the ground. I didn't know what he was doing or why he was doing it, but I absolutely loathed what it was doing *to* him.

"Chin up, Buttercup," Bodhi said, his arm wrapped around my waist so firmly I didn't doubt that he would catch me if I fell. Lips pressed to my head, he added, "Lean on me, we're getting the fuck out of this circus."

The smoldering layer of hot ash beneath those words didn't disguise the heat consuming everything in its path. But could you call it passion? Somehow, I didn't think so.

"I—"

"I got you," Bodhi insisted, loosening his arm from around me and taking my hand. The strength in his fingers, threading through mine, had my chin lifting. He wasn't going to walk me out of here like some woman on the verge of collapse. Nor did I need him to *rescue* me. The crowd around us surged forward, applauding in their eagerness to congratulate the newly-engaged couple.

The wedding would be the event of the season. Likely one for the year, since he was the Grahams' only child and heir. I didn't know much about Oksana's family, but I did know the circles they traveled in. As Bodhi headed for the door, I moved with him. We didn't rush, if anything, we took our time following a circuitous, if steady, path to the exit.

"Miss Benedict." Mrs. Waldemar's greeting paused me mid-step, and Bodhi shifted his stance. It was rather adorable how he put himself a half-step ahead of me so that he was more or less providing a blockade.

"Mrs. Waldemar," I greeted her. Bodhi had my left hand in his grip, so I offered her my right. She gripped it gently. "As always, it's lovely to see you."

"And you," she murmured, glancing toward the crowd that had thickened on the other end of the ballroom. "May I say you look absolutely stunning, my dear?"

"Thank you. I think your gown is also lovely." The prompt made me actually look at her. The gown was simple elegance, the long-sleeved red sequined dress a measure of understated beauty.

"Did you know?" she asked with a kind of blunt charm that my grandfather could also pull off. "About the engagement? It seems such an odd time to announce—you know before the clock turns as they say. One might also see it as bad luck to announce a marriage on the day the year winds down."

"Maybe," I said, fighting for and maintaining my neutrality for all it was worth. "It's already next year for three-quarters of the world. So one could say they are starting the new year off with it."

Whatever one wanted to call it, the whole concept nauseated me. He promised no more lies. He promised no more running. He promised that he loved me.

Tonight, his *parents* announced his engagement. The kiss though—that had been all him.

"If you'll excuse us," Bodhi said, the steadiness in his voice looping the life raft around me more effectively. "I was trying to steal Miss Benedict away while everyone else was distracted."

"Oh my goodness," Mrs. Waldemar said, a smile curving her lips and a cheery twinkle in her eyes. "Don't let me hold you up then. Be safe dear, and watch yourself with this one, he's tricky."

"Good evening," I told her. Practice kept my voice pleasant, my expression easy, and my chin up with my shoulders back. As I turned, I caught Pretty Boy's eye and half-sighed. What I wouldn't give to just walk up to him in the middle of the ballroom and steal him away from all of this.

Worry flickered in his eyes, but King was standing not even two feet from him. While I hated the reasons Milo had chosen to do this, I also respected his choice. I summoned the politest, if distant smile. Adam's thunderous anger was hard to miss in the granite line of his jaw and the hardness of his face. He wasn't that far from Pretty Boy either.

Oh, Ezra. I shook my head internally. Whatever prompted this choice wasn't going to end well for anyone. Bodhi had us moving again. More than once, he murmured a vaguely polite, yet very firm "excuse us" each time someone looked like they planned on stopping us.

The cold air of the courtyard felt good against the flush of my skin. It was like someone had dragged my flesh on too tight and I couldn't loosen it. Distantly, it registered that Bodhi was speaking to me as we crossed the courtyard. Shaking off the malaise, I forced myself to focus on his words.

"...prefer them right out of the fryer, super hot with extra salt. There's no point without the salt," he was saying. "Although, I had them once with a chocolate shake, and I don't know who decided to try that combination, but it was decadent."

"Salt? Or fries?" Because "from the fryer" seemed to suggest french fries. I thought. Maybe.

"Do you put salt on your milkshakes, Buttercup?" Amusement decorated the words but couldn't quite disguise the deeper anger. Still, he wasn't focusing on it so I wouldn't either.

"Never tried," I mused. "Could be fun."

Then we were across the courtyard and stepping into the foyer. Security and valets straightened at our arrival. The majority of the party was going on much further away. "Car," Bodhi said to the valet, handing him a card. "And the lady's coat."

Oh. Car. "Wood is going to be here somewhere... I should message him to wait for Tally." My phone was inside my clutch. There were a series of messages on the screen. I dismissed them all. Including the one from Tally asking me where I was. She must not have seen us slip out.

I'd message her after we were gone. Currently, I didn't want to linger any longer than necessary. After sending the note to Wood, I tucked my phone back in. One of the footmen returned with my coat, and Bodhi took it from him and went over it before he draped it around my shoulders. It wasn't a proper coat because the dress wouldn't allow for it, but it was thick and luxurious and chased away the chill.

"It will just be another minute for the vehicle, sir."

None of the staff spoke as we stood in the there, and none of them said a word about our leaving early. They wouldn't. Not with us *present*. Later, though? Later there would be gossip. Gossip. Rumors. Innuendo.

Frankly, I couldn't find it within me to care. When, and if, I had to deal with it, I would. The car the valet pulled up boasted far more muscle than the sweet sports car we'd taken to Philadelphia. A pang went through me. Then again, the roads were icier tonight and the air much chillier.

"Shall we?" Bodhi said, and I summoned a smile. He wasn't pressuring me or demanding answers. If anything, he was being exceptionally kind. But then, he was always kind to me. Always had been. I needed that kindness at the moment.

"Yes," I said, but before I could take a step, Bodhi's head snapped up and a hand closed on my arm to tug me backward. Three things registered with me during the blur of motion.

The first? The hand on my arm belonged to Karagiani. I guess not listening to me was part of the job. I hadn't wanted him escorting me at the party. Maybe I should have told him I didn't want him waiting for me outside of it either.

The second? Bodhi peeled his hand off of me like it was butter. He gripped his thumb and did something to wrench the offending grasp that had Karagiani grimacing. Then staggering backward when Bodhi released him.

The third? Two of Graham's security people rushed into the melee. One went down clutching his throat after one blow from Bodhi, and the other just sprawled. I hadn't even seen Bodhi hit him. Then Karagiani pulled a gun.

"Don't—" I started forward, but I needn't have bothered. Bodhi disarmed him, taking the gun and fixing it on Karagiani. All the oxygen seemed to evaporate as the men faced off. Bodhi's arm was rock steady, and he'd barely even mussed his hair.

"Don't ever touch the lady again," Bodhi warned him. "Bodyguard doesn't mean you get to touch her. It also doesn't mean you get to grab or drag her off. Attack her again and it will be the last thing you do."

A moment later, Bodhi lowered the weapon, then stripped it down, flicking bullets out of the magazine like they were candy until the gun was just scattered parts.

Without glancing at me, Bodhi said, "Do you want the bodyguard to go with you, Buttercup?"

"No," I said slowly. "I didn't want him here at all."

"Then those are your marching orders." The air was frozen, and around us the security guards stirred, the valets gaped, and the footman looked stunned. Still, no one else tried to intervene.

"Miss Benedict," Karagiani said but I shook my head.

"Not tonight. I'd like to go now."

"Of course," Bodhi said, then shifted to motion me toward the door. He barely acknowledged Karagiani, but he also didn't give the man his back. The valet bolted out ahead of us and opened the passenger door for me. Bodhi waved him away when it came to getting my skirt in and helped me with it.

The whole time, I was violently aware of our observers. Once he closed the door, the heat from the car began to penetrate my icy core. A shiver broke through my facade, but I only allowed myself one. Bodhi waited for a beat, his focus on Karagiani and the security guards who were just now making it to their feet.

When he finally slid inside, he gave me an easy smile. "Buckled in?"

No, but I reached for the seatbelt and dragged it across my outfit before locking it into place. He snapped on his own and then hit the accelerator.

"Want some music?" The banal question pulled a faint smile to my lips, but it wasn't much and it didn't last long.

"No," I said. I really didn't know what I wanted. "I'm fine. Thank you."

An hour later, he was still driving and we'd left the island via the Verrazzano-Narrows Bridge to Staten Island then New Jersey. It wasn't until we got onto 95 heading south that I roused from the chaotic stutter of my thoughts.

"Where are we going?"

"Do you care?" Bodhi said, and I considered it.

"No," I said slowly. "Not really—but I might need a bathroom break at some point."

"Maybe a change of clothes?" Bodhi suggested, and I glanced down at my dress and tried to not laugh.

"Think I'm overdressed, Trouble?"

His soft chuckle was what I was going for. "I think you're perfect, Buttercup."

Leaning my head back, I closed my eyes. "Thank you, Bodhi."

"Anytime," he answered, not even asking me what I was thanking him for, and I didn't look at it too closely when he covered my left hand with his own or when I dug my nails in to hold on tight.

THREE

MILO

S ome distant part of my brain acknowledged the moment Adam appeared at my side. King had gone to "congratulate" the groom-to-be. I'd pass. If I went anywhere near that self-loathing asshole right now, I might actually rip his head off and to hell with the consequences. Ezra Graham had just burned Mayhem badly.

Very badly.

Pain had rippled across her face before she could quite exert control over her expression. The mask that slipped into place was one she'd cultivated while growing up in this world. A world I'd once admired but had learned was no less dark and depraved than the streets where I'd been raised.

Frankly, the wealthy were far worse in my opinion. They reveled in their corruption. Mayhem was an exception, not the rule. Awareness of King's attention rested on me like a hot branding iron. It didn't matter that he wasn't looking at me.

His men were.

We'd arrived with four guards, and they were ranged out in the room "blending" in with the pomp and the circumstance. King's focus had been uncomfortably narrow the past several days, particularly since Ivy had called *me* at Christmas and not him.

That was fine by me, he didn't need to be anywhere near her. Ezra nodded to the next man in the line to shake his hand. He barely seemed aware of the petite little blonde clinging to him. Her eyes were wide, her smile almost brittle and perhaps a little on the shy side. The enormous weight of so much attention seemed to be collapsing in on her.

"Thank you," Ezra said abruptly just as he clasped King's hand. "If you'll excuse us, Oksana's a little overwhelmed. We'll be back out shortly." Then he swept her away from the gaggle of humanity. His father frowned then murmured something to his wife before he strode out after the couple.

"Well that explains some of this," Adam said in too soft a voice that sounded more like the gritting of his teeth than a whisper. "Lose King and meet me for a smoke."

He didn't wait for my response, and I wasn't in a rush to offer him one. King looked *very* pleased when he returned to me. "That's excellent news, don't you think?"

"Was I supposed to care?" Manufacturing a neutral attitude wasn't as difficult as it may seem. I really didn't give a shit about Graham at the moment. What I hated was the harm his actions had caused. Harm, he'd sworn he didn't want to do again, yet, there he went and Mayhem was gone.

She'd left the ballroom, head high, like a goddamn queen, and she'd had Bodhi at her side. As much as I'd rather it were me, I trusted the crazy son of a bitch with her. His affection for Ivy and Lainey was not something he manufactured. Frankly, the guy couldn't be bothered to make polite conversation with "allies." So, no, as much as I wanted to be with her, it was a relief to get her out of the line of fire.

"About Graham?" King said, a faint smirk on his lips as he accepted two glasses of champagne. He handed one to me and then raised his glass with an expectant look.

I didn't quite roll my eyes. "What are we drinking to?"

"To Ezra and his marriage, it will be profitable for all of us."

Right. "You know, I'm going to regret asking this. How is it profitable for all of us?"

King smirked then tapped my glass lightly with his. "That, my son, is part of your lesson. You will find out, and you will learn to trust my decisions. Particularly when I tell you to do something."

Before I could respond, a couple approached and King was all grifter smiles and conman slick as he greeted them. Then they moved away, and that left me with the champagne I didn't want, and under the scrutiny of guards I wanted to lose. I made a show of drinking the champagne as I "worked" the room. My path would take me out a pair of side doors. When I asked one of the waiters where the restrooms were, he'd given me a polite smile and pointed to the doors I'd been scoping.

With that, I slipped out into the hall and made my way toward the bathrooms at the far end. Rather than hurry, since I had maybe three seconds before one of the guard dogs made it into the hall, I slid into the first room on the left. It was dark and empty. Once inside, I turned the lock and leaned against it to wait.

It didn't take long. The footsteps in the hall behind me weren't particularly loud, though they sped up when they didn't spot me right away. I did a mental count to sixty and the follower returned before I hit fifty-eight.

The doorknob wiggled. That made sense, he probably checked all the doors on his way back. A moment later, a muffled voice came through. "Does anyone have eyes on the pup?"

The pup?

I snorted.

While the responses were inaudible to me, I didn't press my way free. Better to wait.

Then, he said, "Trent, move to the driveway, keep an eye on incoming and outgoing vehicles. The rest of us are back on the ballroom. I'll report to King myself."

Chances were, he wasn't going to enjoy King's response.

Not. My. Problem.

Leaving the door locked behind me, I did a quick scan of the room I'd chosen. It was a small sitting room of some kind. But it did have doors on the far side. They opened onto the interior courtyard. That was useful. I scanned the security that was present, then tracked—there he was. I knew all of King's people. Once Trent was out of sight, I let myself out into the courtyard.

First guard spared me an idle look at my approach. "Can I help you sir?"

"Looking for a spot to smoke." While I didn't, my long acquaintance with Jasper's habits meant that no matter where you went—there was *always* a smoking area. The guard studied me for a beat. Considering Adam's suggestion and his long acquaintance with the Grahams, I didn't doubt that there was one. Just a matter of where it was.

"One moment." He turned away briefly. "C3 on the move. Five minutes."

Then he glanced at me again and did a quick jerk of his head. He moved east *away* from the ballroom and through another pair of double doors and then into a hallway and across it and out to a walled garden with heaters, chairs, and amenities.

"Take your time, sir. When you want to return to the ballroom, this hall goes directly around to it, or you can travel back to the courtyard." The guard didn't linger.

"Drink?" Adam said from where he leaned against the bar.

"Beer."

"Make that two," Adam told the bartender. After we had them, he motioned me toward the corner. It was as far from the bartender as we could get, put both of our backs to a wall and gave us a sense of relative privacy.

Once we were seated, he pulled out a case with small cigars in it. At my bland look, he shrugged. "When in Rome…"

Yeah. I took one out and I didn't have to inhale to puff on it. The scent reminded me of the old clove cigarettes Jasper had flirted with for a time. Blowing out a long stream of smoke, Adam studied the garden around us.

"Are you keeping me in suspense or do you actually need a minute?" I asked after another three minutes passed in silence.

"I'm debating the issue," Adam admitted, lifting his bottle of beer and tipping the top toward me. "Now ask me which issue."

I snorted. "You're debating whether you want to sit here and wait for him to stick his head up long enough for you to knock it off, or whether you should go and hunt him down."

I didn't bother to expand on which "him" I was discussing. There was only one person right now that had managed to earn Adam's ire. Or maybe only one currently deserving it.

"She left," Adam told me unnecessarily.

"I saw."

"With Cavendish."

That didn't require a response, so I took another drink of beer before puffing on the thin cigar. There was no real temptation to take a deep breath and inhale it. The three times I attempted smoking as a teenager where it didn't involve actual weed had left me sick to my stomach and with a headache.

It wasn't for me.

But it was a good cover.

"She's safe," was all I said when Adam shifted his stare from the garden to me.

"You trust him?" The marked surprise in his voice indicated that he clearly did not. Then, I knew that. I'd seen his and Ezra's reactions to Bodhi back at the clubhouse when he'd shown up to help us—help *Ivy* again. They didn't have to trust him.

He'd earned it with me.

"He'll protect her." That was all I was saying on the subject. He didn't have to like it. I didn't give a fuck.

Adam let out an aggrieved sigh, then the door to the house opened and the man of the moment put on an appearance. His tie was loose, his hair disheveled, and there was lipstick on his mouth. He was already dragging out a handkerchief to wipe it as he went to the bar.

"Triple shot of whiskey," he told the bartender. "Neat."

Laser-focused, Adam didn't take his gaze off Ezra. As if suddenly aware of it, Ezra tossed a glance in our direction. The moment hung, suspended, as though he weighed his own responses. Finally, he turned and carried the whiskey over to us.

Arrogance filled his expression, and his eyes were cool. The handkerchief decorated with the lipstick smears disappeared back into his pocket, and he raised his glass to us. "To me and my bride."

Then he tossed back the full measure.

Dumbass chose poorly.

"You stupid mother fucker," Adam said, pushing to his feet after he put his cigar out. "You told me you had this shit taken care of."

The cold rage simmering in the air around Adam didn't seem to even touch Ezra. The other man chuckled. "It is taken care of—didn't you see the announcement? It's going to be the wedding of the season. My mother is beside herself with the planning. Probably have to ask some cousin or some shit to be the best man so don't get your boxers in a bunch when you just get an invitation. You know how it goes."

Cavalier attitude in place, Ezra looked at his now empty glass.

"Definitely tasted like more. You gents want anything?"

"Ezra..." I said it almost on a sigh. Because whatever game he was playing, this wasn't the way to do it.

"Ease up there, Hardigan. You and I don't do touchy feely unless fists are involved." He winked then sauntered away.

Next to me, Adam curled his fingers into fists, but he didn't follow.

"He's trying to bait you," I warned him, and Adam shot me an incendiary look.

"Thanks for the insight. I think I know him better than you do. I know all of them better." The implied "so you can *fuck* off" resonated, but I just leaned back in my seat. It didn't take Ezra long to return anyway. Despite being a well-appointed outdoor smoking area with the heat lamps to chase away the chill, we were alone out here except for the single witness working the bar.

"You need to lighten up," Ezra drawled toward Adam. "Maybe if you got laid, it would take the stick out of your ass."

I shook my head. He wanted the fight. He was deliberately trying to provoke—

"I'd suggest Lainey, but she's already got big boy over here, and I almost like him these days. Besides... you're not good enough for her," Ezra told him and his eyes were fixed on Adam's. There was no way he didn't see the reaction he was setting off. "As someone who has been there and savored that, I speak from experience."

Rather than punch him in the face, Adam cocked his head to the side. "So that's your game..."

"My game?" Surprise flickered across Ezra's face before he could quite suppress it, then he tossed back the whiskey to cover. But I'd seen the slip.

I didn't doubt that Adam had as well.

"I don't play games anymore," Ezra said, seemingly sober despite the alcohol consumption. "You need players for a game. You need people. I don't have those. I did—but they're a burden or maybe I was...doesn't really matter anymore. In a few months, I'll be married and moving on to take my rightful place and all that bullshit. Where are you going to be, Adam? Still pretending that you aren't desperately in love with the girl you truly believed was your sister for the first few years of her life?"

I didn't move.

Ezra laughed, and it was a cruel, empty sound. "That's the irony, you know. You thought she was your sister, and you had a thing for her anyway. Even when she was little— or maybe that was your thing, you liked 'em young. Couldn't quite reconcile it when she grew up into that beautiful body and those sweet lips..." He touched his tongue to his teeth as he stared at Adam. "You told yourself she was your sister so you wouldn't want her. So you would keep her at arm's length, but that didn't stop you wanting her. No... I was there... that day you realized that little thing had become a woman and I saw it, you know. Saw the want in you and realized...I wanted her too."

"Ezra," I warned because he was truly playing with fire now. Maybe he wanted Adam to beat the shit out of him, but this wasn't the way to do it.

"Don't worry, Hardigan. He never touched her. Hell, he proposed to your sister to protect her and to keep himself away from Lainey. How fucking funny is that? He wanted King's eyes off Lainey and damn near threw his own daughter under that bus." Ezra laughed. "Twisted, fucked up world. But—Lainey isn't waiting for either of us, and that's the way it needs to be, you know. She's got you—oh wait, she does."

Ezra focused on me now.

"You should go find Daddy, there, Hardigan. Make sure he doesn't notice anything *else* amiss. Elaine Benedict's paid enough of our debts." He stared into his empty glass then turned and threw it at the wall. The heavy tumbler broke apart, but it didn't quite shatter.

With that, he stalked away from us and back inside.

Adam started forward and I sighed. Goddammit. "You sure you want to do that?" I asked him.

Adam Reed paused for a bare second. "No, but he needs me too. Do what he said. Make sure King doesn't think this barb landed. He didn't want to warn us, but he did. I'll find you later."

Then he was gone, leaving me with my beer, my cigar, and a bartender who moved out to clean up the mess.

The whole damn thing was fucked up.

CHAPTER
FOUR

LAINEY

The New Year came and went as we continued south. Somewhere in southern Maryland, Bodhi pulled the car into a rest area. He needed the restroom, and at the mention, I sighed. Because so did I.

"C'mon," he said, unlocking his seat belt and popping mine before he slid out of the car. He'd already circled it to open the passenger door. The flood of icy air into the cheerful warmth of the vehicle's interior was a reminder that it was still winter. The world hadn't just spun off its axis, nor had the seasons changed.

Accepting Bodhi's hand, I let him help me out of the car. The pavement wasn't icy, but it did glisten. There was also the grit of gravelly sand and salt across the sidewalks. I'd fled the ball in a gown and four-inch heels. Not exactly practical. Bodhi stripped off his own coat and wrapped it around me before he gripped the bottom of the dress and began to tie it up and then looped the train around my wrist.

Surprise flickered through me.

"You still with me?" The quiet question provoked a much deeper sigh.

"I'm sorry, Trouble. I'm terrible company."

"Not to me." He put a hand at the small of my back before he closed the door and then walked me toward the bathrooms. The rest area was empty, save for some idling 18-wheelers. I didn't do a lot of road trips. The vehicles were dark, parked farther away from the small buildings.

Em told me Jasper had slept in his truck and she'd done it too. The enthusiasm in her voice when she detailed the "adventure" had pulled a smile to my lips. Not something I could easily imagine. Still...

When we got to the bathrooms, Bodhi opened the door to the ladies' and stepped inside. It was the first time I really caught sight of the gun he wore. It had been hidden by his coat. But it wasn't now.

"Doesn't smell the best, but it's clean," he told me. "And relatively warm." I'd gotten chilled on the walk from the vehicle to the restrooms, and I appreciated the warmth. "Go ahead and use the facilities. The handicap stall at the end has a double lock, and it'll be big enough for the dress."

That was the first time I had a pause. He'd tied the dress up so it wouldn't drag the ground. But it was not exactly the easiest for bunching up.

"I really should have brought a change of clothes," I muttered.

"Don't worry, Buttercup. I'll get you taken care of...Now can you do it or do you need me to help hold your skirt?"

There was nothing remotely sexual about the offer. Bodhi didn't leer or shoot me a flirty grin. He was very matter-of-fact. The directness settled a disquiet I hadn't even been aware of until this moment.

"Attractive as the offer is," I murmured, "I'll manage. Are you staying in here?"

"Yes, and when you're done, I'll take my turn while you hold the gun." More directness, and at the same time, I found my first smile in hours.

"Thank you." I didn't explain it.

Nor did he ask me to. Instead, he just folded his arms and nodded his head. It took a little maneuvering, but I'd had to pee in a ballgown before, so I made do. Thankfully, the room wasn't freezing and the paper shield on the toilet seat itself definitely helped. The fact I only had to pee was a winner in my book.

Trouble was being exceptionally gracious, but I didn't think we needed to stretch these new intimacies any further tonight. Once I finished, he waited for me to wash and dry my hands before he removed the Sig Sauer from his holster. The four-inch barrel gave a nice balance to the grip. It fit my palm neatly.

"Do I need to explain anything?" Bless him for asking and not assuming.

"I've got it," I told him. "Are we expecting trouble?"

"Well," he said, the corner of his mouth drifting upward. "I'm here."

"So, we've already got enough trouble then."

A real grin ghosted over his lips. "You could say that. Three minutes. I had a lot of coffee."

Then he disappeared into one of the stalls. He didn't close the door all the way, but I didn't mind. One could hardly block the sound of a stream of piss hitting the toilet. Three minutes seemed generous, at least I thought it had, until he seemed to go for far longer than I suspected.

When he finished, I was trying not to laugh at the direction of my own haphazard thoughts. "Should I apologize?" I asked as he walked over to the sinks.

He quirked a brow in my direction. "It depends. Did you do something you need to apologize for?"

Arguably, no. And as relieving as it had been to use the bathroom— "You let me go first."

"Ah," Bodhi commented with a chuckle and then finished washing and drying his hands before joining me. Even in my heels and at my height, I still had to tilt my head back to look up at him.

Bodhi wasn't domineering or controlling like Adam in his approach. He wasn't overwhelming either, filling every part of the room with his presence like Pretty Boy, nor just over the top bombastic that made being around him electric like Ezra. Pain spasmed around my heart at the thought of the last. No, he wasn't like any of them. He was himself. A quiet, almost deadly calm at the center of a tumultuous storm.

"You never have to apologize for me taking care of you," he told me. "I am a very patient man."

"Are you?" I could see that.

"Yes," he said, then narrowed the distance between us. This close, I couldn't escape that darkness in his eyes. The shadows that seemed to exist as a layer upon layer. The inky blackness a texture unto itself. "Very patient."

The brush of his fingers against my hand sent shivers racing over my skin, and I forgot to take a deeper breath. "Trouble..."

"Just taking the gun," he murmured, his lips so close to mine that his breath feathered against them with each word. "You took a hell of a hit tonight. Anything else I might want to take from you, I'll need you to be onboard and invested in..."

Surprise rippled through me. "I didn't know..." But it wasn't an unattractive offer in the slightest.

He chuckled. "To be honest," he said, as he closed his hand over mine and then slid the gun from my fingers. "I didn't either. You've always been something of an enigma, Buttercup. But I like you."

The moisture in my mouth fled.

"I can't say that about many people." He leaned a little closer, brushing his cheek against mine before whispering against my ear, "But our first kiss is not going to be in a bathroom at a rest stop in the middle of Maryland."

Laughter burst out of me. The reminder of our location cut through some of the intense sorrow and the unexpected wonder. It created a gash that helped give the bleeding in my soul a place to go while staunching it at the same time. "I like you, Trouble," I admitted.

"I like you too," he said. "For now, let me look after you, and we'll get some things done. Then revisit this."

"Revisit, hmm?" I adjusted his jacket on my shoulders as he holstered his gun.

"Yes, revisit." He studied me for a beat, but for once I couldn't really read him or his expression. "Come on."

He held out his hand, and I clasped it easily. He pulled the door open, and then we were back out in the icy air. While we hadn't really lingered in the restroom, the world out here seemed to have shifted, despite the fact I didn't see any obvious changes. Bodhi's head was on a swivel.

There were no new trucks in the parking lot. Bodhi's car waited for us, giving a casual plink of cooling metal. At the passenger door, he opened it and helped me climb in again. After closing the door, he took another long look around before circling the car.

I didn't say anything until we were back on the road.

The flow of traffic increased the nearer we got to DC despite the time. Partiers were still on the road or just now getting on it to head home.

It was hard to believe that it was New Year's Eve—well, New Year's morning really.

"Phillip..."

He glanced at me.

"Will you tell me about your mother?"

It was a question I had left alone, but something had changed between us tonight. Some indefinable boundary had been crossed. Maybe it was just that he'd been there when humiliation had threatened to swallow me whole. Or maybe it was the way he'd *listened* to me when I didn't want Karagiani coming along or that he didn't try to tell me what to do or what to feel.

In some ways, my history with Bodhi was as complicated as it was simple. I didn't think I could explain it to anyone else, and I didn't want to. Not really. That said, I wanted to understand him. I wanted to do for him what he'd done for me.

Though, I couldn't imagine him needing saving. Not like Ezra... who was currently determined to set fire to his own life. Pain expanded the bruise around my heart. Maybe I shouldn't have left, but I couldn't breathe there and I didn't think I could breathe now if I focused on it for too long.

"Yes," Bodhi said after a long protracted silence that had me almost forgetting I'd asked the question. "But let's get more comfortable first."

We passed the exits for DC, and he continued into Virginia, then bypassed Alexandria and headed into Fairfax. I'd been down here a couple of years earlier. "We have friends with a horse farm here," I murmured.

The boost of adrenaline had faded, and it left me fighting the urge to yawn.

"The Harringtons," Bodhi said. "They have some good Arabian stock, but their business is in warmbloods, especially with King Tut standing stud the last four years."

Amusement crept through me. "You know your horses."

"I go to a lot of parties," he retorted in a dry tone. "Conversations tend to surround what horses or heirs are standing stud."

I laughed. The sound escaped even before I could put a hand over my mouth. It was a burst of pure humor, and Bodhi flashed a smile at me.

"I'm not sure I want to be considered the mare they are looking to cover..." Pure devilment inspired me, but his easy smile accepted the comment without an ounce of censure.

"Well, there are a lot of studs being paraded around you," Bodhi said, though he pursed his lips. "But you were definitely the talk of the town two summers ago during your official cotillion."

"Oh kill me," I groaned. Grandfather had insisted. It was what all proper young women did. He would be my escort, and we would set the tone. Adam and Ezra had both danced with me that night, but since I had to dance with nearly every eligible bachelor present... "I didn't see you there," I said abruptly. "How did you see me?"

Bodhi chuckled. "My secret. Think about it. I bet you did see me, you just didn't realize it."

Like the masquerade. Eventually, he pulled up to a set of gates, entered a code that opened them, and then headed up the driveway. I didn't know what I expected, but a country estate in Virginia was not what I pictured. The house wasn't large or overly ostentatious. It had some southern charm to the wide verandah with a pair of Ionic

columns framing the steps, but the rest of it was just
—cozy.

He passed me a gun and then said, "Stay in the car
while I check everything."

Then he was gone. I barely even saw him moving. He
circled the building and disappeared, and then five minutes
later the lights came on inside and he pulled the front door
open.

His tie was long gone and his shirt unbuttoned at the
collar. The whole image was rather rakish as he descended
the steps. I reached over and turned off the car and picked
up the key fob he'd left as he opened the door for me. He
accepted the gun and the key fob both, then gestured to the
front doors.

"Welcome to Red Hill."

I had to contain my curiosity as he gave me a brief tour.
Then he showed me upstairs to a guest room. It had an
adjoining door to the master suite, but neither of us
commented on that. There was a lovely bathroom with a
huge clawfoot tub. The idea of sinking into that and
escaping was very tempting.

"Clothes here," Bodhi said, pulling open the closet. "An
assortment of sizes, and they are stocked in case of
company that didn't have a chance to pack a bag."

I slid off one heel and then the other as he spoke. "Do
you often bring women here with just the clothes on their
backs?"

"A gentleman doesn't kiss and tell," he said with a wink.
"If you don't like anything in here, go next door and help
yourself to my things."

Smooth.

"But no, the only people I've ever brought here have
been in trouble or on the run. I give them sanctuary and

then move them along. Come down when you're ready. I'm going to make food—if you still want to talk. If you just want to sleep that's fine too."

"I thought you didn't kiss and tell," I teased, still turning over that sliver of information he'd given me.

"I'm not a gentleman," he said, then pulled the door closed behind him.

Maybe not.

But he was something else... and I rather liked who he was.

CHAPTER
FIVE

ADAM

Ezra didn't run away from the garden, but he didn't linger either. If he followed typical behavior, he would be leaving Harrows Park either through the front door or the garage. The announcement had been made. He'd put on a show, but he wouldn't stay. Not when his inclination would be to get falling down drunk.

Wallace Graham had a chokehold on his son. More than once I'd wanted to put a bullet in the man for the shit he pulled where Ezra was concerned. Tonight was the first time I actually reached for the gun. The only thing staying my hand was the desire to make sure the old son of a bitch suffered.

Ezra had already vanished from the hallway, and there was no sign of him in the courtyard. The most likely exit would be via the garage. He had a slew of cars here. Unlike me, he didn't have an apartment in the city. His parents had never allowed it, but he had friends.

He had me.

"Adam." My father's voice was not high on my list of priorities for the evening, so I straightened my jacket, spared him a look then nodded once before I strode away. "I was speaking to you..."

The annoyance in his voice almost made me smirk.

"And I'm ignoring you," I threw over my shoulder, since we were apparently stating the obvious. While Ezra spent more time at my home when we were growing up than we did here, I knew the layout. For once, I wished Hardigan had been able to take Lainey and go. I knew exactly how far he would go, but he was tackling a different burden.

I didn't have to like Lainey leaving with Cavendish because as much of a wild card as that asshole was, he was also fond of my girl.

Fond of her, and based on recent experience, extraordinarily deadly.

Cavendish would protect her.

If none of us could be there, I guessed he was an acceptable substitute. Even as I descended the steps to the garage, I grimaced. The screech of rubber on cement echoed from beyond the still-open door.

Goddammit.

Going right to the lockbox where the keys were stored, I entered Ezra's code. That idiot had taken the damn Bugatti. The roads may not be icy, but the conditions weren't great either. The McLaren was the only other vehicle here fast enough to keep up with the Bugatti.

Keys in hand, I slid into the midnight blue car, locked the seatbelt into place, and hit the remote for the garage door that had already begun to close. The engine purred to life, a beast, ready to be unleashed.

Pulling the hatch closed, I was already accelerating. The McLaren's cockpit had always reminded me of a fighter jet.

Flipping the automatic to manual, I took care of my own clutching and gear shifting as I followed the back drive leading away from Harrows Park. I wanted the control back here, particularly on the hairpin turns.

The garage opened away from the front of the house, and the route took a winding turn through the woods and around the lake. None of it was lit, and you had to know the route or you risked spinning out, or worse, leaving the road entirely.

We'd done some damage back here in our day. It was an escape when the front was filled with guests or we wanted to avoid the parents. A flash of headlights ahead told me I'd made the right call. I put my right foot down, trusting the car to respond.

Mentally mapping the curves ahead, I kept accelerating to close the distance. There was only one way out, but I didn't want him taking advantage of a lead to lose me.

The engine growled as the gears shifted. I followed the road smoothly, barely noticing the increasingly sharper turns as she handled smoothly. Then we were out on Old Beryl Road. Two narrow lanes and less than a mile to a state highway.

The Bugatti surged ahead, taking the turn onto the road a few seconds ahead of me. But I didn't lose sight of his tail lights. We were already cruising past eighty, and he wasn't slowing down.

Aware of the possible dangers ahead when we reached the state highway, I stayed fixed on his ass. He wanted my attention, he had it. The alternative was to pull ahead of him and do a slide drift stop across the road and hope he didn't plow into me.

I didn't like our odds for that. So, if he needed a drive to blow off steam, then I'd be with him. He'd been hiding for weeks now, avoiding me. I'd allowed it. Instead of helping, however, shit had gotten worse.

We hit the state highway and he passed a hundred. I kept pace with him. His mind was not on where he was, because it took him too long to notice me following him.

The hiccup in his speed, the sudden faltering as he dropped, had me easing up before he put the pedal down. The aggressive driving wasn't going to lose me. If he needed to take the edge off, fine. But one way or another.

We were talking.

Tonight.

It was almost two hours later and somewhere in fucking Vermont that he left the highway. The area was vaguely familiar. Ten minutes later, I recognized it. He pulled up to a private gate and entered a code.

I was right behind him and followed him up the drive to another house, this one a lot more comfortable and cozy. Snow was piled everywhere, and the place looked like something out of a winter wonderland photo spread.

Instead of pulling into the circular drive, he led the way around to the side and into a garage where two doors slid open. I parked and climbed out of the car before he finished shutting off his engine.

The cold bite of the air was bitter in my lungs. Ezra didn't leave the car right away, and then an interior door to the house opened and the man standing in the doorway registered.

Dominic Walsh.

I hadn't seen him in a few years.

"Coffee is on," he said, eyeing me before he glanced to where Ezra finally opened his car door. "If there's gonna be a body or blood involved tell me now, and I'll go. Plausible deniability only goes so far."

The dry sense of humor and directness hadn't changed.

"We're good, Nicky," Ezra said, the weariness in his tone made me tired. "Give us a moment?" For the first time since he put on that farce at the house, he glanced directly at me. "Maybe a half hour."

"Yep. Come in when you're ready. Adam." Ezra's cousin nodded to me.

"Walsh," I replied, barely sparing him a look, and waited until the door closed, leaving us alone with the sound of the engines plinking and cooling.

Ezra shoved the door to the Bugatti closed and then leaned back against it. Somewhere he'd lost the ice blue tie, and he'd undone the waistcoat. The cool colors weren't his favorites. They lacked the drama he preferred.

The drive had taken the edge off of him and given me time to consider my options. I could punch him. Fuck knew, he deserved it.

But he'd finally stopped running.

So that had to be worth something.

"How pissed at me are you?" Ezra asked finally as he raked a hand through his hair.

"Tell me what happened." Because all the anger in the world wasn't going to solve this problem. I was fucking furious with him. Furious with the announcement, with going forward, and with the shit he'd been pulling for weeks. Yelling wasn't going to do it.

He frowned. "Tell you..."

"Yes," I said, adopting patience with a deep breath and a fixed stare. "Tell me what happened. Let's start with Oksana. That seems to be the major play at the moment."

The searching look in his eyes warned me that he didn't believe me.

"I said let's start there," I informed him, answering the

unasked demand in his gaze. "We will get to *all* of it, but tell me what happened with your father and the engagement."

His shoulders dropped. "I thought I was out of it. I delayed it, got Oksana to go along with it. I don't think she's any more interested in marrying me than I am her."

For some reason, hearing him say the words offered a kind of profound relief I refused to examine too closely.

"The problem is, she isn't going to fight her family. She wants out from under her father's thumb, and she is fairly certain I'll be a reasonable husband and let her do what she wants."

She wasn't wrong. Especially since he didn't want to marry her.

"You told me it was taken care of..." I kept the accusation out of my words. "We made arrangements for her and that boy... Raoul?"

"Raoul is dead," Ezra told me, his tone flat. "She tried to run away with him last year when everything was going sideways. I provided them with the funds. Got them out of town and wished them a happy life."

"The stupid bitch called her family, didn't she?" I wanted to groan. The first rule of escape—cut off all ties. Lose everything.

Another shrug from Ezra. This one more defeated than the last. I wanted to slap him.

"I wasn't really paying attention. Her father brought her back, Raoul was dealt with, and negotiations resumed...sometime around when I took Lainey to the island."

It was my turn to rub a hand over my face. My head hurt. "When did you know?"

"I thought I had more time. I just needed to get Oksana to leave this time and not look back... but after Raoul, all she wants is freedom from her father. So she'd very much prefer I marry her and give her that."

So, without kidnapping and killing her myself, she was a player on the board who wasn't going to cooperate. Fuck. I turned away from him to take a breath and pace off some of the fresh agitation.

"Why the announcement tonight?" Because this damn engagement had been in "negotiations" for over a decade. What made tonight so special?

"Does it matter?" Ezra said. The loss and the emptiness raked over me.

Pivoting, I strode up to him and fisted his shirt. Nose to nose, eye to eye, I glared at him. "Yes, it fucking matters. Tonight was a show. One you put on that *hurt* Lainey for some goddamn reason, then you went out of your way to provoke me."

He cut his eyes to the side.

Yes.

I was right.

Forcing my hands to unclench from his shirt, I pushed him back lightly then gripped his shoulder. "Look at me."

"Adam..."

"Fucking *look* at me," I ordered and his gaze snapped to mine. The sadness lurking in the defiance killed me. But beneath all of it was fear.

Fear of me?

"What did that sack of shit we call your father do?" 'Cause Wallace Graham had done something. Another reason I really didn't want to hit Ezra: I had no idea if he was hiding new injuries.

Even if he really did deserve a punch in the mouth.

Ezra opened his mouth then closed it again. He made a choked sound.

"Trust me," I told him. I wanted to shake him and demand that he do it, but he had to reach out to take the hand I was offering.

He blew out a ragged breath. This whole thing was a battle for him. Wrapping a hand around the back of his head, I pressed my forehead to his. There was nowhere for him to look or go that he wouldn't see me.

"Let me help you." I didn't add "like you should have already," because he didn't need those recriminations.

"He killed Genevieve," Ezra said slowly and I frowned. The name meant nothing. "She—was a fuck buddy. Just—a casual fling. He had her tortured—raped, disfigured, and then killed."

Why the fuck... "A warning."

Ezra attempted to nod, but he couldn't with my grip on him. Instead he licked his dry lips and whispered, "Yes. He said anyone could be gotten to—Lainey Benedict could just as easily be a victim as Genevieve."

I was going to kill that son of a bitch.

"He found out about...others." His throat bobbed. "Just...a couple of very casual experiments. They—he didn't even care about who they were, just that they were more indiscretions to be removed."

Understanding settled in my bones. "Men?"

Discomfort flickered over Ezra's expression, but he couldn't hide it. "It's—yes. I—It was—we've never talked about this."

No. We hadn't. "We haven't talked about a lot of things," I said slowly. "That changes now."

I gripped his head a little tighter when he would have pulled back and waited for his gaze to fix on mine. I kept my eyes focused on his for a long moment before allowing him to pull back.

"You've been fighting all of this like you're on your own. That stops. Now."

"You don't—"

"Yes," I said, shutting him down. "I do. Because you're right. Some of this is my fault. Some of this is my single-mindedness. I accept that responsibility. The rest is you're my best friend. You go. I go. He comes for you. He's coming for me."

"Adam..." Ezra swallowed hard. "If I just marry her, then it protects Lainey. It protects you. She's probably better off without me...you too."

"Okay, see I wasn't going to hit you."

He blinked at me. "What?"

I punched him and he staggered back against the car. The blow made my hand ache, but it definitely rocked him. "I said I wasn't going to hit you, and then you said something really fucking stupid. Now...we're going in to see your cousin for whatever reason we're here for and after that, we'll figure out the next step."

The next conversation.

Because there was going to be a much longer one, when we were alone.

"New Year, new start. Together."

The shock on his face was a punch in the gut. I'd really fucking let him down if he thought I'd abandon him.

Yeah. Shit was definitely changing.

"Adam—" He threw himself at me and I caught him in a hard hug. The tightness in his grip betrayed just how much he thought we were done.

Changes.

Changes and repairs.

"I got you," I told him. I had no idea where the fuck any of this was going but... "I got you."

CHAPTER
SIX

LAINEY

As promised, there were plenty of clothes in the closet and dresser in a variety of sizes. All of it was new, the tags were still attached, and frankly, I appreciated that. Borrowing a shirt or pants was one thing, but I didn't really want to wear someone else's panties or bra.

The shower helped. The hot water left my cold skin flushed and chased away the chills. It also allowed me time to rebuild walls and regain my composure. Ezra was engaged to be married.

I barely registered the name of his fiance. Like I should know the name, but I couldn't quite place it. Pretty Boy was stuck with King until we figured out his play. Adam was—doing whatever he was doing.

Ezra was engaged.

That thought seemed to keep chasing its tail like a serpent that couldn't quite settle. When he came to dance with me, he wanted to tell me something. It had been all over his face and in his eyes.

For the guy who could eviscerate with his tongue and never seemed at a loss for words, he'd said *nothing*. Then his father called him up there. Then and only then had he found something to say...

"I'm sorry," he whispered before he turned away. At first, I thought I'd imagined it. His voice had been so low, barely there, and then he was gone. I'd still been turning it over in my mind when Wallace and Dinah Graham announced the engagement.

While I didn't think I'd ever had an out-of-body experience before, that moment was the closest I might have ever come. Pain scraped through me. It *hurt*. Him kissing her hadn't hurt, but the look of determination on his face...

I swiped away any tears with the water. Free of all the cosmetics and my hair freshly washed, I half-considered just collapsing on the bed in the guest room. My energy seemed to have drained out of me.

As much as I thought I could sleep, I didn't want to face my dreams. Not when so much was unknown. Too much was happening that I needed to figure out. I chose a comfortable, soft pair of gray sweatpants and a loose, over-sized matching sweatshirt. The plain bra and panties were cotton and new.

It was kind of like putting on armor, while not fresh off a designer's rack and outfitted with all the right accessories, the soft thickness with the light fleece lining helped. I found a pair of thick socks to pull on over my icy toes before I headed downstairs.

The rich aroma of coffee filled the air along with hints of onions, garlic, and... other spices. Was he cooking?

I found my host in the kitchen. He'd also changed. Like

me, he'd chosen sweats, but he'd skipped a shirt. The scars on his back riveted me. Pretty Boy had scars, some old and some more recent, including burns delivered by Emersyn's uncle.

Ezra bore scars too. Some were older that he never talked about, and the others were from being shot almost a year earlier. Adam—did Adam have scars? He'd never let me see him shirtless.

Maybe he did.

Phillip's scars, however, weren't just from gunshot wounds. He'd been stabbed in the same incident that Ezra had been shot during. There were older scars, graveled marks like he'd gotten torn up with rocks and sand. I'd had a burn from a riding accident once when I slid.

My grandmother had treated it with a gel. You couldn't even see the marks on my thigh anymore. No one had done that for Phillip.

"Coffee is ready," he said as I lifted my gaze to find him watching me in the mirrored backsplash over the stove.

"Sorry," I murmured. He'd caught me staring, and beyond anything else, it was rude.

"You can look at me, Buttercup. I'm not shy." He pointed me toward the carafe. There was an espresso machine right next to the tall coffee maker. "Mugs are in the cabinet above. There's sugar on the side and powdered creamer. None of the good stuff, I'm afraid. But you generally drink it black."

"I do," I admitted. "Would you like a cup as well?"

"Probably not going to sleep any time soon, so might as well."

It registered with me that the clock read after seven.

Seven in the morning.

"I need to call my grandfather," I said, pouring each of us a mug. "And you take it black, right?"

"I take it however you want to give it to me."

The bland delivery pulled me up short and I cut a look at him. The barest hint of a teasing grin touched his lips. "Flirting is weird."

He shrugged. "You flirt with the wrong people, Buttercup."

I passed him the mug, and he nodded toward the table. "Your purse is there. You left it in the car."

Touching his arm lightly, I carried my coffee over to the oak table in the corner of the kitchen. Like the bedroom upstairs, it was clearly well-appointed, and everything had a newish look to it, well-tended and cared for... at the same time, it was cozy.

As I pulled out my phone, I caught him watching me again, and a smile pulled at the corners of my mouth. This was not the type of place I imagined would suit him and yet —he really seemed at home.

Three messages waited for me on my screen.

Adam: Tell me where you are.

Adam: Tell me you're alright.

Adam: Don't make me turn on the tracker on your phone.

I rolled my eyes. The messages were at different times throughout the night. I needed to make sure he didn't have a tracker on my phone. For now, I just sent him a message that said I was fine and I would talk to him later, then put his thread in do not disturb before I switched to the phone and called home.

The butler answered on the second ring. "I'm sorry for calling so early, Branson, but I wanted to leave a message for my grandfather."

Grandfather was not up yet; he liked to sleep in on New Year's. That was a relief. After letting them know there'd been a change of plans, I said I'd inform them when I was heading back.

The butler didn't question me, and I didn't offer any explanations. I sank down into the chair and sipped my coffee before I switched to the app I used to talk to Pretty Boy.

One message.

I'm here.

Two words, but they were an embrace and even as I stared at them, they vanished. I wrote back my own response.

I'm safe.

It was true. I was safe. Closing the app, I moved to Ezra's thread and there was nothing, but Emersyn's had a cheery message for a *Happy New Year* with a crazy picture of her and three of her guys kissing her cheeks.

She looked—ridiculously happy.

"You should call her," Bodhi said as he slid a plate onto the table in front of me. I hadn't even realized how close he was. Thankfully, I didn't throw my phone away when I gave a little start.

"Not right now," I said. "But maybe later. She's happy and things are going well for her. I don't want her to worry."

He pulled out the chair across from me and set his own plate down. The food smelled amazing. Ham and cheese omelets, fried potatoes with onions and peppers, and toast.

"She'd want to worry, Lainey B."

I sighed. "I know she would. I also know she'd show up here armed for bear if I needed her. But she's happy—for the first time in a very long time, she's happy and she's safe and I want her to stay that way."

Bodhi locked eyes with me.

"So, let me choose when to tell her?

"I won't lie," he said, "if she asks me. I doubt she will, but if she does, I won't lie to her. She's tougher than you think."

"She's tougher than anyone I know," I told him before I took another sip of coffee. "But this involves her brother and she adores him. Her father—" I thought about King. "—a man none of us really understand and she is *not* a fan of him."

Pretty Boy blamed him for what happened to Em. I got that. If he hadn't abandoned them, if he'd been an actual father, maybe she'd never have been adopted by the Sharpes.

Then I'd never have known either of them.

Another sigh escaped me... "Just, let me figure out what is going on, and then I'll talk to her." Right now, I had more questions than answers.

"She'd want to help."

That I knew.

However, he didn't continue to pursue that line. "I want to help."

"I got that," I said, before I used the fork to dig into the food. It tasted—amazing. As soon as I started eating, it hit me how hungry I was. "I appreciate it," I told him in between bites. It took discipline to not shovel it in at speed. Especially with how hungry I was. "Thank you for making this. And thank you for getting me out of there."

He met my glance with a nod, then we were both quiet as we ate. Only after we were done and we'd traded coffee for water did he say anything.

"You should sleep."

I shook my head. "Probably," I admitted even if it was at odds with me shaking my head. "Not sure I can right now."

Or even if I wanted to.

"Sleep is vital. It helps cognitive function. Lack of sleep begins to erode it and damages your decision making facilities." The dry recitation had me lifting my brows.

"It also makes me a grumpy Lainey, or so I've heard."

That earned me a flicker of a smile. "I don't mind grumpy."

"You've never seen me grumpy."

"I saw you the night of the masquerade in the library."

I opened my mouth then closed it again before I nodded. Touché.

"Come," he said, holding out his hand.

I didn't ask where we were going, I just took his hand and moved with him. He set the alarm on the doors then shut off the lights.

The sun was up—well if you could call it that—but the skies were a deep, leaden gray. As dismal and mournful as I felt.

Bodhi led upstairs and to his room. When he pushed open that door and guided me inside, I eyed him.

"This isn't about sex," he told me before he closed the door and locked it. With a brief kiss to my hand, he let me go and walked over to the adjoining door then locked it too.

I stood there in the middle of the room as he made a circuit, closing the heavy curtains and blocking out even the weak light. The darkness was a warm blanket.

"Sex would be nice, but that's not what you need right now, or what I want to take." He was behind me, resting his hands lightly on my hips as he pressed against my back. The heat of him stole through me and some distant, primitive part of me reminded me that Bodhi was a dangerous man.

A very dangerous one.

He was Trouble, in so many ways.

But he was also Phillip.

He'd never been anything but kind to me.

"No?" I said into the silence. Because now that he'd brought it up, the idea sent a wave of tingles through me.

"No," he murmured, his lips next to my ear. "You see, sex should be earth-shaking, life affirming, and even fun. It can be a comfort and a celebration. It can also be a rage and a demand to survive—proof of pleasure in the face of agony..."

Shivers went through me.

"No matter the reason, it should always be focused on the person you choose. Right now, you're worried about three others that I can think of. Preoccupied with their choices and what is happening. More, you're playing a game of chess on a three dimensional board with more players than you even know are in the game..."

Every single syllable was a caress, winding my body higher and higher.

"As sexy as that is, Buttercup..." His lips were against my skin now, teasing my flesh with a combination of touch, breath, and vibration. "When I make love to you, the only things you are going to feel, see, hear, or experience is me. Those others may have a part of your heart, but when you're in my bed and in my arms, the only thing you will know is me."

My eyes closed as he wrapped his arm around me and pressed his hand against my abdomen.

"Like I told you earlier," he continued as if he hadn't just sent wild shudders eddying through my system. "I'm a patient man. You need to sleep. I need to hold you and keep you safe. There will be no sex in that bed today. Will you stay?"

All of that and then he asked just that one question. Relaxing back into him, I blew out a long breath. "I feel like you just seduced me with your words."

I swore I could feel his smile against my cheek before he nudged me forward. I had to trust him because I couldn't see shit.

"Just wait until I use my hands," he teased and a laugh escaped me. "We might have to wait on my lips and my cock. I wouldn't want to overwhelm you."

Then I tumbled onto the bed and he followed after me. We didn't climb under the sheets or change. I was still in my sweats, and he dragged a comforter up to lay over us before he wrapped me up and tucked me against his chest.

My eyes burned at the nearness, the shelter.

"Sleep, Lainey B," he said. "Nothing will bother you."

The oath resonated.

"Phillip," I whispered. "I love them."

"I know," he said. "We'll make sure they survive. Now sleep."

Could I? Between his sensuous words and caring, he'd woken up an ache in me even as he soothed a much more jagged wound.

The sound of his heart beat beneath my ear lulled me even as he wrapped me into a cocoon that kept the world out.

Sleep should have been impossible, but I slipped away so fast I barely had time to marvel at it.

What I'd said to Pretty Boy was the absolute truth.

I was safe.

CHAPTER
SEVEN

BODHI

Hours after I closed them to sleep, my eyes snapped open. Awareness swarmed me, and I cataloged the differences immediately. I was in my bed in the house in Virginia. A house I brought *no one* that was a part of any world I occupied to visit.

The only visitors allowed were those in transition. When I brought them, it was usually for no longer than a night or two. Then they left and never returned. Those arrivals never even saw where the house was, much less the route to get here.

The night before, I'd left the Graham Fire and Ice party after putting Lainey Benedict in my rental car then took her out of New York entirely. I might as well have been on autopilot. She had an apartment in the city, but otherwise she typically lived at Der Sonne on Long Island with her grandfather.

Either might seem to have been a reasonable destination. Take her somewhere away from the machinations and plotting of the Grahams and whatever they were doing with the Dovzhenkos.

The name had registered during the announcement, but I hadn't quite pieced it together until the drive. A shift of weight pressing against my side and a low sound escaping her throat reminded me of my guest.

My guest.

The description didn't even deserve a mental scoff. Lainey B was far more than a "guest." Another sound, this one closer to a whimper, had me pressing my lips to the top of her head even as I tightened my arm around her.

The tension threading her muscles eased, and gradually she relaxed against me once more. The soft feather of her breath teased over my skin. Lainey Benedict was in my bed, and I couldn't say I'd ever pictured her there.

Yet, now that she was, I had zero intention of letting her be anywhere else. I rolled my head from side to side. It cracked and released some of the aggravation as I turned the previous day over in my head.

Not just the party. Not just the flight. Not just the revelation the Grahams had purchased that girl for their son or maybe negotiated it. Arranged marriages happened far more often than most of my generation liked to admit.

My father's marriage to my mother had been one. Isla Cavendish hadn't stood a chance against my family. She never stood one against my father.

Anger struck a match inside of me. I forced my hands to open their grip rather than dig my fingers into her side or her hip. Flattening my palm to that curve, I let myself soak in her nearness.

Discipline kept my breathing slow and even. A glance at my watch showed it had only been four hours since I brought her up here to sleep. To sleep and to make a promise. The way her pupils dilated when we'd been at the rest stop and the hitch to her breathing here—the interest I had developed in her was mutual.

However, I meant what I'd told her. She wasn't ready for me yet. Her heart had been bruised and battered. Her fighting spirit choked. The signs were there—not all cages needed bars. Hers didn't.

Control the ones she loved and you could cage her without closing a single door or barring a single window. I should have seen it sooner.

Unfortunately for all of them, I was looking now. Another hour passed while I soaked in the feel of her. Savored the closeness and the peace. It was quiet here. No sounds of the city beyond the windows. No movement. No people.

Just us.

The only noises came from the soft notes of her breathing. The occasional rasp of her hair moving against my skin as she shifted her head. The fact I'd been listening so closely was probably why the shift in her breathing, and the faint increase in her heart rate and the subtle but perceptible bit of tension alerted me to the fact she was awake.

"You're still with me," I said softly. The bedroom had blackout curtains. I liked it dark when I slept. Not only did they block the light, but they also helped to muffle the sound. It kept it warmer in the winter and cooler in the summer.

"That wasn't a dream," she whispered against my skin. She curled her fingers where they rested against my abdomen and I smiled into the dark.

"No, I'm real. You can pinch me if you need it."

A gentle laugh escaped her and she lifted her head. I

missed the weight of it almost immediately. "How does pinching you prove that you're real?"

"Cause I pinch back," I offered and that earned me another chuckle. Little by little, she sat up. I kept my arm loose around her, but she didn't try to move away.

The shift of movement told me when she rubbed a hand against her face. I could imagine her, sleep-rumpled and maybe a bit disheveled, but still possessing that innate poise she'd had all her life.

I gave her a moment to collect herself. "How did you sleep?"

"Hard." Her voice held a note of bafflement. "I didn't think I'd even be able to go to sleep, much less stay there. Thank you."

"You're welcome." Another beat and I slipped my arm from her waist. "I'm going to sit up."

"You're being very careful with me," was her only comment as I braced my hands against the bed and pushed up.

We'd slept under the weight of a comforter, so I just scooted back, then adjusted the pillows so I could sit against the headboard. "I'm a careful guy."

"No," she said slowly. "Not always."

"It's a little early to call me out."

"You can take it," she said and the bed shifted and moved as she came to sit next to me. The warmth of her shoulder brushing mine settled something inside of me.

"I like confidence in the people around me."

"You like to control the narrative too." Twice in as many minutes.

"What happens when I get you coffee?" Because now I was curious.

"I don't know," she said with a long sigh. "I don't know how I'm going to do a lot of this."

"I'm going to turn on the light—"

"Wait," she said, halting me. "I—I'm not ready for the day yet."

I let my hand drop back to the bed. "You're ready for anything."

"Sometimes," she admitted, and a smile touched my lips. I liked that she didn't downplay it or try to pretend a modesty she didn't need. "Not sure about today. I'm still trying to wrap my head around last night."

"What part is still troubling you?"

She didn't answer immediately, and I didn't press. Instead, I just leaned there in the dark, aware of her sitting right next to me. Somewhere inside of her, she pulled at the different threads knotting inside and keeping all bound up.

"I want to know why he did it."

"You know why..." Even as I said the words, I recognized the plain truth in them. Ezra Graham was an idiot. He'd been an idiot in school, and he was an idiot now. Hot-tempered, high strung, and very much a victim of abuse.

I recognized the signs.

Wallace Graham was a shitty man. His secrets had teeth.

Reed was always looking out for Ezra. His family was every bit as corrupt and shady as Graham's own. Their money wasn't that old, but it had been dipped in blood. Soaked in it.

Still all but dripped with it.

Like recognized like.

The Cavendishes were the same.

"He's sacrificing himself."

"Possibly," I offered, and she huffed.

"You just said I knew why."

"I did," I agreed with her.

"Then why are you saying possibly?"

"Because you give Graham far more credit than I ever could." Then, because I could almost feel the tempest in her rising, I continued, "He wears his weakness for everyone to see. The drunkenness, the reckless affairs, and the desire he has to have everyone punch him in the face a few times."

"Phillip..."

I didn't smile, but the scold in her voice as she said my name almost made me not mind it. "It's the truth, Lainey. You can love the man and he can still be flawed. Just—see the flaws before you forgive and accept them."

She thumped her head back against the padded headboard. "I hate this."

"I know. There are a few things that I know, truths if you will, that are important. You need to know them too. They'll protect you when you have to wade into this war."

Because it was a war. Everything those assholes were doing to keep her out of it was not going to work. She'd always been in, they just hadn't seen it. To be fair, I'd let my own obsessions preoccupy me.

I'd need to be more focused on the present.

"What truths are those?"

"Everything comes down to money and power. It always has." My family. Their families. Hers. Her grandfather might be a good man *to* her and *for* her, but he was a power broker. He wielded his influence and his wealth like a hammer when necessary and like a scalpel when the situation called for it.

Leopold Benedict knew more about where the bodies were buried than just about anyone else. The trick was, he kept his own secrets carefully secured, and the only weakness he had—a daughter—he'd cut off. Until she provided him with another heir.

"I've heard that before," she said with a sigh.

"You were probably weaned on it, just as I was—as Reed and Graham were." I doubted Hardigan suffered from a similar upbringing, because of his background. Then again, he doubtlessly understood the power of wealth and influence. Power offered freedom and the man had his freedom curtailed not that long ago.

"Grandfather..." She didn't finish the sentiment, and I smiled.

"Has schooled you well," I suggested. "But he hasn't given you a hunger for that power, or a driving desire to take it away from everyone around you so that they must turn to you."

"No." Her frown positively echoed in her words. "He's only ever taught me to protect myself. Protect those I care about."

"He taught you loyalty." I sighed. "That loyalty is why I was in your grandfather's house that night."

That night.

The night we met.

"He kept a secret for someone I cared about. A secret I needed to take, but he'd given his word to never tell me."

She didn't ask, but curiosity would be there. It would fill her hazel eyes until the green peeked through the brown like the dance of summer escaping a cloudy day.

"My mother trusted him with a letter and a journal. He saw her three days before she died. She gave it to him then." Learning that had taken time. When I'd asked him directly, anger had coursed through me. Anger and outrage. How dare he keep something of my mother's from me, but old

Leopold Benedict had merely given me a sad smile and put his hand on my shoulder.

"Son, she didn't want this fight for you. If I hadn't given her my word, I would give this to you. But all I can do now is honor that word to her."

I'd hated him. He'd had the information for two years. Since before her funeral.

Before she died.

He'd visited her at the hospital and if not for the wrong log being stored in her things when they were returned to us—I wouldn't have known.

As much as I wanted to rage at the man, I'd respected his candor. He didn't make excuses or false promises. Just told me it was all he could do.

Then I began to plan.

A week later, I broke into his corporate office.

A week after that, his apartment.

The third week, I'd gone to Der Sonne and into his office there. I'd found the letters and the journal. I'd taken more than that from his safe, rather than point him in my direction.

The only thing that could have given me away was the little girl on the stairs who'd caught me coming out of his office.

Who had never betrayed my secret.

"You asked me about my mother," I said. "I have a story to tell you, and it'd probably be better over coffee. Then we can compare notes and make plans for Graham, Reed, and Hardigan."

She blew out a breath, but then I brushed my fingers along the side of her hand.

"Trust me?"

When she slid her fingers through mine, I had an answer.

"Light," I warned, then reached out to snap it on. When I glanced at her, I found her blinking away from the light but not from me. She was every bit as beautiful and poised as I imagined, even with her hair in a wild disarray.

Someday soon, I promised her silently, I was going to break through that poise and control, until we were both wild with need.

Then I would drink in the sight of her like that too.

I wanted her more than my next breath of air, and the longer I was around her, the more firm my conviction became.

CHAPTER
EIGHT

LAINEY

In the kitchen, the light of day waited for us, even if it was still leaden skies and dreary. At least it was snow that had begun falling while we slept and not rain. It was just after lunchtime, and Bodhi went to work preparing food.

Since he had an espresso machine, I took that over. Regular coffee would be fine for after food. At the moment, I wanted something to soothe myself.

There was a kind of quiet comfort in working together. He prepared grilled ham and cheese sandwiches with slices of tomato in them. At my questioning look, he said, "A different story for a different day."

That seemed fair. The sleep had done more than just let me rest. It had allowed me to gain some distance. Bodhi had been right, I did know why Ezra had played along with that announcement the night before.

He'd martyred himself.

Was he following in Pretty Boy's footsteps, or had something else happened?

As soon as the milk finished steaming, I filled both of our cups and then carried the lattes over to the table. Bodhi followed and set the sandwiches down. As with earlier in the day, he sat next to me rather than across from me.

We ate in silence; however, my appetite was minimal. I favored the coffee more. Still, I needed the fuel. I wasn't going to survive if I let my moods dictate when I ate.

Even that mental shake wasn't enough to encourage more bites. When I'd finished at least half, I leaned back in my seat only to find Bodhi studying me.

"Done?"

At my nod, he rose and then pulled back my chair as I stood.

"Leave the dishes."

Coffee in hand, he guided me toward the sitting room we'd barely glanced at—I kept wanting to say the night before but it really was only a few hours earlier. All sense of time seemed fleeting.

Time...

"Happy New Year," I muttered the belated greeting even as I took a seat on the sofa. In the casual clothes, I worried less about decorum and curled my legs under me.

"That remains to be seen," he told me. "But as starts of years go—this one hasn't been too bad."

The barest hint of a wink pulled a huffed laugh out of me. "I'm almost afraid to ask about those."

"You don't have to be," he assured me before he moved over to the fireplace to get the fire started. "Some years, I barely even notice that it's changed. Others... well, they weren't important. This one is different."

"Why?"

"You."

With that cryptic answer, and the fire beginning to lick along the wood, he returned to the sofa and took a seat next to me. Like me, he turned partially, one leg folded so he could face me.

"My mother died when I was sixteen."

Sorrow unfurled beneath those words, an ache of old pain.

"She was—a good woman," he said slowly. "Beautiful. Kind. But always troubled. I was an only child. Raised—typically, nannies, a governess, tutor, then boarding school."

He listed off the details like they were the expectation, and I couldn't fault him. I'd had a nanny when I was younger. In addition to my grandparents, Nanny Kota had been one of the primary beacons of my early childhood.

She returned when I was home from school, and for a time, she transitioned to being a companion for my grandmother before the dementia grew to the point of hospice.

A wry smile turned up the corners of his mouth. "My mother was an incredible woman, far too fragile for our world, but she was always incredibly kind. She treated life like an adventure, and when I was home or around her, we would play."

My heart twisted at the wistfulness in his description. The ache of missing her seemed to decorate each word.

"I was away at school a lot, so I didn't see the early signs. But she was committed when I was eight. I should say, she was committed again. The first time occurred the first year after I went to boarding school—within months."

When I reached a hand over to place on his, he caught my fingers and squeezed them gently.

"Forgive me, Buttercup. It's been a long time since I spoke about her."

"You really don't have to tell me," I promised him. When I'd asked, it had been to assuage my own curiosity. He didn't, and shouldn't, need to open a vein.

"I don't mind telling you," he said, tracing a thumb over one of my nails. "I just—haven't spoken about her in a long time. Not the full story. No one in my family mentions her any longer. In truth, I would accept it, except that I know lies were told. I saw the truth with my own eyes."

"I'm listening...and whatever I can do to help, I will." I wasn't sure what I could do. Not really. Sometimes, however, the mere act of offering assistance could help someone else. At the same time, I meant it. I would help him, and I listened with an ear for what I could do.

"When I was first sent off to boarding school, I didn't want to go. It was far away from her and our home. I wouldn't even see her on weekends. It would be ten long weeks before the first break came that let me go home.

"What I didn't know then, but I learned later, was she spent eight of those ten weeks in her own boarding situation. She'd had an emotional breakdown. Apparently, she hadn't wanted me to go either and grew rather hysterical when I was put in the car and taken away."

His mouth compressed into a thin line, and I waited him out. The night before had seemed almost impossible in some ways and he'd been a rock for me. I could do no less for him.

"But I didn't know that. When I came home, she was excited to see me and we spent the whole week 'adventuring,' and then I went back to school until the winter break. That set the tone for the next few years. A few weeks at home, the rest at school."

His grip on my hand was infinitely light, yet I could feel the weight pressing down on him.

"She did well, after the first year. But I think she missed me as much as I missed her. She would write me letters. I got them nearly every day, sometimes every other day. Funny letters. Sweet letters. Letters with games in them... they were our secret. The letters, the code we wrote them in."

My heart squeezed tight for the loss hanging off each syllable.

"When I was eight and came home for break, it was the first time she wasn't there. The letters had still been coming, but fewer and farther apart. I was busy, I'd made friends, and I was doing well. I didn't need them as much. No one would tell me where she was, my father didn't have time for it or me. One of my aunts came by to get me, and she took me to the sanitarium—or I should say the latest one—and Mom was so overjoyed to see me.

"I can't say it was the reunion anyone planned. She was so much quieter than normal and so tired. I was worried she was ill. But she brightened while I was there. Before I left, she gave me another letter. I asked my aunt if we could go back the next day—" His smile turned almost bittersweet. "It was a kindness she showed me, taking me there. She and my step-grandmother, Sophia, were the only two who never made any judgments about my mother's condition or my need to see her."

A long sigh escaped him, and he tilted his head back. The darkness in his eyes seemed to writhe, shadows layering upon shadows. Dark secrets and hidden pain boiling up to the surface.

"After that visit, she was in the hospital more than out of it. Every time I came home, she seemed to have grown worse in the interim, but she always showed improvement when I was there."

I frowned. "You were worried she needed you." What a burden to put on a small child.

"She did need me. I didn't understand how much then as I do now—nor did I have the capacity to see past the games being played all around us. The illusions. The gaslighting." He shook his head. "Mother was never as strong as I imagined—or even as she did. In our games, she was always the princess or the queen who needed to be saved. Sometimes, she was the wise one who gave her young knight a quest to retrieve something magical for her... What I didn't see then was that she was never the hero of her own story."

Then his mother died. I was trying to remember the dates, but I didn't think I'd been very old at the time, and it was a wisp of a memory I couldn't hold on to.

"As her stays in the hospitals grew longer, she was moved. Different facilities, different doctors, different treatments. My father couldn't be bothered, thought she was showing the weakness in her aristocratic blood. Clearly, it was better no one else saw it—because what if she'd passed it on to me?"

Only his snort and scoff kept my temper in check. What an absolute bastard.

"When I was fourteen, I discovered I was very good at slipping out of school unnoticed. I'd been tapped for the Royals, and I'd told the recruiter at the time to go to hell. The second time, they tried to beat me into submission. Three of them left with broken hands and the fourth had to drive them."

A mirthless smile touched his face.

"In all my years in school, I'd pursued the attributes my

mother said a knight needed to have. Intelligence. Cunning. Combat." Then he lifted his gaze to mine. "The ability to be absolutely ruthless. For eight years, she'd been in and out of institutions. Almost never at home. But that year was the first time I got to go and see her without anyone being notified ahead of time."

My stomach dropped.

"She was not well, and she was so out of it. They kept her on drugs for compliance, but it was more than that—she had bruises. Marks—some self-inflicted," he continued and sounded almost reluctant to say so. "But not all of them. The doctors didn't think they had to answer to me, but I made such a stink that Mother was moved to another facility. This one was harder to get to... not impossible."

"Phillip," I said softly. "Bodhi, I'm so sorry."

"That was not the worst of it. At least when I saw her, she would be lucid, but I got a better idea of what they were doing to her. On my fifteenth birthday, she told me she was pregnant and she was afraid."

I froze.

Oh my god.

"She didn't want me to tell anyone, she said she was trying to keep it a secret because last time, they made her terminate."

Last time...

Horror crawled out from every corner.

"I made a point of visiting every chance I got, and when they wouldn't let me in—I broke in." Grim pride echoed in his voice. "She was pregnant, Buttercup. Growing more each month. She hid it with her clothes, but toward the end there was nothing that could be done to disguise it. She wasn't a small woman."

I didn't want him to finish. Nothing in this story cried happy ending, and yet, he needed to purge this too.

"Then I got a call at school, pulled out of my classes because Mother had died. A car would come for me, the service would be private, and there would be no public spectacle."

He shook his head and the sadness in his expression transformed. It became anger.

"I asked about my brother or my sister, what happened to them?" Disgust curled his lips. "I was told there was no baby. She'd never been pregnant. When I pointed out that I'd been there, I'd *seen* it, my father told me it was all a lie she'd concocted. Another part of her delusion."

"Your father—"

"Didn't give a damn. He just wanted to erase her, and he was fine with pretending none of it ever happened. He scoffed about her even being able to get pregnant. How would she in the hospital?"

I was no fool and clearly, neither was Bodhi.

"Everyone lied. The doctors. The nurses. The orderlies. Everyone. They swore she was never pregnant and that maybe I was imagining things because I couldn't accept her illness. Maybe I was delusional...who knew, her condition could be hereditary."

"Those sons of bitches." I wanted to slap the shit out of them. He'd just lost his mother and they...

Bodhi lifted my hand and kissed it. "That night when I met you—your grandfather had a letter from my mother. One she'd made him promise to never give to me. A last quest, but one she didn't want to give me. Still...she'd written it all down in a code that we'd always used..."

I was almost terrified to ask. "What was the quest?"

"To find my sibling, because she knew they were going

to take him or her away. She'd heard them. She didn't want to lose another child. Not after they'd taken me and terminated the other pregnancy. She had a baby before she died... and *everyone* lied about it. Everyone."

"That's why you had to speak to the nurse..."

"It's taken me more than a decade, but I've hunted most of them down. Gotten the bits and pieces they had. One of her doctors was at Pinetree—"

Where he'd met Em.

"Another at Shady Oaks." He shook his head. "I knew it was an impossible quest from the day I read that letter, but I have to finish it. I have to know if they're out there—my little brother or my little sister. Mother wanted them safe."

I wanted to cry for him. "But she made Grandfather promise to not give you the letter?"

He gave a little shrug. "Maybe she thought I was too young or maybe she thought it was too dangerous. All I know is that it was the last thing she ever asked me to do— I refuse to fail."

"Then you won't," I told him. "How can I help?"

There were already so many battles being waged around me. I could do something about this one. I *wanted* to do something.

"You've helped me all along," he told me. "You kept my secret." His whole expression gentled.

Putting the coffee aside, I moved to climb into his lap and then I wrapped my arms around him. He shuddered, one long, body shaking shudder, as he tightened his embrace around me.

I'd never needed to give someone a hug so much, and the trembling in him suggested he needed to receive it as much as I needed to offer it.

I had no idea how we were going to do any of this. But

we were going to find his sibling, find out what the hell was going on with Ezra, defeat the damn man King, and find a way to put all these disparate pieces back together.

CHAPTER
NINE

EZRA

As promised, Nicky waited for us inside. My cousin rose when we came in and gave me a long look before he flicked a glance at Adam. They knew each other, but Nicky needed to know it was all right to talk with Adam here. "We can trust him," I said despite the cost of pushing the words out.

"You sure about that?" Nicky said, his gaze pinned on Adam. "Last I heard, he'd abandoned you for his own plan."

Adam let out a sigh, but his expression turned to granite. Before he could take a step forward at Nicky's blatant challenge, I raised a hand. "I know what I said. Things have changed."

"You mean, things have changed *again*?" Nicky returned his attention to me. The questions in his eyes, I got it. He'd been doing a lot of work for me behind the scenes. Our relationship wasn't one most knew about, and he could do things I couldn't.

I spared Adam a glance. The fact he'd followed me from

the party meant something. As angry with him as I'd been, I needed proof he was in my corner. Assurance he hadn't fucking forgotten, especially when it felt like he'd abandoned me. Abandoned Lainey. Abandoned *us*. My heart spasmed at the thought of my sharp-clawed kitten.

No, not mine.

Not anymore.

I'd probably severed any right I had to call her that tonight. I'd done it willfully, right down to the kiss with Oksana. It had startled her, but she'd returned it enthusiastically. The fact I felt nothing for her at all was not her fault.

Adam clasped a hand on my shoulder. The contact was too much, and his fingers seemed to burn all the way through my jacket to leave an imprint on my flesh. We still had a lot to talk about. Dread crawled through me at the idea, but I couldn't just keep standing here. Not knowing was hell, but rejection would be so much worse. I stepped forward and Adam's hand fell away.

Good. I needed a clear head. "Let Adam pay you a retainer, then he's your client too. That should shield all three of us?"

Nicky frowned as he pushed the chair back. The kitchen was done in dark green tile, but lighter green curtains for the windows. There were decorations on the walls and a photo on the fridge of Nicky and...

"It might work," he said. "But we should be careful. I'm going to draw up a contract. Give me five minutes." Then at the door, he paused to look at both of us. "Get coffee. Sit down. Don't talk until I'm back."

That earned Nicky a dark look from Adam, not that my cousin seemed to give a damn. Then the door was swinging as he vanished through it.

"You got Dominic involved in this?" Adam ignored the

advice first thing as he stripped off his coat and tossed it over the back of a chair before he headed to the coffee pot.

"He's been involved for a while." Arms folded, I studied the woman in the photo with Nicky. Her expression was bemused and his besotted. He'd never introduced me. Then again, she kept him on his toes so maybe that was a good thing. Nicky deserved the best. "You can trust him."

"I'm struggling with trusting you at the moment," Adam reminded me. "But I *know* you."

"You know him too," I said, forcing myself to pivot and face Adam. The air seemed almost too heavy to breathe. Heavy with everything we weren't discussing. Maybe we should never let it out. Words couldn't be taken back. Once they were out, they were out.

I should never have kissed him.

What the fuck had I been thinking?

Clearly, I hadn't been. "He's helped before, remember?" I fought to get us back onto this topic and stay away from the darker, deeper waters.

Adam filled a second mug with coffee then held it out to me. If I wanted it, I was going to have to go to him to get it. Dick.

He didn't so much as twitch. His eyes looked more purple than blue-violet in the light. Dark and demanding. If I didn't need the coffee so damn bad... I crossed the room to take it. Just as I wrapped my hand around the body of the mug, the door pushed back in with Nicky's return.

Relief had my shoulders dropping as Adam released the mug to me. Instead of commenting, all he did was shake his head before he shifted his attention to Nicky.

"Papers for me to sign?"

"Yep." Nicky set them down on the table. "Ezra is going

to have to witness. Retainer is five thousand and I bill at five hundred an hour."

"I don't even get the friends and family discount?" Adam asked as he set his coffee aside, scanned the documents, and began signing.

"That is the friends and family discount," Nicky informed him. Once he was done, Nicky slid a card over and Adam transferred the retainer while I signed as a witness.

"Good, are we done with the bullshit excuses now?" Adam asked while Nicky stacked the papers together.

"C'mon," I said. "They aren't bullshit. Nicky is looking out for both of us."

"No, he's not," Adam said even as Nicky announced, "No, I'm not."

Fuck, I needed more alcohol for this. I took a drink of the black coffee. It was strong, more like jet fuel, and burned its way down to my stomach.

What the doctor ordered.

"Fine," I conceded. "He's looking after my interests. Let's not be pedantic, shall we?"

"We should be pedantic," Nicky said, shaking his head. "You've been taking risk after risk after risk. Now you bring him here after you told me you weren't sure you could trust him anymore?"

The dry comment coupled with the bland look put me in my place. I got it. "I know what I said," I replied, not looking at Adam. "I—I've said a lot of things."

"And I've made decisions without involving you." The concession from Adam yanked me around. "I get that," he said, focused on me and not on Nicky. "I'd apologize, but I believed in my choices at the time."

I sighed.

"Look, you made some of your own calls," he pointed out. "Did you think they were right at the time?"

Calls about Lainey.

The island.

Now dealing with this shit from my father.

"You have a point." Grudging as it was, I could admit it.

Adam chuckled. Actually. Fucking. Laughed. "You really hate being made to agree with anything."

I opened my mouth to deny it, then clamped it shut again so hard my teeth clicked. Asshole smirked at me.

"Yeah, you'd rather bite off your tongue than admit that someone else is right," Nicky added. Traitor. I glared at him, but my cousin seemed no more impressed than Adam.

"Right, you two do not get to team up against me. I refuse." With that, I yanked out a chair and sat down. "That's also not the point of this meeting."

Nicky took the papers and his mug to the counter where he poured himself another cup of coffee. "How much do you want him read in on?"

Adam pulled out the chair next to mine. It was like he had to keep invading my space. Not that I could escape the presence of him.

"Everything," Adam stated. "I can't help if I don't have all the information."

"You planning on putting your cards on the table?" This wasn't a one-way street. Frankly, I didn't want to rely on him to "save" me. Not anymore. I dug this damn hole...

"Yes," Adam said. "I told you. We're doing things differently. Now, why are we here?"

"Because a few years ago," Nicky said as he finally claimed the seat opposite us, "Ezra asked me to do a favor. Some guy in another city was on the hook for a crime, I helped him cop a plea. It took some doing, I wasn't even a barred attorney then, but I knew people. I knew how to grease those wheels. It was a calculated risk, and it undercut something the king had ordered him to do."

"You sent him to Hardigan," Adam exhaled the words, fresh shock on his face as he twisted to look at me. "That was you who got him the deal."

"He got it for himself," I said, shaking my head. "I was the one who took out the rapist though...it was my fault he was set up. I was just—doing a job. I didn't even really care, and then King told me to make sure the evidence would bury him."

"But they accused him of the rape..." Adam scrubbed a hand over his face.

"Another smoke screen," Nicky told him. "Cop to a lesser charge, avoid manslaughter. It got him three years and he would be out. If he fought it..."

"They had enough," I said. It was not one of my proudest moments. Back then Hardigan had just been a name. I'd barely connected him to Liam until it was too late. To know him now? "It was my fault he was in that position. I got it, King wanted to wreck this guy—but I had no idea why."

"He went after his own son," Adam muttered even as Nicky shrugged.

"Whatever he was doing, it took Hardigan out of the game and kept him alive. It also gave him the chance to get out of jail while you worked on figuring out more about King." That was as good summation as any. "The problem is—King has his hands in everything. He's connected—too connected."

From there, Nicky launched into the breakdown of his companies, corporations, and shell entities. King really did have tentacles everywhere, including at Reed, Graham, and more. No family that made up the core of the Bay Ridge Royals was untouched by him.

"Wait," I said. "Go down that list again?"

Nicky paused, then started again at the top.

"He's in negotiations with the Cavendish firm, but the board hasn't authorized them to go any further. So while he's pursuing them, he's not in bed with them," Nicky concluded.

"And he has no ties to Benedict...*at all*?" Adam had caught it too.

"Not that I've found. Leopold Benedict doesn't do a lot of business with *any* of the families. No deals even get presented to his board without him agreeing, and he doesn't agree with anyone or anything." Nicky folded his arms as he leaned back in his seat. Despite the fact he was up in the middle of the night by my request, he looked more impressed than tired.

"He's a cagey one," Adam said, rubbing his chin. "But how has he avoided the connection to King all this—"

"Us," I answered for him. "Otherwise, Lainey would have been tapped for the Royals. It's generational, you and I both know this. At some point, our parents have been a part of it. I don't know when King perverted it fully to his own entity, but I know he and my father have other dealings."

That was the hardest part of realizing *who* Julius King was. I *had* met him before. Seen him during social events and moved in the same circles around him. It was how he always knew what we were doing and who we were doing it with—he was one of us and not at the same time.

"That still doesn't clarify what he wants," Nicky said. "I mean if all he wants is power—then he has it. He's also amassed quite the fortune. Breaking it all down and tracing it could take a lifetime. He's got offshore accounts for sure.

I've already been to the Cayman Islands twice, but their banking laws are very specific. Without real fraud, I have no other way to get to them. It won't be easy to crack into their systems."

"I know someone," Adam said abruptly. "Give me the banking data. I'll get it taken care of."

"That sounds illegal as hell," Nicky said as he rose again. "I don't want to know anything about it."

"Done," Adam said. "What else have you two been working on?"

Nicky caught my eye when he came back with the carafe. He refilled my coffee, then Adam's, before he drained the rest into his own mug.

"We've been trying to get Oksana away from her father. There might be a way to get her into Witness Protection. Nicky's been negotiating for her. She'd be able to go, start a new life somewhere else, and never have to see him again."

"But she hasn't been cooperating the past few weeks," Nicky said with a pointed look at me. He'd warned me. Twice. And I'd tried to talk to her, but she'd always changed the subject.

"She's afraid," I pinched the bridge of my nose. All at once, the shock on Lainey's face surged into my mind's eye. It had been there, a split-second before blankness rippled over her expression. She wore an expert mask, hiding her feelings from everyone else present.

I'd wanted to warn her. To invite her to leave before it happened, but I should have known better. Someone had betrayed us, told them about her. Maybe it was my own damn fault. It didn't matter, I had to get her as far away from me as possible.

"She's surrendering," Adam said, grimly. "There are other ways to get rid of her."

"This isn't her fault," I told him. "She doesn't—didn't want this any more than I do."

"But she agreed to it," Nicky said. "She's withdrawing from the meetings I set up for her and she doesn't return my calls. Granted, I only call her on the burner but—" Now he held up a hand. "Is it possible that the phone was compromised? And she can't answer the calls?"

Fuck. A headache nested behind my eyes. "Maybe. I've only seen her a few times the past few weeks." All meals with her parents, my parents, or both present. We'd barely even been left alone.

My father had been eroding what little of my freedom had been left day by day. Did Oksana have even that much after they discovered her lover?

"I'll figure it out. We're engaged now, and he wants me to get her pregnant as soon as possible. One would think that'll earn me some privacy with her." I ignored the snap in Adam's gaze and the tightness of his mouth.

"Just remember," Nicky said. "At any time, they can be recording you. So don't have a conversation with her unless you're sure she's clean and not bugged."

I groaned. "The only way to be sure of that would be to get her naked." Not a prospect I wanted to pursue. Particularly after her reaction this evening.

"We'll figure it out," Nicky said. "Are you guys staying tonight?" Then he glanced at the windows. "Today?"

"Do you mind or is it going to bother..."

"I'm here alone right now or I would have come to meet you. I don't mind if you stay, but I do need to know if it'll be longer than a day."

Fair enough, he liked keeping his life far away from mine. Yet it had never stopped him from helping. "Thanks, Nicky."

"No problem. I'm going to my office here, I have some calls with Japan and they aren't taking today off. You know where the guest room is." With that, he saluted us. "Ezra. Reed."

Then he was gone and it was just me and Adam.

"I really fucked this up, didn't I?" I had to know, because I had. I kept seeing her face. But how the fuck did I warn her with my father watching my every move. He'd already threatened her.

"We fucked it up," Adam said, bumping my shoulder. "We'll fix it."

Exhaustion tore at me. "Adam..."

"You're tired. I'm tired. You need to sleep." So did he...

"I thought you said we would talk?"

"We will, but we're not doing it when you can barely keep your eyes open. Tomorrow—" He spared a glance at the windows. "Later today will be here. Now come on, let's find this guest room and crash."

Just like that I let him bully me up the stairs, and I headed toward the room that was over their garage. It was on the far side of the house and worked as a guest space. I'd only ever slept here twice before and always alone.

"Is she really okay?"

The door closed behind me and I turned to find Adam leaning against it. "She will be."

I frowned. "You sound certain."

"She's tougher than we think—a lot tougher than I ever gave her credit for. While I wish she was here right now where I could see her..."

Fuck did I understand that.

"...I know she's with someone who *will* keep her safe. At the moment, you need me more."

I dropped my chin to my chest. "Adam..."

96

"I told you, later. Now, bed. You care if I share it?" He motioned to the queen-sized bed in the room, and I forgot how to breathe for a moment. Fuck my life. Was he really...?

There was just the barest spark of a smirk and I groaned. "You're such an ass."

"Sometimes," he said. "But we're still sharing the bed. Nothing else—"

I braced for it.

"Nothing else," he continued. "Not tonight. Not sure about tomorrow. And in the interest of clarity, I'm not saying never. But you're emotionally compromised as hell at the moment and I'm—not much better."

"So—we just do what we've always done?"

"No, we're trying something new. We're talking. I'm aware. You know I'm aware. I've got your back." He'd said that before but, gaze locked on mine, there was no disputing the raw honesty there. "Whatever happens—I've got you."

Letting out a long, shuddering breath, I focused on him and nodded. "Well, don't get touchy feely with me now, I'm an engaged man."

Adam rolled his eyes. "You just wanna get punched again..."

Maybe, but some of the stones that had been sitting on my chest since my father dropped that bomb on me eased off.

"Flirt," I said, testing the waters and Adam just shook his head. But there was a hint of a smile there before he turned away.

That'd do.

I dragged out my phone and checked it. I ignored the other messages and checked Lainey's.

Nothing.

"She's okay," Adam said, giving me a nudge. "Get in bed."

I wanted to believe him, so I held onto that fact for now and half fell on the bed. I didn't even bother to get undressed. Who cared if the suit got rumpled? But then Adam was tugging my shoes off, and I glared down at him.

"Not my first time looking after you," he reminded me. "At least you're not throwing your guts up drunk."

I snorted.

No, I really wasn't.

And this was... kind of nice.

CHAPTER
TEN

LAINEY

As much as we could have lingered at Bodhi's place in Virginia, we didn't stay there long. At first, he indicated he had plans to tackle a different issue. While he didn't specifically invite me, he didn't reject my offer to join him. When I asked him where we were going so I could dress the part, he'd merely studied me for a moment.

"A sex club." Succinct.

"Evening wear or underwear?" I had no idea if it was my bland tone or the actual wording, but the corners of his mouth twitched.

"If I said lingerie, you'd wear it, wouldn't you?"

I shrugged. "Not sure I'd select anything with open access, but there's nothing wrong with some strategically placed lace and garters."

Playing with fire? Check.

That said, Bodhi's huff of soft laughter rewarded me for the attempt. "I'd very much like to see that," he told me.

"But an evening dress, something simple, will do. I don't plan on performing and no one will touch you that you don't allow."

He really hadn't needed to tell me the last part, but I appreciated it. It did seem like just a few hours after arriving at the hidden farm, we were on our way again. The car we'd brought down from New York was gone. A different one waited in its place. The Mercedes was classic, a restrained demonstration of wealth compared to the sexy beast I'd driven to Philadelphia.

Like the dress he'd had delivered for me, it was just another part of the world we both occupied. I was amused at how accurate he'd gotten my measurements. Instead of heels, though, he'd selected black leather boots, which seemed utterly feminine but not fragile. At my raised eyebrows, he'd just grinned.

"They emphasize how slender your legs are and the strength in your thighs. Keeps people guessing—and lusting." The compliment sent a wash of heat straight through me. It lacked any kind of flowery poetry, but I preferred the directness. A leather coat, a duster, completed the look.

Bodhi had gone for a standard tux, though he hadn't bothered with a tie and left the top two buttons open. Between those choices and the tousled nature of his darker hair, he looked every inch a rake. Once we were in the car though, I checked my phone.

I'd been avoiding messages, except for my grandfather —he just wanted to know I was well. He'd heard about Ezra's engagement and wasn't sure what he thought of it but did want to know if I'd noticed anything during the party. I'd carefully edited my answer but kept it honest when I told him I left early.

The other message I checked was from Pretty Boy.

Another check-in. I swore, I could practically feel his glower through the three words he'd typed.

How are you.

The heat of it had given me pause while I considered my actual answer. I'd showered, and made use of the new cosmetics that Bodhi had provided. I would have to compliment him later, because he'd actually found most of my favorites and in short order, though the delivery had not come directly to the house that I was aware of—he'd gone out briefly to collect them.

"I prefer to keep this house private," he'd said. I could respect the desire. It took me the time until I was in the car to come up with an answer for Pretty Boy.

Miss you. Still safe. With a friend.

He had to have seen me leave with Bodhi the night before. As much as Pretty Boy seemed to understand my relationship with Ezra—something I struggled to understand, and with Adam, despite Adam's attempts at the contrary—Bodhi was not a discussion we'd had.

"Where are you?" Bodhi asked after a beat, and I glanced over to find him casting a quick look at me before he focused on the road again. It was already dark. The sun set so early in winter. We were on a state road heading toward an interstate. I thought we might be angling toward D.C., but I hadn't specifically asked.

"Wondering when it became all right for me intellectually to be involved with several men, even if I can't define it." As blunt as that might sound, it was also the truth.

"You love them," was all he answered. "Your heart is not limited. PPG probably doesn't hurt either."

PPG.

A laugh escaped me before I could stop it. The origin of the nickname was a story I knew, and it still amused me.

Freddie, one of Em's boyfriends, called her Pretty Pussy Girl, and as awkward and mouthful of a nickname as that was, it suited the pair of them. It was how Bodhi had met her in Pinetree.

That reminder sobered some of my humor. "Just thinking about you being at Pinetree and that's how you met Em."

He nodded. "Yes. The doctor in charge of the facility had actually run one of hers. I didn't get a chance to question him the way I wanted."

Because Em had killed him.

"She didn't know," I told him. I had no idea why I wanted to apologize for her taking that chance from him, but all he did was shake his head.

"She didn't have to know. She protected herself. If I'd gotten there five minutes sooner, I would have done it for her." The absolute certainty in his tone lacked even a hint of regret or hesitation. "Don't worry, Buttercup. I like PPG. I am glad she saved herself. She didn't deserve what was being done to her there."

No more than his mother had, I suspected. When I put my hand over his on the gear shift, he flashed me a smile.

"As for your earlier question, you care. You're loyal. You don't have to justify your feelings to me or anyone else." I could almost feel the heavy underline he struck under the last two words. "PPG is in a relationship with several men and you don't think less of her."

Never. I frowned. I would never judge Em that way. "She also keeps our world at a distance," I reminded him. I would defend her right to the relationships she'd chosen to my dying breath. The Sharpes had been powerful and influential. She was the last of her family, save for Moira, her mother, or rather, her adopted mother, since Em and Milo had the same birth parents. Still, Moira wanted nothing to do with the Sharpe name. Last I'd heard, she'd cut ties with it.

"You don't have that luxury," Bodhi said as we merged onto one of the roads known as the Beltway.

"No," I told him. "I also don't pay much attention to gossip. But I can't afford to ignore it either." Then, because I understood the conversation might be discouraging, I added, "I'm not trying to tell you I'm not interested."

Heat flushed through me again at his low chuckle.

"I'm more concerned with you being safe than I am you justifying your feelings, Buttercup. I'm not going anywhere. Perhaps I should have expressed my changing interests in you before now, but you've always been—a lot younger, and it was never appropriate before."

"You're not that much older than me."

"I'm a decade older than you," he said dryly.

"What I hear you saying is you're a ten."

His snort was everything. I grinned.

"Buttercup," he said, turning his hand over underneath mine and locking our hands together. "I'm not a serial dater. I've never had a relationship. You could call my social connections limited to family, hunting, and a string of periodic one-night stands where I didn't want to know them and never made the attempt. I've never slept with a woman more than once, and I never saw a point in making an emotional connection. I've never had anything for anyone else...not while I have this quest."

His mother's quest.

"I get it," I told him softly.

The silence between us deepened, but he didn't release my hand until we exited somewhere in the district itself. I thought we might be near Georgetown. He followed the streets like he knew where we were going. When he turned onto a very quiet block, he parked at the end, then turned in his seat to meet my gaze.

The darkness with just the subtle hum of the engine and the lights from the dashboard, enhanced the sense of intimacy. "That's why you are going to be the exception for me."

Because I understood.

"Thank you for letting me help."

One corner of his mouth edged a little higher. "You never have to thank me, Buttercup."

"Maybe I want to, *Trouble*." That earned me a real grin. "You aren't treating me like I'm fragile and I shouldn't be anywhere near the danger."

"Danger is half the fun," he said, then kissed my hand before he slid out of the car. I watched him as he scanned the street before he circled around to open my door. Once there, he leaned down to lock gazes with me again. "Understand, anything coming for you is going to have to go through me."

The quiet ferocity in his tone made my stomach bottom out and sent chills rippling over my skin. It wasn't fear. No, I wasn't at all afraid. When he held out his hand to me, I took it and slid out to join him.

Bodhi had always been a safe place.

I was intrigued.

Eager.

And a part of me wanted to find out what would happen if someone made a move on me.

Bloodthirsty?

Maybe.

He canted his head. "That smile tells me you're enjoying the thought of violence."

"Maybe," I demurred with a wink. "A girl needs to keep some of her secrets."

"Hmm. Ready?"

"To visit this sex club?" I flicked a look to the quiet row of townhouses and the absolute lack of people. There were plenty of parked vehicles and the occasional light on porches, but—it didn't seem like a busy area. "I can't wait."

He threaded my right arm through his left. "In the event of a challenge, always move to my left if you can."

He was right handed, so I nodded.

"I have a second weapon in an ankle holster. If necessary, grab that."

Another nod.

"You are skilled with swords, I hear."

That surprised me.

"How are you with knives?"

Our steps made no sound on the pavement as we walked. The soft shush of my boots didn't click. The icy air around us seemed to wrap us up in a silky bubble. We traveled most of the block before he turned to a tall iron-wrought gate that blocked a path between the townhouses. A handful of them had been present.

He lifted the latch and it swung open almost noiselessly. Curiosity threaded through me as he guided me through then closed the gate without making a sound. He moved to put his hand at the small of my back. The path between the townhouses was very narrow and barely lit. I could see light on the paving stones only, not quite visible from the sidewalk.

That was fascinating. We walked nearly the full length of the townhouse to where I would expect a back patio, but instead, he opened another door and lights came on to illuminate steps leading down. Lips pursed, I glanced at him.

"It's a very good thing, I trust you, Trouble."

It was like we were all alone and no one in the whole world was around us. Still, I didn't miss the flash of his grin before he pressed his lips close to my ear. A shiver skated through me at the tickle of his breath.

"It's a very good thing, Lainey B. You have nothing to worry about. The dark should be afraid of you."

While it wasn't the most romantic thing I'd ever heard, it definitely made me want to swoon. Together, we descended the steps to another door where he lifted a huge brass knocker and banged it three times.

Suddenly, light filled a sliding door peephole, revealing a masked face that stared out at us. "Password?"

The challenge sent another thrill through me. I had no idea where Bodhi was taking me, but I couldn't wait to get in there.

ELEVEN

BODHI

"Password?" The man in the window challenged.

"Klimt." The key had been offered in the invitation I'd managed to obtain. The painting had been The Kiss by the aforementioned artist. Not one I would go out of my way to own, but I understood the meaning. The man on the other side flicked a look from me to Lainey B then back again. Good for him. He kept his inspection neutral.

The Underground was known for its catering to the specific needs of its clientele. If they didn't offer it and you desired it, you only needed to let them know and they would find it for you. This wasn't my first visit. Nor even my second.

However, it was the perfect location to be seen and never mentioned, so it allowed me to make contact with various individuals who had information I needed. They didn't want to be associated with me and felt safer behind the anonymity of the clubs. The amusing part was that it also allowed them the sense of mutually assured destruction.

Not that I gave a damn if I was associated with a sex club, but I had no problems letting them think so.

The door locks tumbled open and then the man stood back to allow us entry. "Masks are available," he rumbled. The dim lighting and his averted gaze allowed us another suggestion of privacy. "Do you have a reservation desire?"

"Not at the moment," I assured him before passing him five one hundred dollar bills. The doorman offered a layer of security, but only a layer. I liked having those layers grateful to me. He nodded once and then motioned us ahead to where a curtain waited.

Saying nothing, Lainey moved with me through the black curtain. There was another entrance, because no sounds drifted this way, but this room allowed us to choose from a selection of masks.

The Underground thrived as a warren of kink, secrets, and deviancy. That was just getting through the door. I studied the options then used a code to open a different box. These were new and not for reuse. When I turned to Lainey, she raised her eyebrows.

Fearless, she met my gaze with her guile free eyes, yet seemed moderately intrigued. "We have a thing for masks, do we?" The question in her low, teasing tone stroked through me.

"Not particularly, but then I think you're beautiful in everything." When I held up the simple silken mask, she turned to let me tie it over her eyes.

It would wrap around the upper portion of her face, leaving only her eyes and mouth visible even as it teased over her nose. The silk slid through my fingers as I tied it just under her hair. When she turned to face me again, I had to admit...

"I was right," I told her, cupping her chin as I studied her eyes. "You're beautiful in everything."

Her smile offered me a reward I hadn't truly earned yet, but I soaked it up anyway. "What do you need from me in here?"

"I won't say obedience, but if I tell you to do something, I will need you to do it without question for now. I promise to explain later. No one will touch you..."

"Are they going to touch you?"

As amusing as that thought might be, I shook my head. "No, we'll take our time and make our way through the various galleries. Nothing is off-limits in here. The only boundaries are set by the individuals." Her pupils dilated. "Men and women alike, the fewer clothes they wear, the more open they are. You will see some sex partners are literally free use. Others are treated as pets. Still more are pleasuring themselves while watching others be pleasured."

A shiver went through her. "I don't know whether I should be embarrassed by my interest or not."

Chuckling, I stroked my thumb over her lower lip. The gloss she'd chosen didn't wipe off easily. I found myself intrigued by what I would have to do to remove it.

"No reason to be embarrassed at all. If you want to explore these interests, we will make time for it—later." Because tonight was about business. Unfortunately. "There is still time to tell me no. I can take you back then return..."

She snorted. Somehow, I suspected that would be her answer. When she rested her hand against my chest, I pressed a kiss to her silken clad forehead.

"Stay close to me. Remember... no one in here is allowed

to touch you." A rather unreasonable urge to keep her to myself threaded through me.

Our first kiss wasn't going to be in a sex club either. As much as my body rebelled at the decision, I firmed on it. Lainey B deserved so much more.

Ready or not... I made myself take a step back, then I added my own mask, tying the silk against my face and savoring the way her lips curved as she watched me. When I held out my hand, she settled her palm against mine and we moved to the next set of doors.

I pressed a button, and a moment later, the interior door was opened by another attendant. He bowed with a sweeping gesture to welcome us inside.

A combination of sandalwood incense, musk, sex, and hints of sanitizing products flooded the senses as we stepped inside. Lainey moved with me. I wasn't surprised by the gazes trailing over her or me. But as I'd assured her, no one approached and no one would.

In addition to being practical, the boots were also another sign to the guests. She was unobtainable. She'd arrived with him. She would stay with him. It was subtle messaging. Most of the women were barefooted. A casual few were in high heels. Few wore boots.

Those in boots were not to be touched. Simple, elegant communication. We needed to pause periodically so I could scan each room. There were various partners enjoying themselves—some on stages, others on beds, still more in their chairs.

The freedom of The Underground, nothing was too taboo. A man crawled along, a good little pet, and rubbed against the leg of his mistress. Another patron was on her knees, swallowing around a cock as her master fucked her mouth.

Sex was everywhere. There was a freedom in The Underground to be as primitive or as open as you wanted to be. A single woman writhed between three men, their bodies pumping as they filled her. From her moans, she was very much enjoying the experience.

A slight hitch in Lainey's breathing made me smile. Did she want to know what that was like? I was sure we could arrange something. First, we'd need to sort out the other assholes.

When I squeezed her hand, she pulled her attention from the public display. We left the pleasure rooms behind and ventured into pain. This was not my kink nor would it ever be. When I inflicted pain, I wanted it to hurt someone. I couldn't ever imagine—even as a transfer of power— harming Lainey.

I supposed if she wanted a spanking, we could discuss it. Still, that seemed more Reed's speed or maybe Hardigan's. If they could give her that, I'd allow it. The moans and cries here varied from the sharp surprise at blows, to the moans and sobs.

Lainey stiffened at some of the more brutal acts. The caning. The woman being teased with an electric tickler. The sharpness of electricity could be a definite enhancer, but you really needed to know what you were doing.

The deeper we traveled, the variety of kinks increased. Lainey nearly missed a step when we passed two men urinating on a third. Everywhere you looked, there were asses, tits, and dicks galore on display. Some were toned, some were saggy. Some were erect and others limp.

Generally, though, everyone seemed to be having a good time. The alcohol rules were limited, as were the drugs, though we passed by a group each doing a line of cocaine under the supervision of one of The Underground's infamous monitors.

The monitors were always masked, no one knew who they were, and their identities were kept secret on purpose. They made the hard calls if someone broke the rules. They could inflict violence, a lifetime ban, or even just make the troublemaker disappear entirely.

One did not piss off the monitors.

It wasn't until we reached the peach room with its soft colors and relaxed atmosphere that I found my target. I should have known he would be in the bowels. The peach rooms were scattered about, a place to relax from the sexual escapades, hydrate, cuddle, and sometimes even sleep.

The man I wanted to speak to sat at a table alone, his attention on the woman writhing on the stage, to some song only she could hear. I guided Lainey over to the table in the corner.

Unsurprisingly, the man seated there didn't wear a mask of any kind. The cell phone ban in The Underground provided another layer of security. Besides, if anyone announced that a member of a now-defunct royal family was at a sex club in Washington D.C., I rather doubted many would care.

If his family were still a power, he'd likely be a prince, or an elector as they were once known. The prince-electors decided on the Holy Roman Emperor, but that power faded with their titles and eventually crumbled to nothing following the unification of Germany and her subsequent defeat during World War I.

I pulled out a chair for Lainey, and while she gave me a brief look of question, she took the offered spot and crossed one leg over the other. The prince studied her for a moment before he lifted his wine glass to sip, then turned his attention to me.

"You're late," was all he said in accented English. I knew enough German to get by, but I preferred to keep our communications in English.

I shrugged. "Explains why you're all the way back here."

The man smiled. "It could." He glanced at Lainey again. "Friend?"

"Yes."

He wanted to know if he could speak freely in front of her. Not an issue he needed to worry about; however, I understood his concern.

"I told you that I did not have any more details on the three doctors you were looking for. As far as I can tell, they've never been employed by any of the facilities in Switzerland, Austria, or Poland."

I waved a hand. "I'm aware. Tonight's issue is someone different entirely."

"Oh?" Curiosity flashed in his eyes. One thing Hans was terrible at was curbing his own boundless need to know everything. Gossip. Intelligence. Intellectual property. He didn't even need to *use* it. He just wanted to acquire all of it.

It made him a good resource.

Especially since he didn't mind sharing what he knew —at least with me. His family had tried to remove him from the board a long time ago. I got him out of the hospital they'd dumped him in and he'd dealt with the troublemakers. Now, he spent his life doing what he wanted and his family kept their noses clean if they didn't want to be cut off.

It was an equitable arrangement.

"Then don't be a tease. I was bored of trying to find the doctors anyway."

I didn't laugh at the careless tone or the thrill in his eyes. While I trusted the discretion of The Underground, I waited for the waitress to bring a fresh drink for Hans, and when she looked to me and Lainey, I only ordered, "Water, lime, fresh-squeezed. No ice."

That would take her a moment. If Lainey disagreed, she said nothing, instead, she just leaned into my arm and I lifted it to let her slide in a little closer. When we were alone with Hans again, I focused on him. "Julius King."

He paused, glass halfway to his mouth then looked at me with a blink of surprise before he took that sip and lowered it again. "King."

Lainey stiffened faintly, but she didn't interrupt. I didn't think it possible to enjoy her more, but her trust—it was a gift.

I would not squander it.

"Yes."

Hans studied me for a long moment, then nodded. "He is a dangerous man. He also does not like his past to be dug into."

"No one does. After all, when you dig up the past—you tend to find the bodies that have been buried."

"True," Hans mused then glanced at Lainey again. His expression was speculative only and he settled back in his seat. "How soon do you need the information?"

"Tell me what you know now and then I'll consider what else you might find out." Because Hans knew something. He was terrible at hiding his excitement and the name had given him significant pause.

Lips pursed, he appeared to consider his answer. When the waitress returned with the water, she smiled at me and then at Lainey but I waved her off. We were not interested in anything else.

A bit of a pout escaped her, but she left us alone, and Hans sighed. "Who is your companion?"

"No one you need to know," I told him. "That's not how this works."

It was Hans' turn to pout. "You aren't very much fun anymore." Despite the complaint, he continued, "Julius King was once Jeff Hardigan. Before that, he was known as Jacob Knight. Before that, John Hennessy. He's had many names, Hennessy, I believe is the oldest. As far as I know, he's had three biological children, though he has no contact with any of them."

The names would be useful. "Why so many identities?"

Hans shrugged. "He makes enemies. He moves. He has many enemies. But he has also amassed power with each move. The last one was almost twenty years ago? Give or take? That is when he became King. He attached himself to one of the Bay Ridge families, rumors abound about how he took over certain aspects, but I have no idea which one is accurate. I doubt anyone does, most people from that time have died or disappeared."

King was cleaning up behind himself. I glanced down to Lainey and saw the question clearly in her eyes and nodded.

"What are the rumors?" she asked.

"I can't guarantee their veracity," Hans said, even as he leaned forward.

"That's why they're called rumors," I reminded him. But we had names. That was as good a starting point as any.

"The first rumor is that he was born on the wrong side of the bed, hardly the first heir to be fathered on a mistress."

If he were an heir though, he would go after that family specifically... wouldn't he?

"Another is that he isn't the heir at all, just took the place of that heir. I tend to favor that theory... It seems a little darker and more deceitful. Fitting for a man like him." Well, if I'd wondered his opinion about King, I didn't anymore.

"You don't know the family," I said, and it wasn't a question. If he knew, he would have told us. "I want to know though, I want to know what families he's attached to and how..."

"That's a lot of details," Hans protested.

"You said you were bored," I reminded him, and his sulk gave way to a laugh.

"I did. Very well..." Then he eyed Lainey again. "Next time, I want to know your name." With that, he winked and rose.

After he left, I glanced down at Lainey again. I could practically read her frown through her pursed lips. "He'll do his best. If it's out there, Hans will find it."

"You're looking into King."

"Yes," I told her. "Milo asked me."

Fresh surprise filled her eyes.

"I like him. He's PPG's brother. He's also important to you. You want to know...because King is why Milo isn't with you."

She let out a shaky breath. "Yes."

"Then we'll find out." I took a drink of the water. "Now, was there a room here you wanted to explore or should we go?"

Her slow blink made me smile. Tempting for her. For me.

"You really are trouble," she said, a little breathless. "And I like that part of you far too much."

"Good," I said. "It keeps life interesting."

When she brushed her lips to my ear, I went completely still. "Thank you," she whispered.

Yes, definitely time to go. I wanted Lainey B.

I wanted her very much.

Especially when she slid her hand into mine and moved with me, her trust a badge of honor I got to carry.

TWELVE

LAINEY

M y mind whirled with the new details, the names, and the uncertain knowledge behind his declaration that Julius King had *three* biological children.

Three?

Pretty Boy and Em had another sibling? King had ties back to one of the families? Which one? Why so many rumors? Where the hell had he come from that he managed to wedge his way inside a circle that didn't open easily or often?

"Watch your step," Bodhi ordered gently as we reached the exit. My pulse seemed to thunder in my ears as my thoughts raced to the various possibilities. I couldn't even really enjoy the sexual displays around us.

The location was going to require more time and thought at some point. I didn't even know if it was a place Bodhi actually enjoyed or if this had merely been secure for a meeting. I could see arguments for both.

Once we were out of the galleries and back into the antechamber, he slid the silk from my face and paused to study me. The intensity in his eyes arrested the syllables burning on my tongue.

Packing away the distractions, I focused on him. "I'm fine," I told him.

"No," he said slowly. "You're not. What he told us troubled you."

It had. "We can discuss it later?"

I wasn't sure of the security in here, and he nodded. Instead of putting the silk mask back into the box he'd retrieved it from, he pocketed mine and his.

"Later," he murmured with a hint of a smile. Bodhi was the wildest combination of primitive, enigmatic, and elegant. I wasn't entirely sure which part of him attracted me the most.

Our exit was every bit as peaceful as our entrance. The ascent took a minute. I hadn't realized how many stairs we'd actually descended. The air outside was bitter in its coldness, a sharp knock to my senses that helped to chase away the headiness of sex, musk, and the lingering perfumes and scents that filled The Underground.

When Bodhi held out his hand to me, I clasped it, and the walk along the darkened street seemed to be blanketed in a hush I didn't want to pierce. I didn't miss his watchfulness or the way he kept himself between me and the street.

He put me in the car before he circled around to the driver's side. Still, we didn't speak until we were out of the district and back on an interstate. He put his hand over mine before he turned up the heat and then covered my hand again.

I didn't think I was that cold, but a shiver worked through me. "Are we going back to your house?"

"We can," he offered. "Or I can get you back to Manhattan. You're upset by what Hans told us."

"Not upset," I said, with a shake of my head. "Disturbed. King is Milo's and Emersyn's biological father." I was fairly certain he knew, but better to verify.

"Hans mentioned three children."

"Precisely." Milo adored Em. He'd given up so much for her. There was nothing he wouldn't do for his sister—a feeling I shared—yet I'd seen the same devotion in Em. She'd not known about him for so long. Though getting to know him had been a struggle, she loved Milo. "They don't know about another sibling."

"Not impossible. He left them a long time ago. The child could have come along after." He shrugged. "Though with his different identities, maybe before."

"King hasn't mentioned another child to either of them." If he'd told them, they would have told me. I had zero doubts on this front. "So this is something he doesn't think is important—because why would his children be something he cared about?" Clearly, he'd abandoned the two we knew of.

"Or it is very important and a chink in his armor." Bodhi saw exactly where I was going. "We'll figure it out, Buttercup."

"I need more details, because they are going to have a dozen questions." I wouldn't keep this from them.

"Hans will dig. He lives to ferret out information. He likes having material on everyone and everything. His reaction about King tells me he has some personal vendetta there. That will motivate him."

"You trust him?"

"I trust his desire to know," Bodhi answered, stroking

his thumb along the side of my hand. "I trust his hunger for knowledge."

"There's a chance he could sell the information elsewhere, then?" The last thing I wanted was for him to alert King to our hunt. The man had to know, but I didn't want him taking out his rage on Pretty Boy, Ezra, Adam, Andrea, or anyone else.

"I told you I've spent years hunting down all the caregivers and anyone associated with my mother's time in her various facilities?" The quiet question held not an ounce of censure.

"Yes. That was how you met Em."

"And Freddie," he agreed. "Yes. It's also how I met Hans. His family had tucked him away, determined to have him declared incompetent then take over his wealth, properties, and more. Inheritance laws dictated everything went to the eldest son, so there was something of a conspiracy amongst his relatives."

I made a face. "That's—awful."

"Yes, now, I'm not saying he isn't a little cracked." He flashed me a smile. "The best people are. But I got him out. Helped him deal with a few recalcitrant family members and secured his position once again."

"So he owes you a debt."

"Debts require collection. I like to think of it as I did him a favor for no other reason than I wanted to and he does me the same courtesy. When I want something, I get it. When he needs assistance, he asks." It sounded so very simple. But at no point did Bodhi say he *trusted* him.

I didn't like it, but I could accept it. Head back against the seat, I stared at the darkness. "I want all the info you have on him."

"I can do that."

"Thank you," I said, squeezing his hand. "If he ever betrays you, I want to know where to find him."

His soft chuckle was in no way dismissive. "I'm not the only one who gets to be protective?"

I slid a look toward him. "Does that surprise you?"

He gave me a brief look then lifted my hand to kiss it. "No, but it does impress me. I usually look after myself."

"Then it won't hurt if I'm also looking after you."

"No," he said slowly. "It won't."

As much as I needed to go back to Manhattan, I chose the house here in Virginia. I wanted one more night. One more night to put the walls back up, to put my defenses back together, and to arm for war.

The fact neither Adam nor Ezra had reached out since their first round of messages concerned me. Hopefully they were together and working out their own issues. Dread curled in my stomach as it hit me that I really didn't know if they had worked that out.

Should I be there?

I hadn't spoken to Adam, not directly, since Ezra's announcement. What if he blamed him? He had the night of the masquerade. A headache surged behind my eyes, and I barely paid attention as Bodhi pulled into the garage and parked the new vehicle.

Still wrestling with that, I reached for the door handle, but Bodhi had already circled the car to open the door and let me out. When he wanted to move, he was like smoke. Swift and unstoppable.

Inside, I shrugged off my jacket and let him take it before I unzipped my boots. I didn't even know what time it was...

"Come on," Bodhi said, hand out to me again. He

snagged the boots from me before clasping my hand. Up the stairs we went and straight into his room.

I didn't comment, especially when he led me straight into his bathroom and turned on the tub. At my raised eyebrows, he fixed me with a steady look.

"I want to take care of you this evening. Will you let me?"

The directness took my breath away and I shivered. The reaction wasn't lost on him but he didn't move as the water thundered through the taps, the sound of it steady in the bathroom. It wasn't long before the water turned warm, then hot. The steam curled up from it.

I could have said a lot of things in that moment. I could have told him he didn't have to, but he already knew that. I could have said I didn't expect it. Yet, no doubt existed within me, he was well aware of it. Maybe he understood me better than I did myself right now.

At the end of it all, he said he wanted to take care of me. He was asking me to allow it.

So I gave him the simplest answer of all, "Yes, please."

A smile softened his mouth, and he pulled the stopper in the tub so the water would begin to fill it. "I think a scent of honey and chamomile will do." After he added the oils to the tub, he nodded to me. "Make yourself comfortable. I'll be back in a few minutes... Do you want wine? Or would you prefer a hot tea?"

The depth beneath each of his actions and words seemed endless, and yet I didn't fear sinking into them. "Maybe whiskey," I suggested. "In tea?"

He chuckled. "That's a good thought." A brush of his lips to my cheek and then he was gone. I caught sight of myself in the mirror, the flush to my cheeks and the bright-ness to my eyes.

He hadn't turned on all the lights in here. If anything, the glow was warming without being too bright. I slipped out of the dress and pulled my hair up and pinned it atop my head before I wiped off the make-up.

By the time I was ready to slip into the water, the tub was more than three-quarters full. It was huge and designed with perfect depressions to sit against. I stretched out in the water and leaned my head back.

On one hand, I was vibrantly aware of my own nudity. Aware that Bodhi was going to come back in here and find me lounging in the tub. Maybe he would even join me. Anticipation coursed through me. I curled my toes against the bottom and let out a long sigh as the temperature began to warm the ice at my core, and I gave another shudder.

The scuff of a foot dragging pulled my eyes open and I found Bodhi stepping back inside. He'd lost his clothes somewhere between leaving and making the tea. A dark blue towel wrapped his hips, and I let my gaze skim over him.

Scars marked his chest and his shoulders. Wounds made by knives. Others by bullets. Still others I didn't know what caused them. One side of him was almost pebbled like he'd been dragged through gravel. The twists and folds in the skin a roadmap of his past, and his triumph over it.

When my gaze struck his, I found him staring down at me. He seemed to soak in the sight of me as I had him. As he lifted his eyes to mine once more, he smiled. "I brought tea and snacks."

The corners of my lips twitched as he set down the tray with the mugs of tea as promised. There were also crackers, cheese, slices of meat, and bits of fruit. Not quite a charcuterie but enough to eat.

"Hmm," I said. "And here I thought you were the snack."

"I'm sure we can arrange something," he murmured. "Do you mind if I join you?"

"Not in the slightest. I was about to insist." When I sat up so he could slide in, I had a better view for his tug of the towel, and it pulled free. Long, lean muscle shaped his legs and torso. Like his chest, his legs also had scars. The line of his cock, half-stiff and leaning toward me had me smiling.

Even more when he made no pretense of giving it a squeeze. When his knuckles whitened briefly, I frowned. "Uh uh," he told me before he stepped into the tub and then we maneuvered so I could lean back against him. The press of his cock against my ass was right there and my head rested on his shoulder.

"Tonight," he said. "I am taking care of you. Tea. Food. Hot bath. Comfort."

"That sounds like no sex…"

"Not yet, Buttercup," he murmured before he pressed a kiss to my throat. "Anticipation is good for us. When we have sex, it's going to very much be about us. About what we want. About me having you and you having me."

Another shiver went through me. He said when, not if.

"A lot like our first kiss then?" I tilted my head back to look at him and he smiled.

The man was going to drive me crazy.

"You deserve to be romanced," he said, before trailing his fingers down my arm. "And I deserve to romance you."

That…I couldn't and wouldn't argue with. Though my pussy clenched and my nipples tightened, I could hardly miss the steadily growing firmness in his cock. Tonight wasn't about sex. It was about intimacy. With that in mind, I reached over to the food and selected a bit of cheese.

With care, I pressed the food to his lips in an offering, and he smiled at me again before he sucked the food from them then nibbled my fingertips.

I was right. He was going to drive me mad.

Absolutely, totally mad.

CHAPTER
THIRTEEN

MILO

The phone vibrated on the dashboard of the treadmill as I finished my run. I'd gotten up early and hit the gym well before King or his men. The man's home offered a lot of amenities, but it reminded me more of prison every single day.

Panting, I stared at the name on the screen. She shouldn't be calling me. Fuck. Head down, I debated sending her to voicemail. The moment the thought hit me, I quashed it. If my sister was calling, I would always answer.

"Hey, Ivy," I said by way of greeting after scanning the room to make sure no one had walked in while I was distracted. I slung the towel around my neck and retrieved the water bottle.

A part of me wanted to do some heavy weights until my muscles burned and the noise in my head died down. But that wasn't an option at the moment. In the three days since the New Year's party, I hadn't seen Mayhem at all.

She was safe and she was with Bodhi Cavendish. I had to trust the man to keep her that way. But the time spent here was wearing on me. Two months with King was like a life sentence, and they kept adding time to it.

"Hey," she said, her tone far to somber. "I'd say Happy New Year, but Jasper just told me why I couldn't show up to surprise you and Lainey."

Fuck.

"It probably sounds worse than it is," I told her as I headed down the hall, head on a swivel. Living with King meant there was no relaxing here. Fortunately, I had years of experience in watching my own back and never allowing anyone to approach me while unaware.

"Are you or are you not *living* with the man who *abandoned* you?"

You. Not us.

The corner of my mouth curved upward. Not just at the language, but at how genuinely incensed she was. Ivy hated King because of what he'd done to me. Not because of what he'd done to us.

"I'm doing what needs to be done," I answered as I made it back to my room without running into anyone. That was preferable. I particularly didn't want her on the phone if our sperm donor made an appearance.

Once back in my room, I locked the door and headed into the bathroom where I turned on the shower. I periodically searched it for bugs, but I couldn't be sure I found them. Did I think he would invade my privacy?

Without question.

"Milo." The way she sighed elongated my name. "Please tell me you're not... that you didn't leave Lainey to live with that—asshole."

"Then don't ask me about it so I don't have to lie to

you," I told her and then sat on the closed toilet lid. The coolness of the porcelain was a relief to my overheated skin. The shorts and t-shirt were sufficient for running, and I'd pushed it.

"I hate this for you and for her."

My heart twisted. "Can't say I'm a fan either. The last thing you need to be doing is worrying..."

"Have you met me?" The open challenge in her tone pulled a grin to my face. "Of course, I'm going to worry. You tried to turn my life upside down when you came home. All roaring and growling at everyone. Thumping them and beating up poor Jasper."

"... he did not beat me up," Jasper muttered somewhere near her.

"The hell I didn't," I commented even as Ivy said, "I adore you, Jas, but he absolutely did. He was very mean to you."

Mean to him. I groaned even as a laugh shook free. "Ivy, sweetheart, I love you."

"I love you too," she said. "Tell me how I can help. Do you want me to talk to him?"

The hum of conversation in the background ceased. So she wasn't just with Jas. That was fine. "No," I said slowly. "In fact, what I want is you far away from any of this."

"He's been leaving me messages. Not a lot...but more than he did in the past."

Dropping my chin to my chest, I frowned. "Ivy, I don't know what he wants from you or from me." That wasn't totally true. I was almost dead certain he wanted to punish me. Whether it was over not choosing him when I was seven or some other imagined sin, I didn't know. "The problem with someone like him is they don't usually want something because they care or have any kind of charity in their heart."

"I know." Her sigh tore at me.

"Listen to me," I told her. "You are the best sister. I wouldn't trade you for anyone. What I'm doing right now, I need to do. I miss Mayhem." Saying that didn't cost me anything, and I could almost picture her warm eyes watching me from wherever she was. "I miss her like I'd miss my arm. But I need to do this. It'll hopefully keep her safe. Keep you safe. Eventually..."

Eventually get rid of King. One way or another.

"I want to help," she stressed the last word so hard. "I *hate* that you are there."

"I know, sweetheart," I promised her, trying to cajole her. "If—*if*—I can think of something you can help with, you will be the first person I call."

"You will not," she said with such a scoff of disgust, I had to laugh. "Don't think I haven't figured you out. Fine, you have to do this, I accept that. But you're my big brother and she's my best friend. I'm calling her next and if she needs me..."

My heart twisted. "I know." I also knew Mayhem. She'd never let Ivy walk into this mess. "I love you, kiddo."

"I love you too," she muttered unhappily. "Kel wants to talk to you."

I bet he did. "Okay, let me talk to him. Go poke Jasper with a stick or something for me."

She snorted a laugh, but it was still a laugh. "Be nice, he didn't want to tell me."

No, he hadn't, but he also wouldn't lie to her, and as much as I wished she didn't know, I couldn't fault the guys for their devotion to her.

"Hey," said Kellan Traschel, who along with Jasper were

two of my oldest friends. When I'd been in jail, they'd worked to protect the Vandals for me, and when I got out, Kellan took over to save them and me from myself. "I'll be right back, Sparrow."

I gave it a beat as a door closed and the background noise faded. Kellan had questions.

"Tell me the truth," he said without further preamble. "Do you need us there?"

"Of course, I do," I said, not downplaying it. "But if you come, you're bringing Ivy. If Ivy is here...I don't know what his real interest is. He keeps trying to play dad, but I don't buy it. His interest in power and politics—he could be after anything from her money to her contacts to..."

"Control," Kellan said, summing it up.

"Yeah. I don't trust him."

"Good," he said, blowing out a breath. "She's pissed that you're doing this, and she doesn't want you on your own. You might get a visitor sooner rather than later..."

"You're not going to let her—" Then it hit me. "Fuck, Doc knows."

"Yeah," Kellan said. "Consider this a warning. He was even less pleased than she was. He has his own axe to grind with King."

"Thanks. If you can head him off, I'd appreciate it. When I can, I'll fill you guys in on the rest."

"Holding you to that, and I'll see what I can do. No promises." No, he wouldn't make them. Frankly, if Mickey decided he was going to show up here, he would. I scrubbed a hand over my face.

After ending the call, I threw myself through a shower. Talking to Ivy and the guys made me miss them. But more, it made me miss Mayhem. Somewhere...Braxton Harbor had stopped being home.

Mayhem was.

"The point," King said, one hand in his pocket and the other half-curled at his side as though he was considering punching the man in front of him. "The point," he repeated after releasing a deeper breath, "is to identify the problems *before* they become a problem. You accepted the offer."

"I'm aware."

I would give the older man some props. He couldn't weigh more than a buck fifty. King and the two goons working for him today as his bodyguards towered over him, but Hugo Rutherford seemed neither intimidated nor impressed.

"However," Hugo continued as though being threatened was an everyday occurrence—who knew, maybe it was. "As I stated when we *first* discussed *your* terms, I was not happy with them. I did not think they provided me all the opportunities I would prefer. My new partner was far more amenable to negotiations. I am satisfied with the deal we've made."

"You *accepted* my offer," King repeated. "That does not mean you get to negotiate with someone else, nor take them on and give them what belongs to me."

With nary an eye twitch, Hugo removed his glasses and made a show of cleaning them. "I understand your disappointment, Mr. King. No contracts were signed nor executed."

"You accepted," King just about spit the words out like they cost him for each and every syllable.

"Correction," Hugo told him as he slipped his glasses back on, "I told you that if we could not improve on that offer, I may have no choice but to accept. You were not able to improve." The barest suggestion of a smile crossed Hugo's face, and it took all my discipline not to laugh. "I, however, was able to find a better deal; therefore, I do have a choice and I don't accept your offer."

The absolute lack of fucks on the old guy's face coupled with his genuine pleasure at defying King earned my respect. King's expression darkened further.

"Maybe we should go," I suggested before King could say another word. "If Mr. Rutherford isn't doing business then we don't need to be here."

It was a calculated risk, King didn't want me interfering with his business. At the same time, he'd dragged me to so many of these meetings, and I'd endured the tedium of his "negotiations" over and over. His idea of negotiations was shaking down creators and business owners for all of their hard-earned work.

Then he would cut them out and make profit off of it. He might wear an expensive suit, but he was still a grifter, a con, and what amounted to a platinum-plated thief. He was practically a mob boss, though he pretended he was anything but.

"When I want your opinion," King began, his attention leaving Rutherford and slamming into me.

"You'll never want it," I told him dryly. "Fortunately, I don't care whether you want it or not. You keep bringing me along, so you're going to get it. The deal is off. We can *go*."

Jared and Jock—though their names could have been Joseph and Jimmy for all I knew, still loomed over Rutherford. The tension gathering around them was like storm clouds waiting to erupt.

Despite his cavalier attitude, Rutherford was in a great deal of danger.

"This is the fight you want, son?" King asked in a dark tone that didn't pretend to be anything friendly.

"Bring it," I told him. "You were the one who made me show up. Now you get to deal with me being here."

Maybe it was talking to Ivy or maybe it was missing Mayhem. Or maybe, just maybe, it was watching King get ready to throw his weight around like the jackass bully he was, but I was fucking tired of this.

I wasn't here to kiss his ass.

"Deal with my son," King said abruptly. "If he would like to take on Rutherford's lesson, give it to him."

Honestly? The order pleased me enormously. Rutherford paled.

"You should go," I said to him easily enough, ignoring the blistering look in King's eyes. He'd grown more and more arrogant of late, particularly when it came to me and being under his thumb. I hadn't missed the self-satisfied waves rolling off him at the announcement of Ezra's engagement or how he'd cooly tracked Mayhem's departure from that ballroom.

No, I'd tracked those reactions and filed them away. I rolled my head from side to side as the pair of mismatched goons turned their attention on me. The taller of the pair wore a warier look than his partner. John, or whatever his name was, was smarter than Jack or Jimmy—fuck it, the J twins.

Big J definitely didn't want to rush into the fight. Little J had no such reservations. He charged even as Rutherford retreated from the room. Unfortunately for the man, we were still in his offices. I'd apologize, but he could deal with the cleanup since I was going to handle this beating for him.

Little J didn't seem to fight with any kind of strategy in mind beyond going for overwhelming his opponent. Not my first brawl, and unfortunately for him, I was a brawler. Swift strikes and punishing blows were how I learned to fight. I didn't have Liam's skill in the ring, but I didn't need it.

I took Little J's first two blows while I shifted my stance. I wanted to be closer to the wall. His next strike I caught in my fist and turned his arm out. Pain flickered over his face, and I almost smiled before I yanked him toward me. Between pulling him off balance and using his own momentum against him, he flew forward. I twisted to the side, and he ran headfirst right into the wall.

The crunch of plaster giving as he went down filled me with a kind of primitive satisfaction. Big J was already on me, using my distraction to his advantage. Smart. But even as he wrapped his big arms around mine, I slammed my head backwards.

Rule number one in a fight: If you're close enough to grab me, you're close enough to be hit. I drove my head back twice more in rapid succession. The blows rattled me, but his nose gave on the third blow as he moved his face. The crunch of cartilage accompanied by the spray of blood and Big J's shout of pain gave me a kind of visceral joy.

Little J was staggering to his feet, so I twisted, ramming my elbow backward into Big J's solar plexus. The combination loosened his grip on me, and I wrenched him forward and all but threw him right into Little J.

They collided with pained grunts, and with my foot, I added force to Big J's ass that drove them both into the wall in a shower of plaster. And as much fun as this was, King was at my back and I didn't want to give him any free shots. I fisted a handful of Big J's hair and slammed him face first into the wall before delivering a sharp blow to the back of his head. He dropped onto Little J, half-pinning him and leaving him open to a sharp kick to the side of the head.

Both men down, I pivoted to face King.

Flexing my bruised right hand, I enjoyed the faint click and pop of my knuckles. His expression was cold, furious, and for the first time in decades, I saw the man who had walked out on my mother reflected in his eyes.

"You want your shot?" I invited him.

King shook his head then glanced at his downed men before he focused on me. "Are you out then?"

"I said I'd come to work, I'd take Andrea's place because threatening children and using them to do your dirty work seems to give you some kind of pathetic thrill. I am not going to stand here while you bully, intimidate, and threaten others to get your way. Rutherford outplayed you. Take the loss like a man and not a little bitch."

His head jerked back like I'd slapped him. Fuck, the temptation was right there.

"As for the rest, we're changing a few things. You want me around, you start acting like it. I'm not going to be your fucking hostage anymore. Because your word doesn't mean shit to me."

With every word, I closed the distance between us until we were face to face. He met me glare for glare, but I saw the withdrawal before he surrendered a step. Then another.

Smart move.

Finally, he spread his hands and backed off fully.

"You may regret this, son."

"I've got a lot of regrets," I told him. "You're not that special."

With that, I stalked out of the office and down the hall. This wasn't a move I'd planned on making, but now that I had?

Fuck that felt good.

I pulled up Mayhem's number before the elevator doors closed.

FOURTEEN

LAINEY

I didn't make it back to my apartment immediately upon returning to New York. I'd had Bodhi take me to my grandfather's. I wanted to spend some time with him. He left me with the admonition that he would take me back into the city. The quiet intensity in his gaze seemed to suggest that he really wanted to do it. Which was why he was picking me up today rather than Wood—who, after time spent in recovery, was back to work.

I would rather Wood took it easy for another couple of weeks. He was concerned about missing that much work. I instructed the accountant to make sure Wood received his full pay even while on medical leave. I hoped that would put his mind at ease. I'd also sent Marlene a message that I would be back in the city this week. She was still at her daughter's, but I didn't need her to hurry back.

The apartment had been empty since I left for the "holiday," so I wasn't too worried about it. I could always have my own groceries sent in. Though, I would probably need to pay attention to where everything went because Marlene did not like it when things were put up in the wrong places.

Understandable.

I didn't expect Grandfather to walk me out when they announced that Bodhi was here. Despite the bitter cold outside, Bodhi waited next to the passenger side of his Mercedes. He straightened as the two of us came out. I returned with a pair of small suitcases. I never needed to bring that much out to Long Island when I came to stay at Der Sonne, but I liked having a few of my personal items. I was returning with far more than I brought with me on this trip.

"Phillip," Grandfather said as we descended the three steps to where he waited. The sunshine seemed almost too bright against the snow-covered lawn and gardens, though the drive was completely clear as were the steps.

Grit ground under my heels as we crossed to meet Bodhi. Grandfather let go of my arm when we closed the distance and accepted Bodhi's handshake.

"Mr. Benedict," Bodhi greeted him with a warmth that reminded me of his tale about Grandfather knowing his mother. The letter he'd taken. I never asked if they'd spoken since that incident. "It's good to see you, sir."

"And you," Grandfather said before giving me a searching look. "I wasn't aware that Phillip was your ride back to the city. Where is Wood?"

"I want Wood to keep recovering," I reminded him easily. "Phillip and I are friends."

"Are you?" Was that disapproval? The guarded note made me raise my brows.

"We are," Bodhi answered, pulling Grandfather's attention off of me. "We have been for many years, but I give you my word—it has always been and always *will* be respectful."

Grandfather narrowed his eyes, flicking a look from Bodhi back to me again. "Darling girl, would you step back inside so that Phillip and I can chat?"

I opened my mouth, but Phillip actually took another step closer, "Why don't we let Lainey B wait in the car, where it's warm, and then you and I can move up to the doors?" It would get Grandfather out of the wind and me out of earshot.

Irritation feathered through me as Bodhi gestured to the car and Grandfather looked thoughtful. Finally, he nodded then pressed a kiss to my cheek. "In the car, darling girl. Let us talk as men do."

On that note, I met my grandfather's stare with one of my own. "Do remember, as you *talk* as *men* do, that I am very much my own person with my own mind and the ability to make my own decisions."

"Of course," he murmured, though the downturn to his lips at my chastising tone said I'd hit the mark. "I will do my best," he promised and I pressed a kiss to his cheek before I walked over to where Bodhi opened the door to the car. His eyes practically danced with mischief once he faced me and not Grandfather.

"You be a good little woman and wait in the warm car," he murmured and when I narrowed my eyes, he winked. "We'll talk as men do."

With a huff, I slid into the passenger seat, and Bodhi chuckled as he closed the door. The interior was much warmer, and he had the seat heaters on. Thankfully, it wasn't too hot. As it was, I tugged off my gloves while Bodhi and Grandfather walked up the steps toward the door again. It would get Grandfather out of the wind—a good thing—but also kept their backs to me.

Men.

As annoying as I found it, I understood that Grandfather just wanted to protect me. Still, I was an adult. He didn't need to protect me from my own choices. Before I could stew on that for long, my phone rang. I tugged it out of my pocket, and my heart did a little fist bump to my ribs.

"Pretty Boy?" I answered, uncertain and elated in the same breath. Was he all right?

"Mayhem," he exhaled the nickname and tears flooded my eyes. "How's my girl doing?"

"She misses you," I said without an ounce of reservation. "It's been a long few weeks." So long since we'd last been where we could do more than just exchange a glance. I'd barely gotten to see him at the party. "Are you okay?"

"I'm pretty damn good actually," he said. "I want to see you."

"Same," I admitted. "But..."

"No buts," Milo stated so firmly, I had no choice but to just accept it. "I just informed King that this deal of ours is changing. I'm done with not seeing you."

I was almost afraid to get excited. "Will you be safe?"

"I'll be fine, Mayhem. So will Andrea. I'll make sure of it." The oath fisted around my heart, and I closed my eyes, just drinking in the sound of his voice. "You believe me, right?"

"Of course, I believe you. Even if we had to make changes, I wouldn't care. I want you back."

"How are you doing?" His voice gentled. "Really, especially after Ezra's idiotic announcement."

"I'm—managing. I haven't spoken to him or Adam

since New Year's Eve. I did get a message from Adam, but I wasn't really ready to talk then."

"Are you still with Bodhi?" The care with which he asked the question held not one ounce of judgment.

"I am. We went to Virginia and—oh, we found out some information. I need to fill you in." I hadn't really had a chance. "We didn't stay there long, then I had to see my grandfather." I stole a look out the window where the two men were *still* talking. "Bodhi is driving me back into the city. I wanted Wood to rest."

"Where's your bodyguard?"

I grimaced. "I didn't want to deal with him, especially after the party, so Bodhi made him go away. I trust Bodhi to look after me." And me to look after myself.

"Good. You're heading back to the city?"

"Yes. Will you meet me?" Eagerness threaded through me.

"Soon," he said. "I want to test a couple of theories, particularly because I don't trust what King did as *not* being a test. Do something for me though?"

"Anything."

"That's a lot of latitude, Mayhem."

I chuckled. "You can handle me."

His exhale gave me another thrill. "Damn right I can handle you."

"What favor do you want?" I teased, getting him back on the subject. It was so damn good to hear from him.

"Be safe? Watch your back? Don't take unnecessary risks, and stay close to one of the others if I'm not there?"

One of the others. I looked out the window toward Bodhi and found him watching me as Grandfather spoke to him. A question hovered in his expression. Was I okay? I nodded. I was more than fine at the moment.

"I can't promise about Ezra or Adam until I talk to them. I really don't know what Ezra was thinking...and I'm worried about him."

"So was Adam," Milo told me in a soothing voice. "He was also going to look after him."

That helped.

"But Bodhi is here and..."

"And he's interested in you, isn't he?" The soft question sent a wave of heat through me. "I saw that New Year's Eve. He's a loose cannon in some ways, but Ivy trusts him and so does Freddie."

"I trust him too," I admitted.

"Good."

"Pretty Boy?"

"It's all right, I never thought I'd be a guy who shared, but I want you to have everything you want, Mayhem. I want you to have *who* you want. But they don't get to hurt you. Understand?"

I did. "That goes for you too."

"I'll see you soon. Stay safe."

"Love you," I whispered.

"My life is better for it," he said with a sigh. "And I love you too." Then he was gone, and I lowered the phone with a whoosh of breath. He was making changes. I'd get to see him soon. I was almost impatient for Bodhi to finish with Grandfather. At the same time, I needed a moment to get myself back together.

As if summoned by the thought, he descended the steps and circled the car. Grandfather stood at the door, studying us both, and when I blew him a kiss, he nodded then motioned for a call. I tapped my heart. I would call him later, promise.

With another nod, Grandfather went back inside, and

then Bodhi slid into the driver's seat. "All good?" he asked, concern evident in his eyes.

"Should I be asking you that?" I challenged, trying to wrestle my emotions back into some semblance of order. Pretty Boy understood my interest in others, and he was still with me. He still wanted to be with me, and I got to see him soon. The level of desire and need collided in a wave that threatened to choke me.

"Your grandfather loves you, and he gave me a very pointed and detailed description of what he would do if I took advantage of you in any way."

I raised my brows, and the corners of his lips tilted upward.

"I gave him my word that as long as you wanted me in your life, no one was getting me out of it. If I hurt you, he wouldn't have to hunt me down. That said, I wasn't going anywhere, and the only one who made those decisions was you."

"I doubt he cared for that."

"No," Bodhi said as he put the car in gear. "But like I said, he loves you and he wants only the best for you. In that, we're united."

I shook my head. "Men."

"Yes," Bodhi said, almost too agreeably. "You have many of us in your life now. You're going to have to make accommodations for these types of discussions."

A laugh that turned almost watery escaped me, and I dabbed at my eyes.

"What happened?" Bodhi asked, all traces of humor vanishing.

"Milo called."

"Does he need help?" The fact it was the very first thing he asked made me smile. While we were already heading down the long drive, he took his foot off the accelerator.

"He didn't say that, but he did say he was making changes and I would get to see him soon. It sounds like he might be putting King on notice." I was so ready for that. "I need to tell him what we found out."

Bodhi nodded slowly.

"He's worried about fallout, so I promised I would be careful."

"Good," Bodhi said slowly before he put his foot on the accelerator. "Do you want to reach out to your bodyguard again?"

I made a face. "Not particularly, but it would free all of you up from babysitting me, and I have things to do too."

"We can find you a different one," Bodhi said. "You don't have to put up with him if you don't want to."

"It's not that," I admitted. "It's that Ezra hired him, and I have a feeling that colors my viewpoint on a lot of things right now."

Ezra.

"I need to talk to him too." The last came with its own set of problems. I needed to pack away my emotional reaction so I could find out what had happened. Something had. He needed help, and I needed to help him.

"We'll make sure it all happens," Bodhi said. "I'm not going anywhere."

"I told Milo..." Head turned so I could face him, I leaned my cheek against the seat. "That there might be an us." I chose the words carefully. Bodhi didn't have to be tied down if he didn't want to. Every moment we spent together seemed to bind me to him more tightly, but I—I was already committed, and he deserved to have what he wanted.

"No might about it," Bodhi said. "There is an us. Don't worry, Buttercup. I'll talk to them too—as men do."

"Oh God," I groaned, but laughter still escaped me. "I'm going to end up pummeling all of you."

"Good," he said. "Balance is always good."

The drive back to the city sobered me more. The closer we got to my apartment, the more I accepted that there were more troubling times ahead. I'd let myself run away for long enough. Ezra needed me. He needed Adam too. Hopefully, Adam had handled whatever the issue was between them, but there was still an engagement to be dealt with.

At my apartment, I got Bodhi into the garage and my private parking area. I would need to get him a remote. Clearly, Ezra and Adam already had one each. Still, he insisted on seeing me up to the apartment itself before he had to go handle a meeting.

"I'll come back this evening if you don't mind the company," he offered and I smiled. "Though if Milo is here, you can send me away."

"Or let you talk as men do?" I teased and he shrugged.

"It's going to happen."

The fact he said it as fait accompli sent a quiver through me even as my stomach bottomed out. They were going to talk. About me. About all of us. "I should be involved in that conversation."

"Eventually, there are things that would be better for everyone if we just work it out between us."

I did not roll my eyes at that, but the fact that Adam was standing in the middle of my apartment when I opened the door should have been predictable.

"It's about time," he said without a second look at Bodhi. "We need to talk."

I guess we were going to have one of those talks sooner rather than later.

"Where is Ezra?" I asked.

"That's why we need to talk."

Dammit.

CHAPTER
FIFTEEN

ADAM

Even the awareness that she had been with Cavendish the past few days hadn't soothed the rough bricks of worry weighing me down. The sound of her key in the lock, the opening of the door, and the sight of her calmed the tempest and let me relax for the first time since that asinine announcement.

"It's about time," I said. The profound relief didn't soften my words. I'd been pacing for hours. Hours as I tried to figure out how to fix all of this. As much as I wanted to talk to her, I didn't want to do it without a *plan* of some kind. If nothing else, the past two years had been one clusterfuck after another, and all of them kept pushing her away.

No. Fucking. More.

If that meant dealing with these interlopers and assholes, then so be it. But Lainey had been and always would be *mine*.

151

"We need to talk," I informed her. Cavendish could go, but I wouldn't insist. Not yet.

"Where's Ezra?" Concern flickered to life in her eyes, and it softened some of my own objections. The fact she still cared and worried about him after his choices was a credit to her. He wanted her to stop caring, but I didn't think it was possible.

Not for Lainey.

"That's why we need to talk."

She blew out a breath then glanced at Cavendish, and he gave me a measuring look.

"Do you want me to stay?" Despite the fact his gaze was on me, it wasn't me he was asking.

"I think we should all talk," she admitted, and while she wasn't wrong...

"First, you and me," I said. "Then we can put everything on the table." I wanted my time with her. I needed to know she was all right, and that she could handle whatever the hell came next.

I needed her to reassure me, and the fact I could admit that at least to myself seemed to be a step in the right direction.

I hoped.

"Give us a moment," Cavendish said to her. He had a hand on her lower back and stood far too close for my taste. The fact she raised her eyebrows at him almost made me smirk. The stubbornness and defiance housed in Lainey was legendary.

"Fine," she said, then pressed a kiss to the corner of his mouth. "Thank you for the last few days. I'll talk to you soon?"

"You will," Cavendish told her like an oath. It grated. I

could admit that. She glanced at her pair of suitcases that he'd set just inside the door then at me.

"I'm going to get coffee, then I'll be in the library."

"I'll find you." It was my turn to promise. She tugged off her jacket as she walked away. She looked very together and warm in her leggings, long sweater, and boots. The fact her hair was pulled back into a ponytail added a youthful touch but...

Fuck, she was beautiful.

When the door to the kitchen closed, I faced Cavendish again. His pleasant expression vanished for one of cool appraisal.

"Planning to threaten me?" I asked. There was no love lost between us. While our families moved in similar circles, he'd been ahead of us in school, and the arrogant son of a bitch never had much to do with us either.

Now he wanted Lainey?

That... grated.

"What do you think I'll do if you hurt her—again?" The question was delivered in the exceptionally civil tone held a much deeper menace.

"I don't think I'd see you coming." We'd always labeled him a wild card. I didn't think he was so wild anymore, not when he was on the table for her. That could be a good thing.

Maybe.

"Well, what do you know—you can learn." Cavendish slanted a look around her apartment then back to me. "Is Graham here?"

I shifted my stance, bracing for the possible attack. "If he is?"

"Don't leave him alone with her. He needs to grovel after the crap he pulled."

Asshole. "I don't totally disagree. You don't know all the circumstances."

He shrugged. "I don't need to. I know she cares. I know he is important to her. That means she wants him safe. But I won't allow him to hurt her again. I won't allow any of you to hurt her again." The way he ticked off each item, he might as well have been discussing the weather. Yet his tone was utterly at odds with the look in his eyes.

"I have no desire to hurt her."

"Your desires don't interest me, Reed. You've been punishing her for years because your feelings for her were too intense and too deep."

He might as well have slapped me. Yet I refused to rise to the bait. If I had to deal with this to get rid of him, fine. Then I would. "Then what do *you* want?"

"To trust you with her. Make me believe you."

I frowned. "Are you insane?"

"Unproven so far," he answered with a shrug.

"I'd cut off my arm before I allowed something to hurt her. The problem I've had is I haven't trusted her with her."

"This is true," he said. "Glad you see it."

"Bodhi," Lainey said, her voice a soft lasso wrapping around both of us. He glanced toward her and the corner of his mouth tipped upward. "I'll be fine."

"Yes," he said. "You will be. But I don't like Reed. I don't like how he's handled things." He cut a look at me. "Don't disappoint her again."

"No problem." I meant it sarcastically, but he smiled for real.

"Good, then we won't have one. I'll call you, Buttercup. Be careful." Then he pivoted and strode out of the apartment, leaving us alone.

"Buttercup?" I demanded, slanting a look toward her.

She lifted her mug of coffee and held out a second one to me.

"I brought you coffee."

"Sometimes," I said with a sigh as I met her halfway and took the mug from her fingers, "you are too damn stubborn."

"Thank you," she told me with a wink. "I try."

Then she turned and headed for the library, leaving me to follow. Which I would. I glanced at the door to the hall and paused long enough to rearm the alarm before I continued after her.

She was standing in front of the cold fireplace, the steaming mug of coffee on the mantle. Her gaze was on the wood that had been stacked there, waiting.

"Is he here?" she asked before I made it three steps.

I sighed. "Yes, he's upstairs. Drunk as hell and sleeping it off."

All at once, her shoulders dipped and her head bowed.

I felt like an asshole. "I brought him here to keep him from going home. He didn't want to go back to my place."

Worry filled her eyes as she pivoted to face me. "So, you two just used your keys."

Blowing out a long breath. "I know, overstepping. As usual. But... I needed him to settle down. This seemed like a good alternative. For what it's worth, he didn't want to come here when he thought you were here—and no, I'm *not* telling you that to hurt you."

I put my mug down on the table and crossed the room to where she stood.

"I'm telling you because—they used the threat of hurting *you* to make him cooperate."

A frown tightened her brow. "And you're telling me that...?"

"Because you were right," I said, lifting my hands to her arms and then clenching them before I dropped my hands away. "I've spent most of your life trying to protect you from everything. From me. From the family. From... our world."

Fuck, we should have had this conversation a long time before.

"And I plan to keep protecting you, but I have two choices—I can pursue the definition of insanity and continue to not involve you in it or I can tell you what's been going on. I can..."

The words locked in my throat, and my jaw clenched as if of its own volition.

"It kills you...doesn't it?" The bruises in her eyes seemed to retreat as she lifted her chin and met my gaze. "That you can't just tell me what to do, lock me in a car, or a room—or just make me be a good little girl."

A laugh escaped me. "You have been many things, Lainey," I told her, and this time, I let my fingers trail down her cheek. "A good girl has never been one of them. You are too willful by half, far too stubborn, and you seem to thrive on driving me mad."

"You always wanted to control me."

I dropped my chin and shook my head. "I wanted to control the world so it wouldn't hurt you..." Ezra's cutting remarks sliced at me from the past. "For too long I thought you were my sister and I hated that my reaction to you was as unbrotherly as possible."

Shock rippled across her face, but she didn't pull away.

"They were never quiet about their affair, you know," I told her.

"I know," she whispered, and the sadness that lingered

in her voice pulled me closer. "I hated that they did that to your mother."

"I don't think she cared by the end... she always loved him." Disgust curled in his tone. "I wish I could say he returned the affection."

Cupping her cheek, I pressed my lips to her forehead and closed my eyes. For a moment, I told myself, just drink in her closeness for a moment. I needed it like I needed oxygen.

"I hated him," I continued. "Hated him because I thought you were his child and he ignored you. Mom—my mother—"

"She thought that too?" True grief echoed in Lainey's voice. "But she was always...so kind to me."

"Because she was a kind person," I said, then laughed. "I know, I don't take after her."

Lainey pulled back, but she didn't retreat. "You tried to protect me because you thought I was your sister."

"Yeah..."

"Then you didn't stop when you found out I wasn't."

"No," I murmured. That day had been... a gift and a curse. The complicated emotions she aroused in me. Feelings I should never have toward a sibling or someone so much younger than me. It didn't seem to matter how ruthlessly I suppressed them all. "You've been mine from the beginning... Mine to protect. Mine to keep safe. Mine... to cherish."

"I—"

I touched two fingers to her lips and she quieted.

"You need to let me say this, Lainey. Because I don't know that I'll ever have the words or the wherewithal to admit it again. You have *always* been mine. Even when I thought it made me sick and perverted to want you like that. I was protecting you—from me as much as from the rest of the world."

The softness in her mouth as she opened it in a gentle "o" should not be so tender.

"When I realized there was no taboo to keep me away...I damn near went to find you then. But you were too young. I needed you to grow up, and I needed you *safe* while you did it. Far away from the bastards like Bradley Sharpe and the other cutthroats in our world. It helped that your grandfather didn't want any of us near you either...and I made sure the guys left you alone. If they didn't get the message the first time..."

Well, I'd broken more than a few bones. Busted more than a few faces.

"I'd kill for you." Even as the words broke out of me, I braced for her rejection. Her eyes were clear as she stared at me. "I'd kill a thousand times over. There is no crime I wouldn't commit for you... Do I hate that Hardigan has had you? Or Ezra? Or now Cavendish seems to be falling into your orbit?"

She licked her lips, apprehension flickering to life.

"Yes. I fucking despise it. You were supposed to be mine. Only mine." My hands were shaking when I wrapped them around her biceps. It took every ounce of my control to tug her to me and keep it gentle. "But I learned something over the last two years."

"What's that?"

"My love has no boundaries...and neither do you."

She frowned.

"Keep them. Get rid of them. I don't care. I mean... I'm with Cavendish. No one gets to hurt you again. But you have to accept me, Lainey. You have to take me... all of me.

The good. The bad. The brutally ugly. I *need* you to want me too. I—"

It was like my voice cracked there, pushing those words out; opening a vein went against everything inside of me. I was ready to go to my knees and beg.

"Adam," she whispered and then she surged upward and her lips were on mine. I sucked in the fire and the heat, drowning in need.

Drowning in *her*.

CHAPTER
SIXTEEN

LAINEY

"I need you to want me."

The words played on a loop in my head. The raw, open vulnerability was not something I was used to hearing from Adam. More, the open emotion was all over his face. The blue-violet of his eyes had given way to almost pure purple for the intensity within them.

Need for him ignited in me. I did need him. More, I wanted him. As much as I could punch him, I pushed myself upward in his arms and fused our lips together. I nipped and bit at his lower lip until his mouth opened to me. A violent sound escaped through his as he banded one arm around me and lifted me off my feet.

I sank my hand into his hair, fisting it as he tilted his head back. Wild and wanton was the desire igniting in me. There was something dark and utterly primitive in his declaration about me being his.

Before—it had irritated me with its presumption and demand. More, it was like he wanted to incite a fight with me. The baffling combination of push and pull where he wanted everything and gave no ground frustrated me on every damn level.

This man, who had been my bane and protector, my tormentor and defender, had literally just said every word I hadn't realized I needed to hear. More, he was here and he'd looked after Ezra.

Worry for Ezra collided with the almost feral desperation blooming within me. I dug my fingers into his hair, tugging his head back further. With my legs around his hips, I balanced against him as he dragged his hands down my back.

"Adam," I panted in between strokes of his tongue dueling with mine.

"I'm here," he promised.

"Ezra..."

"Can fucking wait," he snarled, his fist in my hair keeping me close so his breath was like fire licking over my lips. "They are a part of this, I accept that. But right now? It's you and it's me."

My stomach bottomed out. We were in the middle of the library and...

I searched his eyes as he glared at me. Yes, the heat in his eyes was real. The demand—it sent a thrill through me. "You really do want me." There was a genuine sense of wonder at the concept. He was always so damn careful with me. Brutish in his attempts to cut me off, but gentle in everything else.

I didn't want gentle.

Nor did I want careful.

I wanted *Adam*.

"Did you think I just cut myself open for kicks?" He

practically growled and it had my pussy clenching in anticipation. "What do you need me to do to prove this—"

I pressed my fingers to his lips. "I *need* you," I whispered and soaked in the way his pupils dilated and his breath hitched. "I want you."

His pulse sped up, and his nostrils flared.

"Right here, right now—no take backs, no second thoughts...let me have *you*...Adam. Let me have you, and take me, I'm right here."

Those were the last words that I was able to give voice to because when he kissed me this time it was a pure battle for dominance. One I was more than satisfied to let him win —after a struggle. Delight curved through me at the thrust of his tongue.

A moment later, he was on his knees and my back was against...a faux fur rug. This was new. What else...fuck it, I didn't care what else was new. Not when he was staring down at me like he was trying to decide what part of me to eat first.

I had a few thoughts.

Without a word, he tugged my boots off and then my leggings were peeled downward. When he turned away, I sat up and pulled the sweater up and over my head. When it pulled free, all I could see was the way he drank in the sight of me.

Goosebumps rippled over my skin. Not an hour ago, I'd been in a car with Bodhi. He seemed intent on driving me mad and it was working. Now, I was getting naked in front of Adam and hoping like hell he wouldn't leave me hanging.

Ezra was here and at least safe. Pretty Boy was coming home soon. Adam was with me now...

My pulse raced as the air grew almost too heavy to breathe.

"Take the bra off," Adam ordered and the clenched worry inside of me let go. I took my time, stretching my legs out before I reached for the bra.

His gaze traced over me, leaving fire in its wake as I unclipped the bra and slid it off. It wasn't anything fancy. Like the panties he'd stripped away, it was soft, practical, and comfortable.

With his hot gaze drifting over my breasts before coming up to let his eyes lock on mine, I was alive with competing sensations. I wanted to feel his hands, his lips, his teeth... his cock. I wanted to feel all of him on me.

Yet, he stood there, drinking me in, and my nipples were so tight it was almost painful.

"Lean back," he ordered, his hand going to his belt. "On your elbows and spread those legs, Lainey. Let me see all of you."

Apprehension assaulted me, apprehension and nerves. Butterflies filled my stomach, and I swallowed. This was Adam...

This was what I wanted.

He was who I wanted.

His gaze snapped up to meet mine. "You're so damn beautiful, Lainey—let me see you." Even as he spoke, he pulled his belt free and my pussy clenched. I wanted to see him too, and I needed to find out where this faux fur rug came from.

Later...

Focused on his eyes, I took a deeper breath. Then another. The tension coiling through me relaxed.

"Adam," I whispered.

"I'm right here," he said, taking a single step toward me.

So close and yet he wasn't touching me. "Not going anywhere...waited a long time for you. So. Damn. Long."

"You want to see me." The knowledge went from unsettling me to emboldening me. He licked his lips, and my breath got stuck in my throat for a moment. "You want to see what is yours."

His *mine* had always come across as so primitive. And yet, the brand of it resonated. These men made me absolutely insane.

I dropped to my elbows and slid my right leg wider, baring my pussy for him to see. I was soaking wet. I didn't have to check. I could feel the slickness on my thighs. There was a dampness hitting my ass.

The ache of wanting him filled me with every beat of my heart.

"Now you," I said, as I lifted my right foot and pointed my toes at him. "I want to see you—all of you. I want to see what is *mine*."

His hands were already moving to the buttons on his shirt at my demand, but there was no mistaking the pleasure reflecting in his expression.

"Yes, Adam," I told him as our gazes locked. I didn't stay on my elbows, I moved up to my knees so I could unbutton his pants. "I do want you...I've wanted you for so damn long, and all I ever thought was that you hated me."

Was I scolding him?

Yes, goddammit.

"You hurt me over and over with every rejection. Every cutting remark."

His shirt was open and I tugged the zipper downward. The heat of his erection was right there, a bulge that wouldn't be denied. I'd gripped his cock a few times lately, twisted it too, and he'd not been put off.

What had he said when I asked him if pain did it for him?

"You do it for me."

"I thought it would be better for you," he said in a low voice that held elements of regret. "What I wanted from you and how I wanted it... you weren't ready for that. I had to keep my distance, Lainey. You needed to grow up... Then..."

Pain flickered across his face as I curled my fingers into the waistband of his briefs and his pants and peeled them downwards so his cock could spring free.

What was it with the men in my life? They were all hung like damn beasts. His cock was long, thick, and even fatter around the crown. His tip was red to the point of purple, and the veins along his shaft were so pronounced, I swore I could see the blood pumping through them.

"Then?" I asked him as he stepped out of his pants, and I pressed my hands against his thighs. At this angle, I could swallow his cock. I'd probably choke on it, but there was something so damn powerful about feeling them stretch my cheeks, press me past the point of comfort and push into my throat.

"Then... I wanted to be free of all of it," he admitted, his voice ragged and hell in his eyes. "I wanted to be free for you so that we didn't bring all this ugliness into your life. I wish...I wish I'd understood that it was hurting you."

I dug my nails into the clenched muscles of his thighs. "You'd have done it anyway." No doubt existed within me. He would have punished me, pushed me away, threatened me with anything... "To keep me safe, you would have inflicted everything on me. It's why you let me go with Milo."

There...a muscle twitched in his jaw, and I swore his cock flexed.

"Pretty Boy captivated me, and as much as you hated it, you protected him and me. You have done everything you could to keep me safe, even if it meant pushing me to other men."

He closed his eyes and dropped his chin. A bead of pre-cum appeared like a pearl on his slit. I tilted my head to press a kiss to the base of his cock.

His sharp inhale dragged my gaze upward, and I met his dark stare as I teased my tongue along the thickest vein and traced it up to his crown and then down again. With one hand, I cupped his balls and stroked them as his chest began to rise and fall in swift motions.

"Yes," he confessed. "But you're still *mine*, Lainey. You always have been."

"Yes," I said, willing to admit it. "I am." Shock registered on his face, and then I slid my hand up to his cock and opened my mouth. I swallowed all of him, taking him as deep as I could, and it left my jaw aching.

Adam's hand came to my hair, and he fisted it as I continued to struggle to swallow him to the root. I didn't know if I could, but I was determined.

"Lainey," he said, his ragged voice its very own caress. The muscles on his chest moved, and so did the ones on his thighs. I'd always known he was strong, powerful, but I'd never gotten to savor him like this.

I pulled back until his cock rested on my tongue and I lapped up more of the pre-cum. Bitter, strong, with a taste that just made me think of him. I was swallowing bits of him.

"Fuck me, Adam," I said. "Fuck me and claim me." No more holding back. If nothing else, Pretty Boy had taught me how to ask for what I wanted. Ezra had shown me that sometimes he needed to hear the words and have me surrender.

For Adam... I could do all of that.

"There's no gentleness in me," Adam warned, but he didn't stop moving; one moment, I was face to dick with him, the next, I was one my back and my legs were over his shoulders.

I raised my hands to his face, and when he leaned in close, he said, "Open your mouth..." I did as he said and then he spit. The saliva struck my tongue, and I swore it mingled with his pre-cum.

It should be a total turn off, and yet, a moment later, he stroked his cock against my soaked labia and let out a groan.

"You are so fucking mine." He lined himself up and thrust in so deep it shoved all of the air out of my lungs. He swooped in to kiss me, fucking me with his tongue as he began to power his cock into me.

Everywhere stretched. My cunt. My ass. My legs. Then he was gripping my ass, and he teased his fingers along the seam.

I couldn't breathe. I couldn't think. Every slam of his body into mine sent pleasure spiking through me. He seemed to know just how to touch me and where. His chest rubbed against my nipples. Then he dragged his head up.

"Play with your clit," he ordered. "Make yourself come. Now."

I wanted to object, to defy him, because goddammit with the orders. But my hand was already moving....

"Wait," he snapped, stilling, and I jerked. "Give me your fingers..." When I held them to his lips, he spit on them. "Now, rub me into your clit."

Fuck me.

I slid the hand between us, and he pulled himself back far enough to watch as I teased my fingers against my clit. It was swollen and throbbing. My pussy clenched around his cock where he still rested partially inside of me.

"That's it, Lainey. Make yourself come on my cock, I want to feel it, and then I'm going to fuck you through that..." I swore it was his words that triggered the first explosion. I rolled my hips upward, and he thrust into me again, then again.

"Adam," I cried out, and then his mouth was on mine, and the spit he shoved past my lips, I swallowed. Somewhere, a door opened and I gave a little jerk. I was shuddering and when I turned my head, I found Ezra staring at us.

Hips still pistoning, Adam shot a look over to Ezra. "Sit your ass down and wait. This is my time with her."

I shivered and another wave of pleasure crashed down in me as Ezra dropped into one of the chairs. His hands were shaking and his hair disheveled.

"Eyes on me," Adam ordered, and I caught Ezra snapping his gaze to Adam's ass before I looked up at him. "Ezra is going to watch me have you...and you're going to show him how much you want this."

Fuck...

"Yes," I whispered as he leaned in closer.

"Good girl," he said. "Now spit in my mouth."

So fucking gross, and I did it anyway, his smile went purely wicked and then he began to rock into me again. Adam stretched me out, every thrust hitting that perfect spot, and I was going to come.

Again.

"Let us hear you, Kotyonok," Ezra said, his words a demand and entreaty.

"You heard him," Adam growled. "Scream for us." Then he pinched one of my nipples as he pushed a finger into my ass, and I came so hard I swore I blacked out.

I definitely screamed.

CHAPTER
SEVENTEEN

EZRA

Waking up to a thundering headache and a mouth that tasted like ass, I was grateful for the glass of water and pain relievers on the nightstand. Blurred vision and even fuzzier thoughts meant it took a minute to even recognize where I was.

Lainey's.

We'd come to Lainey's. Adam said she was out of town, and I hadn't wanted to go to his place. Fuck, the last three days were in splinters, and I'd spent more time drinking than talking.

I needed the liquid courage, but he wouldn't discuss shit with me while I was drunk. So I'd just gotten drunker. Stalking into the bathroom, I threw myself through a shower and brushed my teeth. At least Lainey's guest rooms were all outfitted with everything. Hell, I'd bet there was new underwear with the tags still on.

It took me almost all of the ten-minute shower to get most of the pieces assembled. There were blank spots, but I figured they were all labeled whiskey, whiskey sour, and more fucking whiskey.

After brushing my teeth, I downed more water. As hangovers went, this one wasn't so bad. I needed food though. Food—and then maybe more alcohol before I talked to Adam. If I put it in the coffee, he wouldn't notice right?

There were clothes in the case he'd dropped at the foot of the guest bed. On my way to the stairs, I paused at the entrance to Lainey's bedroom. There was an imprint on the comforter. Adam had slept in here.

I didn't blame him. I wanted to sleep in here too...it smelled like her. Just the essence of her perfume. Closing my eyes, I filled my lungs with the hints of her. It was a good thing she wasn't here. At the same time, fuck—I wished she was. I wanted to just...

She'd listen. She'd tell me it would be all right. She—she just made everything better. My hands trembled, and the burning need for alcohol had me shoving away from her room. I didn't deserve to be in there.

The last time I'd been here, I made her a promise that I failed to keep within minutes, fleeing instead of staying. The history between us was littered with so many broken promises. I just hit the last step when a genuine moan drifted down the hall from the library.

My cock was almost instantly hard at the combination of masculine and feminine groans. I followed the sexual symphony to the library door.

"Adam!" Lainey's sharp cry sliced through me. Need and desire pumped through the pair of syllables that made up his name. I had my hand on the door and pushed it open before I fully registered the slap of skin on skin.

Lainey sprawled, naked, on a fur rug. Flushed pink and dotted with hints of sweat, she had her knees hooked over Adam's shoulders as he fucked into her. His whole body was one long, rippling muscle from where his ass clenched to the sharp cut lines along his lats.

She took the full weight of him, soaking him based on the squelch of sound released every time his hips jerked forward. His mouth fused to hers but her eyes were open and they fixed on me.

Fuck. My cock was so hard it was painful. I didn't know where to look first. The scent of sex was in the air. Her perfume. His musk. My mouth watered, and I was half-tempted to start stroking myself off as he kept fucking her.

Then those blue-violet eyes pinned me in place. His eyes were practically purple, and I forgot how to breathe. "Sit your ass down and wait. This is my time with her."

The command resonated and I shuddered. I dropped into the chair even as my cock cramped against the zipper. It hurt and it felt good.

"Eyes on me," Adam ordered. I didn't know if he meant her or me, but sitting here, I had the perfect view of his ass, the way his balls slapped at her perfectly pink pussy and flickers of his cock drilling into her. It was—everything. "Ezra is going to watch me have you...and you're going to show him how much you want this."

Holy. Shit.

I forgot how to breathe.

"Yes," she whispered and it ripped through me. I'd had her when her voice trembled like that. The feeling of sinking into that sweet pussy, the wet heat enveloping me and the desire to fuck her raw until I filled her to the brim.

Then I wanted to do it again.

"Good girl," Adam encouraged her, and I had to lick my lips. I got my pants open and my hand in to wrap around my brutally hard cock. "Now spit in my mouth."

The fierce order demanded absolute obedience, and she did it. Then he slammed his hips harder and I was torn between imagining myself as him and sinking into her or being her and feeling him stretch me like that.

Fuck...what if I was right in between them? Fucking her as he fucked me?

"Let us hear you, Kotyonok," I begged, squeezing my cock to the point tears burned in my eyes. I could come just from the sound of them.

"You heard him," Adam growled. "Scream for us." He was all over her, his hands everywhere and when his finger pushed into her ass, she screamed and I let out a gasp of my own.

Pre-cum leaked from my cock. It was slicking up my hand.

"Get your fucking hand off your cock." The command had me letting go before I could push myself to come. Adam had shifted, his cock was still thick, engorged and soaked. He'd pulled out of her and my sweet kitten was mewling as he pulled her up.

"You're having your time with her," I argued.

"I don't care," he said. "You don't get to make yourself come. If you're staying in here, you're doing exactly what I tell you."

Rebellion flexed inside of me. He had her on her knees, in between us and he kneaded and cupped her breasts.

"Spread your thighs," Adam ordered her and she did, letting me see that drenched pussy. "See how fucking wet she is..."

"Yes," I said, shaking with it.

"That's for me," he continued and it was almost a taunt.

Pain and pleasure pierced through me as I dragged my gaze back up to his. "You?"

He slid his hand up to her lips and pressed his finger between them. They were puffy and swollen, and her eyes were so dilated I couldn't see the hazel shade at all. They were practically black.

"Do you want to suck his cock?" Adam asked and I shook as I slid off the chair onto my own knees. Was he...

Lainey lifted her gaze to mine. Tears filmed over them. "He's..."

"Please," I said. "I'll beg if you need me to—or I can eat you out while Adam fucks you."

The chance to be there. To be with them... even partially?

"Get naked," Adam ordered. "And don't touch your cock. You stand there until she's willing to touch you."

It was hell.

It was purgatory.

It was everything.

I shed my clothes so fast, and my cock strained, almost pulsing in its need to be closer to them. Adam lifted her ass and then he pushed into her again. He was fucking her from the back. It blocked my view of him, but I could see her.

"Kotyonok..." It was almost a plea.

"Don't," she snapped in between gasps. Her expression tightened and relaxed. I couldn't tell if his thrusts were pleasuring her or hurting. Both? Maybe? But she was straining back to meet him.

Adam pressed his hands to her asscheeks and he spread them apart before he spit at her crack and a moan tore out of me even as I tried to swallow.

"Please," I tried again. "I'm...I know I hurt you." This time, I dragged my gaze from her to him then back again.

Adam's eyes held no answers for me, and Lainey whimpered as he pressed a finger into her ass and worked his hand around to her clit. Then she was screaming as she came and I dug my fingers into my palms. My cock was desperate, even a single touch and I'd probably detonate.

She was always so fucking beautiful when she came, but the pair of them together—it was art. Pure and simple.

"I couldn't tell you," I said. "I wanted to just protect you —to protect him."

"You kissed her," Lainey said, her words torn between anger and a groan as Adam dragged her up, spread her legs over his lap as he lifted her and sank her down on his cock. Nothing was hidden from me here. "You didn't tell me and then..."

"And then he announced it." I could fucking cry. "I don't want her. I've never wanted her." The only people I truly wanted were right here. "But it will keep you safe."

"I don't want to be safe," she snapped and then it was Lainey who held me in the ferociousness of her gaze. Sweat shone on her skin and her hair clung damply to her cheeks.

Her nipples were tight and her clit was so swollen, I could see it poking out of its hood. She took his monster cock like she'd been made for him.

Made for me.

Made for us.

"You have to be," I whispered and Adam nipped at her throat.

"It's the first thing he's said that he's right about," he growled and the roughness in his tone was its own caress. "But you are done making these decisions on your own."

That snapped my gaze to his and I realized he was talking to me. "You wanted my attention, Ezra. You fucking have it."

Another wave of pleasure went through me. "Adam..."

"Shut up," he told me and I snapped my mouth shut. "You can plead your case in a minute. Lainey... suck him off while I fuck you. I want to hear him come with you."

She tilted her head back to look up at him and she wasn't alone. Was he serious?

"I don't know if he deserves that," she murmured and my hopes crashed, and I went to my knees.

"He doesn't," Adam confirmed. "But he knows that... and he needs you."

Another wave of regret crashed through me.

"Let him have you." The rugged command wrapped around me even as Lainey turned her gaze to me once more.

"You hurt me," she whispered and I bowed my head.

"I swear—I only wanted to protect you."

Then soft fingers were on my face and I lifted my chin to meet her gaze as she stroked my cheek. "Then you have to let me protect you."

There was no wiggle room in that statement. Behind her, Adam watched us both. My gaze went from hers to his then back. She was still stretched over his cock and mine strained out to them.

"I don't know how," I admitted. After all this time...

"Then you'll learn," Adam said like it was the simplest thing ever. "Swallow his cock, Lainey. Give him something else to think about."

She brushed her lips to mine. There was sweat, sweetness, and something bitter. I teased my tongue along the seam of her lips and she opened to me. I tasted him on her lips. That was Adam… and I groaned as she let out a grunt. Adam was fucking her again.

When she pulled back, I almost wanted to retreat, to savor them but I couldn't. Not with Adam watching me. Not with her reaching for me. She was on her hands and knees and I pushed up higher.

The moment her lips closed over my tip, I let out a groan.

"Don't you fucking come," Adam ordered and I dragged my eyes open to stare at him.

Was he fucking insane?

"No, you let her play with your balls, suck your cock, and tease you until you can't see straight. But you don't come until she does—and I do…and I plan to fuck her for a while."

This was death. This was…how I died.

"Do as you're told," Adam said and he was stroking his hand over her back. The feel of her cheeks hollowing as she sucked me deeper threatened every drop of my control.

I had no idea how I could enjoy this if I had to fight coming the whole time, and there was a hint of wicked pleasure in Adam's smile.

The bastard damn well knew it. So I reached over her, sinking one hand into her hair so I could fuck her mouth properly and the other I put over his on her ass.

"Exactly," Adam said before he spit at her crack and I leaned over to do the same, then we worked our fingers against the tight puckered hole. "Together."

She bucked between us, but I couldn't look away from Adam. We stretched her with one finger from each of us and heat licked over my skin as my orgasm kept threatening to burst through me.

First Lainey—then Adam.

Then I could come.

"I'm here," I promised. "I can do this."

"Yes, you can," Adam told me and the pride in his voice gave me a very vicious sense of satisfaction. Then Lainey began to mewl around my cock as she came.

CHAPTER
EIGHTEEN

LAINEY

I couldn't take a deep breath around Ezra's cock as he slid in and out of my throat. It took time to focus on when to breathe, but then Adam would fuck into me and shove all the air back out. A riot of sensation cascaded over me. Adam's fingers bit into my hip; his free hand was on my ass. Ezra fisted my hair. I flowed between them, used and pleasured, and then used again.

It was too much and not enough. I was already shuddering on the edge of an orgasm when they worked their fingers into my ass. Both of them. The burn was intense, the pressure too much, and I screamed around Ezra's cock.

He eased up as tears rushed down my face and a gush of wetness coated my thighs. Then Adam was thrusting again, the rhythm a demand for me to follow. It was like my skin was too tight and the Ezra's cock rested on my tongue, heavy and hot. It leaked pre-cum and I lapped at it.

So different from Adam, and they were both different

from Pretty Boy. Drunk on the taste of them, I wished Pretty Boy was here right now for as long as I could string the thoughts together and then there was a third finger working into my ass and I bucked, both pulling away and pushing back.

Adam's low throaty chuckle threatened me with madness. "So perfect and wild. Can you feel me?"

Could I...

It wasn't like I could answer, the drive of his body into mine rocked me onto Ezra and thrust his cock even deeper into my throat. Between them, they filled me over and over. Even though Adam had ordered Ezra to wait, I teased and tortured his cock every chance I got.

Particularly his piercings. I knew what he liked, how he wanted them tugged and teased. I lost count of how many fingers were in my ass, just that the burn was intense and it continued until it added another layer to this sensual chaos they were unleashing on me.

"Come for me one more time," Adam ordered.

I wanted to sob. I was shaking, focus was impossible. It took all of my concentration to ride his cock while swallowing Ezra's. He wanted *more?*

"Yes you can," Adam growled, stretching against my back, and trapping Ezra's arm between us. His face was next to mine, where Ezra's cock filled my mouth and I could see Adam through the haze of tears in my eyes. "You can do this—you exquisite woman. You're everything I thought you'd be and more. You are beyond all imagining, and I want you to come on my cock, I want to lose myself in you while you feel nothing but us."

I didn't feel anything but—they scissored their fingers and another hand teased right against my clit. I had no idea which of them it was, but I came. I tried to lock my jaw open as the soundless screams escaped.

A soaking wetness escaped me, and then Adam let out a shout and hot jets exploded out of him and I could feel him coming inside of me. It triggered me again and I was shaking as I caught him looking upward.

Ezra swore and he gave a jerk. The first pump of cum hit the back of my throat. He started to pull out but I held onto him. Trusting Adam to keep me up even as we were all shaking.

Choking on his release, I fought to swallow it, and Adam seemed to slide through his own cum as he pulled back and then pumped into me again. I had no idea how he was still hard. One of them pinched my clit and I blacked out.

Awareness floated back through me. A rumble of male voices. One so intensely satisfied and deep, it unfurled a sense of pleasure somewhere in my core. I'd made Adam sound like that. The other voice, rougher, tortured and sad —yet there was an ineffable joy there.

Ezra...

At some point, they'd eased their fingers from my ass, and I was sprawled between them. Ezra ran his hands over my chest, petting even as Adam stroked my hair. We were sticky, hot, and fuck—I hurt so good.

"There she is," Adam murmured and then he nuzzled a kiss to my ear and down my cheek until he cupped my chin and turned my head. He kissed me, tongue sinking in to lap at mine.

The bitter flavor of Ezra's cum lingered on my tongue, but Adam seemed intent on chasing it, and I swore my pussy clenched at the emptiness. He'd slipped away from me and there was so much dampness between my thighs.

A mouth locked over one of my nipples and Ezra bit down. The scrape of his teeth was almost electric, and it was too much. I writhed, but they both had legs over mine, and they were pinning me.

When Adam lifted his head, he stared down at me with so much...love. The depth of raw emotion in his eyes stuttered all the objections as too much. I hurt from how much I was shaking, and my cunt was stretched and my ass bruised. Even my throat was sore.

But looking into his eyes, I'd do it all again. Right now.

"Ezra," Adam said, his voice still commanding no matter how silky and soft.

"Hmm?" Ezra sucked against my nipple and my back arched, but I couldn't escape them.

Adam's gaze drifted from me to Ezra, and then he released my chin to fist Ezra's hair and he tugged. Ezra lifted his head and fire seemed to spark in the air between them as they stared at each other.

My heart beat brutally against my ribs as Ezra started to lean forward, to fall into that kiss that seemed to wait poised between them. Fuck, I could *feel* the tension.

Lust crashed through me. Lust and pure want to see them connect. Ezra needed him so much and for the first time, I saw it in Adam. The need for Ezra—the need and the need to control. Just like with me.

All of my fatigue vanished under the new wave. But just a breath away from his lips, Adam tugged Ezra's head back. Surprise flickered across Ezra's face but Adam's smile filled me with a mixture of excitement and trepidation.

"You and I need to have a long talk," Adam told him. "You took one kiss then ran like hell. You avoided me. You fought me. You made really stupid decisions."

"I'm sorry—"

Adam shook his head, cutting Ezra off with a look. "I don't want your apologies. But you're going to have to earn the right to kiss me. For me to kiss you. You want to be mine, then you're going to learn what that means."

My stomach bottomed out as Adam glanced at me.

"Open your mouth, Lainey."

I didn't think. I just did it. Too riveted by the byplay between them. Adam leaned forward and he spit into my mouth again, and I shuddered. Then he kissed me like he was fucking me.

"So good for me," Adam whispered against my lips. "You're going to be good for me again."

I was?

"Ezra is going to eat me out of you while I have your ass..."

"She promised that to me." The objection from Ezra half-startled me, mostly because Adam hadn't let either of us go. All my life, Adam had been domineering, insistent, and controlling. I should have known he would be in bed.

But he'd gone to his knees for me.

I could be on my knees for him.

"Give me to him," I told Ezra. "I know I said you could try my ass...but Adam wants it too..."

Ezra dipped his gaze to me and the uncertainty in his eyes threatened to break me.

"Trust us," I whispered. "Be here...with us." Then because he had to understand... "Give him what he wants."

He was asking for Ezra to give him himself.

"He *sees* you now."

Understanding lit in Ezra's green eyes. But that enlightenment did nothing to assuage the fear. He looked from me to Adam.

"Is that what you want?" The question sparked tears in my eyes. "Am...I? Are we what you want?"

"You're my best fucking friend," Adam told him with the kind of fierceness that demanded you believe him. "I had no idea you wanted to be my lover, and I've never fucked a man before, but if that's what you need—I'll figure it out."

My heart stopped and Ezra's eyes widened.

"But right now, what I want is for you to earn that trust. To prove to me you want us." Adam glanced down at me then over at him. "I'm going to fuck her ass and you're going to eat me out of her pussy. You want to know what it will be like to suck me off...you'll find out. But from now on, we're doing this my way."

I bit my lip as Ezra shuddered. He searched Adam's face as Adam relaxed his grip on Ezra's hair. Then let him go. He wouldn't force him. He had to want it.

"You need lube for her ass," Ezra said. "She's loose now, but in a minute, she's not going to feel anything but me."

A true smirk curved Adam's lips. "That sounds like a challenge."

It was a—oh shit. They both turned heated eyes on me. I went from sprawling beneath them to in Adam's lap, his cock was against my back and he had three fingers in my ass as Ezra planted himself face-first into my pussy.

I was too sensitive by half, and I was squirming and fighting the urge to scream as his tongue swept over my clit. He delved deep into me, and I knew he was hunting for every drop of Adam and that thought turned me inside out.

An orgasm held me right on the edge then Adam replaced his fingers with his cock and laid my head back against his shoulder as he urged us both backwards. Ezra crawled along, holding onto my thighs as he helped Adam push into my ass.

Thoughts scattered utterly after that as Ezra licked, nipped, and sucked until I was bucking and Adam began to thrust into my ass. At some point, he came again, and then Ezra pushed into my cunt and filled me while he divided his attention between me and Adam.

Wrapping a hand around Ezra's nape, I dragged him down to kiss me. I licked at the cum on his lips and rode the wildness as he thrust deep. Adam was softening in my ass but they were hanging onto each other as they split me wide open between them.

When Ezra let me up for air, Adam turned my head to kiss me, then he pushed me back to Ezra again. They were trading kisses through me, and when Ezra finally came again, we collapsed into a sweaty, soaked heap.

We lay there for—hours. I thought I might have slept. At some point, Ezra eased out of me, and then Adam did. One of them went away, and then there was a washcloth on my thighs, cleaning me up and another on my ass.

Adam picked me up, and then Ezra was moving around the room. It reeked of sex, and I couldn't find the energy to care.

"My room," I whispered. "My bed."

"Shower first," Adam said.

"Bossy," I complained and he nipped my lower lip.

"Yes," he said. "In bed, I will always be in charge."

Right. We'd fight about that later...

"Ezra," I said, and he was there as Adam set me on my feet. I was shaking and there was no steadiness to me.

"I can stay in the guest room—" Ezra began, and I let go of Adam to wrap myself around Ezra. He was shaking as much as I was.

"You're staying with us," I told him. "You're mine too."

It was like someone cut his strings, because he half-collapsed in my arms. If not for Adam, we probably would have both gone to the ground. Still, I held Ezra and cradled him.

We'd figure this out.

All of us.

CHAPTER
NINETEEN

ADAM

S pending a day in bed seemed beyond hedonistic, and yet, that was exactly what we were going to do. While Lainey hadn't mentioned him directly, I didn't doubt that Hardigan might show up. If he did, we'd deal with it. In the meantime, I shuttled them through the shower. Lainey wasn't altogether steady on her feet. Ezra, however, seemed to be doing better while he had her to look after.

As much as I wanted to be the one raining that tenderness down on her, the fact there was a light in his eyes hadn't been lost on me. Nor the wariness whenever he thought I wasn't looking. *That* part pissed me right the fuck off. Still, I let him wrap her up in a towel and cuddle her while I finished my shower.

She was clearly sore, and I hadn't really been gentle. I made a point of pressing soothing kisses to the bruises on her hips and the bite marks on her breasts. Ezra abandoned us for a couple of minutes to head downstairs for "snacks," and when I would have followed him, a gentle hand latched onto mine.

"He'll be back," she murmured, and the light touch tethered me more firmly than a chain. Her lips were puffy from kissing, and sucking cock, if I were honest. Her eyes were lighter than they'd been when she walked in with Cavendish.

Lighter and maybe a little more welcoming. She studied me with a direct, relentless intensity that would unsettle a lesser man. Yet, I found myself lifting my chin and squaring my shoulders for her inspection.

Like I knew the sun would rise each day, I knew she was about to tweak me. "How are you?"

Three words that actually caught me off guard. I frowned. Ezra and I had both pulled on clothes after our showers—well, boxers for me and pajama bottoms for him. Lainey had ignored the shirt I offered her and sprawled on her bed.

Nothing in the world prepared me for how truly beautiful she was. She had a body that had been shaped for sin, but a mind so razor sharp she practically dared me to underestimate her, and a heart...

A heart that was as fearless as it was boundless. Protecting her from the rest of the world was an unceasing task, because she would never hide from it and her loyalty knew no depths she would not plumb to protect the ones she loved.

"What?"

The corners of her lips curved upwards in a slow smile that had me narrowing my eyes. "*How*," she repeated softly, squeezing my fingers, "are *you?*"

I half-twisted on the bed to study her. This was her room, so the colors of the bedding, the soft oak of the wood, and the warmth of the walls all suited her. Her damp hair had begun to dry in waves. It spilled over her shoulders and hid her breasts from me, and I wanted to push it aside.

More, I wanted to spread her out and play for hours. I wanted to taste her orgasms. I wanted to see her fall apart. I wanted to utterly—

"Did I break you?" The question slapped a little reality back into me. The tweak was exactly what I needed, and a soft chuckle escaped me.

"You broke me a long time ago," I admitted. "You just had no idea how much power over me you held."

"Bullshit," she retorted, and the fire in her eyes was everything. "It's a pretty story though. Now… tell me the truth before he comes back. How are you doing?"

"I'm…" The word *fine* would not just roll off my tongue. "I have you," I said and the truth rolled all around those words. Sliding my hand to her cheek, I savored the softness of her skin. More, that I could touch her like this. Touch her. Stare at her. Kiss her. "Ezra is here…"

Though he was taking a hot minute downstairs. I should have followed him.

"And he'll come back up," she told me with a kind of certainty that I envied. "You didn't reject him."

It was like she read my mind, and at the same time, I sighed. When I tugged her to me, she flowed right into my arms, and I moved to sit against the headboard with her in my lap.

"He's always—he's always needed me. I never realized how much." Giving into the need to wrap myself around her, I savored the fact she threaded her arms around my neck. Soft, warm, naked, and holding me tight. "But I meant what I said—I've never had a male lover. Never wanted one."

She leaned back until we were forehead to forehead. The way she studied me told me she was searching for something. "You're a good man, Adam."

It was absolutely the last thing I expected her to say. Moreover, it wasn't remotely true. I was a selfish, greedy bastard, and if I could steal her away from all of them without hurting her, I would do it in a heartbeat.

I'd take Ezra because he needed her too. Needed us. Fuck, I needed to pin his ass down until he talked to me. I hadn't been kidding in the library. If he wanted more, he was going to have to earn it, and he was going to do it my way.

"Be gentle," she murmured, so softly, I almost missed it. "With him and with you...and don't do anything you really don't want to do."

For some reason, that amused me and I chuckled. "Lainey, Ezra's a beautiful guy. He's a red hot fucking mess, high strung as all get out, but loyal to the bone, and I know he's got a talented tongue."

To my delight her eyes widened. "How—"

"He made you come in a very short amount of time," I teased her, and to my utter delight, she flushed a deep shade of pink. It spread down her chest to her breasts, and I nipped her lower lip, teasing her mouth open until she was kissing me.

This was what I'd always wanted. Lainey warm, sated, and ready for more. She bit me, and a real laugh escaped. That was also what I wanted. She was a fighter and always had been.

"You owe me another match, by the way," I reminded her, and surprise flickered across her face. "You are a gorgeous fencer."

The fact her smile took on a shy quality turned me

inside out. The bedroom door pushed in and Ezra returned with a tray of food.

"Oh god," Lainey said, a hint of horror on her face. "You cooked."

"I did not," he retaliated and then stuck his tongue out at her. "I found these in the fridge all with clear instructions for the microwave."

Laughter bubbled up through Lainey, and when she would have scooted off my lap, I looped an arm around her middle and pulled her back. "You're fine here."

Food, as it turned out, was hot roast beef sandwiches with au jus.

"Marlene is so good to me," Lainey said with a happy little sigh, and I chuckled. As much for her delight as for the way Ezra relaxed under her pleasure. "Thank you, Ezra."

"You're welcome, Kotyonok. I made coffee too." He motioned to the carafe on the tray. "Nothing special. But it's still early, and I didn't get any coffee earlier."

"Is that a complaint?" I asked, even as I studied him. Had he gotten something to drink while he was downstairs? Would I even know unless I kissed him? Did I want to kiss him? These thoughts tumbled one right over the other like some kind of avalanche.

Just imagining the feel of his lips and cataloging all the ways it would be different from Lainey's. I'd kissed my fair share of women, never for long, and never enough to commit them to memory. They were always... placeholders.

Aggravation clawed at my belly. Ezra and I had shared a few of those women too. Never at the same time. More I'd watch him and he'd watch me. There was something wholly erotic about how he would throw himself into pleasuring a woman.

I'd enjoyed watching him do it to Lainey earlier.

Those placeholders weren't even understudies. They'd never been the one I truly wanted. It never occurred to me to explore that with Ezra either.

Not until now.

When he pushed into her earlier and I'd felt his cock through that thin wall of her body. It had been...perfect.

That was going to take me some time.

"Not hungry?" Ezra asked, focusing on me, and I shook my head.

"Actually," I said. "I'm not. You two eat. You should both be taking better care of yourselves."

"Pour him coffee," Lainey suggested as she balanced against my gradually stiffening cock. The more I thought about sharing her with him, the more I imagined all the ways we could... "He's going to be more insufferable now."

"I don't think that's possible," Ezra said, pouring three mugs of coffee and offering Lainey the first. He passed me the second. "He was pretty much a bastard from the beginning."

"True," she said, and I glared at him then her.

"I'm sitting right here."

"I know," she told me with a grin that was all mischief. "But come on, even you have to admit you're a control freak. You want to be in charge all of the time."

"In and out of the bedroom, apparently," Ezra said, and I didn't miss the way he ducked his head but kept shooting me looks.

Right. Time to deal with at least part of this. "And you fucking love the fact that I told you what to do and how to do it."

This time when his gaze hit mine, it stayed there. He ran his tongue over his lower lip while I waited him out. Finally, a sigh escaped him and some of the tension evaporated.

"Don't let it go to your head," he muttered. Lainey's laughter polished away the suggestion of his complaint, and his whole being seemed to warm as he looked at her. A familiar, albeit somewhat new, twinge hit me.

He *trusted* her.

Where he used to trust me, now he trusted Lainey and... I didn't hate it, but I wanted that trust back.

Maybe he wasn't the only one who needed to earn it.

"Hmm." Lainey scooted and I frowned. "I have to pee, Adam. I cannot just stay in your lap twenty-four seven."

It sounded nice, if impractical.

"Fine," I told her, then bit her shoulder lightly before letting her up. She was facing me, but she flicked her eyes in Ezra's direction before meeting my gaze again.

Right.

She was leaving us alone to talk

"Don't take too long," I advised, and she grinned.

She was all willowy grace as she strolled into her bathroom and pushed the door closed. My smile faded, and I caught Ezra studying me again.

"Ask," I told him.

"Did you mean it?" He didn't play coy or beat around the bush. "Did you mean what you said about me, down there? Or was that...just in the moment?"

"The earning my trust part? Getting to suck my cock? Or kiss me?" I was being a bit of a bastard, but there was a part of me that wanted to punish Ezra. He deserved to be tweaked for the hell he'd been putting me through worrying about him. "I said a lot of things, Ezra."

"All of the above." He focused on me now, the weight of it so heavy it seemed to turn the air tense. "I mean—I'd get it if you weren't into it. You said you've never been with a guy before."

"I said I'd never fucked one," I told him, clarifying. It would be good if we were absolutely clear. "You have been though."

He ducked his chin. "Yeah... a couple—experiments. They were the ones Dad..."

I nodded. "Were you trying to figure out if you liked guys or just liked me?"

When had it changed?

"A little bit of both," he admitted, then stole a look toward the bathroom before looking back at me. "It hit me...for real...when you disappeared. When you played dead. When I couldn't find you...what I felt...what I feel—I love you."

The words rocked me. More the rawness of it.

"If you don't want more than just this friendship, sharing Lainey—bossing me around when I'm there while you two fuck. I can live with that."

The door opened and Ezra's phone rang at the same time. He scowled and reached for the cell. Lainey shot me a questioning look, but I just held out a hand to her. It was gratifying when she came straight to me.

Ezra glared at his phone then declined the call before he shut his phone off and put it on the nightstand again. "That was Dad."

"You're not going back there," Lainey ordered, and I agreed.

"He won't," I told her, rubbing her arm soothingly as she climbed into the middle of the bed. "We're going to take care of him."

He frowned at me, but Lainey wrapped around him. Where she held him all the hard edges blurred.

"What we were talking about," I told him. "I can't live

with that. We're going to figure it out, you and me—and probably Lainey here. There's a first time for everything."

Understanding crystalized in his eyes. When I moved to wrap my arms around both of them, he shuddered.

I had no fucking idea how it would all work, but I'd make it work. We would.

There were no other options. They needed each other. They needed me.

And goddammit, I needed them.

TWENTY

LAINEY

As the day grew longer, I had to get up. Not that I hadn't enjoyed the hours of just sprawling together and talking. Not that we talked of anything important. They'd tried when I wasn't in the room. Twice when Adam left Ezra and me alone, Ezra whispered his apologies over and over for the announcement.

My heart ached for him. Even more, it ached for the expectation in his eyes. He truly didn't think I would forgive him. The fact was, he had to forgive himself. I forgave him nearly as soon as it happened. I didn't doubt it wasn't a choice, but it was forced on him.

The second time Ezra left me with Adam, he just held me tight and shook his head when I offered to listen. I couldn't imagine how much was going on in his head at the moment. His declaration to Ezra was exactly what Ezra needed to hear—but what about Adam?

"You have to get dressed?" Ezra complained as I pulled a shirt on as well as panties.

"Yes," I told him. "Because I need more food and I want to make some tea." Actually what I wanted was wine, but Ezra hadn't drunk anything all day so suggesting alcohol was right out. "And I'm a little too sore for other activities."

"Is your throat sore?" Adam asked almost lazily, and I chuckled.

"Someone is greedy."

"Where you are concerned? Yes. I haven't had the chance to fuck your mouth yet, and I am very much looking forward to it." His eyes were dark as he spoke. With Ezra facing away, he couldn't see the effect his words were having on him.

Then again, Ezra couldn't see the fact that I wasn't the only one Adam was watching. The openness in Adam set fire to a thrill that rolled through my system like one of those sparklers on the Fourth of July.

"Be a good boy," I told them both. "Maybe you'll find out."

"Fuck," Ezra whispered, his jaw dropping a fraction. With that in mind, I winked and added a little extra sway to my hips as I left the room. Like they were attached by a tether, they weren't far behind me.

Ezra carried our coffee mugs while Adam brought down the tray. If Marlene was here, she'd yell at me, but I went ahead and rinsed out everything and then wiped down the tray. Adam opened the fridge to inspect the meals Marlene had left me.

"Why don't we just order some Chinese?" Ezra's hands were empty; he'd left his cell phone turned off and upstairs.

A fact I was grateful for. Oh, speaking of cell phones, I needed to grab mine.

"Chinese would mean leftovers." I hadn't had leftovers in forever. That would actually be nice.

"Kind of low rent," Adam commented, and I glanced at Ezra, caught his half-smirk and we both turned and stuck our tongues out at Adam. The bemused expression on his face gave way to a half-smile.

"Order from the apartment phone. I have menus around here somewhere. Marlene keeps them for when I'm in the mood, and Pretty Boy is really fond of the place over on Twentieth. It takes longer, but they make the best *youtiao*."

"I found them the first day we were here," Ezra announced as he went into the pantry. That made sense. Marlene kept a file drawer in there with recipes. I left the kitchen and headed for the library.

Adam caught me with an arm around my waist before I could snag the phone and spun me around. The room still smelled like sex. Hot, sweaty sex. It sent a ripple of anticipation through my belly.

Particularly with Adam wrapping around me. He nuzzled a kiss to my ear and then bit down gently on my throat. I slid a hand up to sink into his hair and just held him.

Eyes closed, I leaned back into him. "Everything okay?"

"Yes," he murmured, his breath sending teasing eddies over my skin. "I just missed you."

"I was barely gone."

"I've missed you for years, Lainey," he said and my heart squeezed. "I missed being able to be to you who I wanted to be."

"Well," I said slowly, touching my tongue to my lips. "We're changing that now." Because he wasn't the only one who'd missed being able to have something like this. I half-twisted. At first, he didn't seem to want to let me go, then he loosened his grip so I could face him.

"I think it's going to get worse before it gets better." The admission from him didn't quell any fears. I pressed my hands to his chest. The bare skin was hot, and despite the fact he'd dragged on a shirt, he hadn't bothered to button it. Just like he'd pulled on slacks rather than pajama bottoms.

Now that we'd left the bedroom, he was rebuilding his walls. The relaxed man, even with all his secrets still firmly hidden, had left. I wasn't sure what he struggled with more though. Putting the walls up? Or letting me inside those walls while he put them up?

"Maybe," I said, not disagreeing. "We have a lot of talking to do. A lot of solving. We have—a lot of problems to deal with, but we're not doing it alone. Not you. Not Ezra..."

"Not Hardigan." I swore it cost him to say that, but I wouldn't scold. He was trying. "And apparently, not Cavendish."

While the last wasn't a question, I caught his searching look. "He cares and I care about him," I said. "There is an us. But he also knows that I love the three of you."

Surprise sparked to life in Adam's eyes, and it made me ache to think he didn't *know* that I loved all of them.

"For someone so very intelligent, you can be painfully stupid sometimes," I said and his lips compressed. "Of course, I love you. I've loved you all my life. There have been times when I hated you too. Some days, I hated you and loved you in equal measure."

"Don't hold back," he said with the barest trace of amusement.

"I'm not planning on it. As much as I want this between us—I'm not giving any of them up. So you have to accept me for me and that they are a part of me too." It would kill me if he couldn't. If he pulled away. I'd hate it, but I'd let him go. "I won't force you to accept something you can't—but I won't let them go as long as they want me too."

A soft sigh escaped him and he pressed his forehead to mine. "Elaine Benedict, you...own me. You always have. Even when I didn't understand what it meant—I was yours."

The air backed up in my lungs.

"I will never be happy about sharing you," he continued. "Never. But I won't fight *you* to make you let them go. "

"Are you planning on fighting them?" Because that would not end well.

"That's going to happen sometimes. Ezra and I will fight. Hardigan and I will. Ezra and Hardigan. Cavendish..." He made a face.

"Bodhi will just punch you. I don't see him fighting."

For a moment, real amusement appeared on his face. "I am eager to see how he and Hardigan get along. Maybe they will take each other out."

I slapped his chest. Joke or not, I didn't like the idea. The laughter that escaped him was real, and for the first time in hours, he relaxed.

Genuinely relaxed and there was a smug smile on his lips. I studied him as I backed up a couple of steps and snagged my phone.

There were missed calls from Tally, Mother—I made a face at that one—a couple from the attorneys, and Andrea.

"I missed a call from Andrea," I said, and Adam folded his arms as he narrowed the distance. "She left a message." I pulled it up and hit speaker so he could listen.

"Oh my god," Andrea complained. "You used to answer your phone, now all I get is voicemail and the occasional text. Sometimes, I think you forget you're my favorite sister and I'm supposed to be your favorite sibling."

The absolute outrage in her voice made me smile, and Adam shook his head.

"But fine, I'm sure you're busy doing something with your eleventy billion charities. Did you know that your grandfather invited me to Der Sonne when I am home this summer?"

The last part was a mixture of squeal and utter disbelief.

"He sent me a letter—an actual letter. Like on real paper and stuff. I've been at this school for five years, and I've never received an actual letter before. It was even on *Benedict* letterhead. So fancy."

I bit my lip.

"*Anyway...*" Andrea dragged out that last word with all the angst a teenager could shade onto it. She was almost a teenager. Ugh. I hated the idea instantly. "That's good, right? That he invited me? He's never done it directly before."

He'd never done it at all before. Her invitations had always come from me, but I'd done my best to not let her know about Grandfather's indifference. What Mother had done was *not* Andrea's fault, and his hatred for the Reeds should not also be shouldered by Andrea.

"You'll be there, right? So we could do like a sleepover thing? That would be great. Okay, I gotta go. I'm supposed to be in class and not the bathroom. Also, I might have mentioned it to Mom. Sorry, love you, bye!"

Then she was gone. That was definitely why Mother had called me, and I didn't worry about ignoring her. Grandfather, however, had reached out, and that was huge. I would thank him later.

"Building bridges?" Adam asked, and I glanced up at him. His expression was thoughtful and maybe a bit worried. Before I could answer though, the alarm dinged as it disengaged.

Adam pivoted on his heel and was out of the library faster than me. If Ezra bolted this time, we were damn well going after him.

Instead of leaving, however, Ezra was exiting the kitchen with the menus in hand as the front door swung open. Adam slowed, but I bypassed him 'cause there were only two other people besides Marlene with keys to the apartment.

"Pretty Boy..." I exhaled, and then I half-ran, half-skipped over to him, and he caught me in a one-armed hug as I jumped up to greet him.

Something raw and taut inside of me went loose as I took a deep breath, filling my lungs with him. He pushed the door closed as he cradled me.

"Reed," he said, his tone not hostile but not exactly friendly. "Graham." Hostility edged his voice now.

I pulled back a little to find Milo studying both of them before he swung his gaze back to me. "Everything okay, Mayhem?"

"It's almost perfect now," I told him, cradling his cheek. "You're here."

Ezra coughed, but it was Adam who said, "Are we calling Cavendish too?"

"I can send him a message," I answered, without looking away from Milo. Was he okay with this? With them here? He nodded, a barest hint of motion, before he pressed his lips to mine in a kiss that was one hundred percent present and accepting. More, it was sweet without an ounce of demand.

I sighed as he squeezed me a little tighter. "We might need to work out sleeping arrangements."

"And food," Ezra declared. "We're ordering Chinese."

"I like that place," Milo said, setting me on my feet but keeping an arm around me as he glanced between Ezra and Adam. "Tell me he groveled at least a little."

"Groveled a lot," Ezra answered. "Need to do more. But that's between me and my kotyonok. So button it, Hardigan. What do you want to eat?"

"And how long before King figures out you're here?" Adam looked more thoughtful and cautious than angry.

"We can discuss that." Milo glanced down at me. "We can discuss a lot of things. Is Bodhi definitely a part of this?"

My heart bumped against my ribs, apprehension unfolding, but I nodded. "Yes."

While he and I may still be working out the details, one thing was sure. There was an us. That meant he was one of them.

"Call him then," Milo murmured. "But first..." He ignored both of them to kiss me until my toes curled. I drowned in the scent and taste of him, and only his arm kept me on my feet. Finally, when he let me up for air, he said, "Better."

Definitely better. Heat rushed through me, especially when I found Adam and Ezra both watching us.

"Fine," Adam said with a kind of abruptness. "That was almost hot."

"Almost?" Ezra said with a snort. "You need to work on your standards. That was definitely hot. Call Cavendish and find out what he wants, but we all need food, and we need it now."

He wasn't wrong. Blowing out a breath, I gave myself a

little shake as Milo tugged off his jacket and headed to the kitchen. Ezra and Adam were right behind him, and they were discussing food.

Was this really happening?

I glanced at the phone in my hand and had Bodhi's number on the screen. He answered on the first ring, like he'd just been waiting for my call.

The guys were *talking* in the kitchen. Talking.

Not fighting.

And Bodhi was on the phone.

"Are you free?" I asked him.

"For you? Always."

CHAPTER
TWENTY-ONE

BODHI

After leaving Lainey's apartment, I lingered in Manhattan for an hour to give her time to call me back if she needed me. When she didn't, I took care of some appointments and checked in with Collin as well as the rest of the family.

My father was out of town. That set off little alarm bells, particularly when all I could get from his secretary was a "probable" return date. Probable.

I left a message for Sophia. If he was doing something I needed to know about, she would likely be aware. After that, I returned to my apartment and resumed my research. I needed everything on Oksana Dovzhenko, her family, their connections, and what the Grahams would get out of the marriage.

I'd added a third blank card next to Hardigan and PPG notes and photos. The information said there was a third child for King—but we had no age. Hardigan would know if he had another sibling with the same mother. So that eliminated her.

For a brief moment, I had the unsettling realization that there was no info on Lainey B's father. No name on the birth certificate. No records filed. Her mother had never been married prior to marrying Reed.

I couldn't even find a mention in the social register. But if she were the third child—King would have been after her money already. He did not possess the intelligence or the sophistication to take on Leopold Benedict.

There weren't even rumors that I could find regarding her biological father. She never mentioned him, so...no. It wasn't King. As unsettling as that would be, it would break her heart and I'd kill him for that alone.

So, who was the third child? Was it important?

I was going through the financials on Reed when she called, and her voice was a welcome respite. Even better, she wanted me back at the apartment. Fortunately, she didn't sound troubled or upset.

The drive to her apartment didn't take long. Maybe it was time to invest in another place. One in her building would let me be closer even on nights I wasn't with her.

I used her code to get back into the private parking area in the garage. Then again at the elevator. It was Hardigan who opened the door when I arrived.

"No," Lainey was saying as he let me in. "You are *not* going to talk to him, see him, or *deal* with him without at least one of us there."

"Kotyonok," Ezra said, his expression dark and worried. "You cannot be that person. You have no idea what— dammit." He pivoted away and stalked across the room.

"Welcome to the chaos," Hardigan said before he shut and locked the door behind me. "We got Chinese."

"Excellent." I heard and responded, but I tracked Lainey's reaction as she stared after Ezra with her hands on her hips. "Is this a free for all argument or are you two keeping it private?"

Reed sat at the table with the food and his laser focus on both Lainey *and* Graham. Made sense.

"It's not an argument," Graham snapped, then glared at me. "Why are *you* here again?"

"Yes, it is an argument," Lainey countered. "Private for now, please help yourself to some dinner." The fact she flashed me a smile softened the words some, particularly because it was brief and vanished as soon as she glared at Graham again. "He's here because I invited him. It's time *all* of us talked. But you and I are settling this first."

"Kot—"

"No," she told him. "No more *kitten*. No more *shielding* me. I'm not a child. Something I *know* you are aware of. You don't have to hide the darkness of the world from me. Whatever your father is doing to force you into this, *we* will deal with it, *together*."

As I reached the dining table, I recognized why Hardigan was leaning against the front door, beer in hand. Graham wasn't allowed to leave.

Good.

"Adam..." Graham turned to Reed for help, but he wasn't going to find it there.

"Lainey's right. We have to do this together." He made a face like he couldn't believe he was admitting to the second part. If it was less serious, I'd be more amused. As it was, I preferred the support.

I checked the first container. Spicy beef with peppers. That worked. I freed up a pair of chopsticks and just ate straight from the container as Graham gaped at Reed.

"You finally get to nail her and now you just agree with everything she says. What happened to protecting her first?"

"I thought we'd try something new and listen." The droll comment was acceptable, but I fixed a look on Graham. If he got much cruder or stupider, I was going to involve myself.

With an aggrieved sigh, he threw himself down. "He said he'd kill you, Kotyonok. But it wasn't just about killing you, it was about torturing you and taking you apart so you suffered."

"He's not touching her," I said.

"Agreed," Hardigan tacked on. "No wonder you wanted to get her a bodyguard."

Crossing over to the sofa, Lainey settled next to Graham and caught one of his hands. "I can protect myself. You forget, I have been doing that for a long time."

"You were in a car accident," Graham protested.

"It was an *accident,* and if you'll recall, I was also *fine*." She wasn't quite scolding, but some of her patience slipped. "Do something for me..."

"I'd do anything for you," he told her, and for the first time, I truly believed he meant what he said. Good. Lainey B deserved everything.

"Then *trust* me, right now. Trust me. Trust Adam. Trust Milo and Bodhi."

"Adam and you—yes, but Cavendish?"

"As long as Lainey B wants you in one piece, you're safe with me," I informed him. "No one will touch her. Or you. You should probably eat, your hands are shaking."

I recognized DTs when I saw them.

"It's not about the food," he grumbled, he wasn't looking at me, but at Lainey. The silence elongated. Lainey

B didn't back down an inch or blink. "Okay," Graham said finally and buried his face in his hands. "Okay. But I can't stand the idea of anything happening to you."

"Neither can I when it comes to you," she told him and then she wrapped her arms around him and he all but fell into her and held on tight.

"Think it's safe for me to sit and eat?" Hardigan asked, and Reed chuckled.

"Come eat, I'll take watch. He's probably safe for now. He got his chaos and drama out for a bit."

"Fuck you, Adam," Graham muttered, but he didn't let go of Lainey. She flashed another smile as Reed paused behind the sofa to grip his shoulder.

"Lainey's right. We trust her. But we talk. We plan. We do this together." He glanced toward me then Hardigan. "*All* of us."

"Thank you," she murmured to him.

"I'm trying," he answered with a brush of his knuckles down her cheek. It seemed much had shifted between the three of them in the last few hours. Good.

"I know," she said, then pressed a kiss to Graham's lips, a single brush. "We're all trying. Will you eat now? I know you want a drink, and if you think you can stop at one, I'll make it myself."

"But you need me sober for this," Graham said with an air of resignation. "I'm fine. I'll be fine."

Still, Reed leaned against the front door while Lainey rose to join Hardigan and me at the table. Graham lingered for another long moment then he joined us. Hardigan took the chair next to mine, and when she would have claimed Reed's chair, he tugged her into his lap.

"Sit over there, Ezra," Milo told him. "That way Adam can sit down and eat."

The table could easily seat six, but the spot they were pointing Graham to was the corner. He would have to get past us. That worked.

"You sure?" Lainey checked with Hardigan as she perched on his thigh.

"Yes," he told her. "If we're going to have this meeting, I'm going to hold you." He glanced at Graham who merely raised his hands in surrender. I had to wonder how long this conversation had been going on if they were all confirming he understood.

Still...

"Who starts?" While I was asking, I presumed Lainey would begin. Her apartment. Her rules. For now, I used the chopsticks to pick the spicy beef out of the container.

"I think," Lainey said, opening her own pair of chopsticks and glancing at the different containers until she found the one with the pot stickers. She picked up one and held it. "We need to put on the table what we're after...and I'm not talking relationships between us, yet."

"We all want you," Hardigan told her. "You want all of us. There's something going down between Adam and Ezra, but that seems to be fairly personal so we'll leave it tabled for the moment."

A half-smile flirted with her lips as she twisted to look at Hardigan. The adoring him with her gaze was a good look on her. I was cataloging all of them. He was good for her.

Of the three sitting there with me, him I liked. The jury was out on the other two.

"More or less," she murmured before offering him the pot sticker to eat.

"Focus," he told her but accepted the bite and the kiss she dropped on his nose before she pulled out another.

"I am focused," she argued, lifting her chin, and the softness, while still present, melted away for the fierce woman beneath. "We have common enemies. Initially, I thought it was only King, but that's disingenuous. He's definitely one of them... but there's also Wallace Graham."

Graham—Ezra—I should probably get used to their names. Ezra sighed.

Lainey flicked a look at Adam. "Mrs. Waldemar?"

"I don't know that she's an enemy precisely—at least for us. She seems quite fond of Milo." Adam shrugged. "She wants King dead. Or she did."

"I'm still wrapping my head around the fact *she* was the one who had Ivy and Rome kidnapped," Milo said with a grunt. "We're positive it's her?"

"She seems too nice to order something like that?" I asked, because my interactions with her had been limited. But the older generations only seemed benign. It afforded them a great deal of latitude. "Power buys a lot of influence and access. She doesn't have to do it herself."

"No, I get that," Milo said. "But they took Ivy and Rome because they thought Rome was Liam—"

"She wanted access to King." Adam eyed the containers before he picked out one with noodles. "Access to take him out. She's never mentioned why she wants him gone. She doesn't rant or rave or lose her mind. She merely...interrogates me for everything I know. She did tell me to kill him at one point."

Adam locked gazes with Milo.

"Then she decided to wait. She wanted me to befriend you instead."

"Shocker, you weren't interested in me for my witty conversation." The dry remark amused me.

"You're not bad, but I think she still wants access to

King. Whatever her hate-on for him is, it's very—intense. Yet, I can't tell if it's 'personal' to her or not." Adam shook his head. "She controls the narrative, and she's—not to be discounted."

"I've been pulling apart King's business interests," Lainey said, and that earned her sharp looks from Adam and Ezra both.

"You wonder why we want to protect you?" Ezra demanded.

"No," she said, pointing at him with her chopsticks. "I don't wonder. But here's the thing...he's got shell corporations hidden and tucked away behind others. There are so many that it's a series of Russian nesting dolls to find. Nothing is in the name Hardigan..."

"Julius King is on some of them." Milo shrugged, and Lainey glanced at me.

"We know Julius King isn't his given name. He assumed it sometime after he abandoned you and your sister."

I understood why she wanted me to direct this part. My emotional investment was minimal, and she didn't want to hurt Milo. We weren't the ones who would be hurting him with this information, however.

"When Lainey and I were in Virginia, we met with a contact. I've been looking into King, feelers for where he came from. He's also approaching Cavendish and other families about going into business—spreading out his tentacles. Jeff Hardigan doesn't appear to have been his birth name anymore than Julius King."

That gave Adam, Ezra, *and* Milo pause, and I had their full attention.

"Rumors suggest he was born on the wrong side of the sheets. That he's actually a member of one of the families, just a discounted, disowned, and forgotten one."

"Well, at least he would know how it feels," Milo muttered, and Lainey put down her food to curl into him. "I'm alright," he murmured. I gave them a moment before continuing, because we had more.

"According to my contact, he also has three children, not just two."

Milo frowned.

"We're pulling that thread. I have nothing concrete to offer you." It was the only apology I had for him.

Scrubbing a hand over his face, Milo scowled at the table. "Older than me or younger than Ivy?—Fuck, he could have one my age. How would we know?"

"We wouldn't," Lainey told him, her expression offering comfort that her words could not. "But, we'll find out."

"We need to find out who his girlfriend is too," Ezra said. "But my question is, if we find out all of this, what do we do with it?"

"We begin by taking apart his power base," I said. "Then we take apart anyone else who is supporting him. Identify the threats."

"Then eliminate them," Adam stated, and when I met his gaze, I read determination and agreement there. "If they threaten us, we get rid of them."

His gaze flicked to Lainey. I wasn't the only one nodding. No matter what else happened, we had Lainey in common.

King might rule his little fiefdom, but our queen was going to be safe.

"We can't just off everyone we don't like," Ezra said. "I mean—I can't just kill my own father."

I could and, based on the look on Adam's face, so could he.

"One step at a time," Lainey said. "We need to know

friend from foe. That's part of where we start. You staying away from your family is another part." She focused on Ezra. While he nodded, he also sighed.

It might be prudent for the four of us to have another conversation.

We should talk as men did.

CHAPTER
TWENTY-TWO

LAINEY

By the time we finished with food, the discussion over planning turned to more tangible elements—like where people were sleeping tonight. Ezra and Adam exchanged a loaded look that I wasn't up to interpreting, not right now.

My head hurt. My heart ached. Yet, I was happy as hell all four of them were here, no matter the circumstances. We'd talked—*really* talked, and Ezra had confessed at least some of the terrible things that had been happening.

I hadn't missed the new marks on his back. The scars—some of them had been there before, but I hadn't realized the significance. Now?

Well, now, I could kill Wallace Graham.

Adam opened up—to me, to Ezra, and while we may not be on solid ground yet, we were no longer on broken ice and drifting apart. That was something.

Bodhi was here. Bodhi came when I called him, and Pretty Boy was home. The last settled something deep inside of me. Having all of them here was what I needed more than I realized.

"Actually, I don't care where the three of you are sleeping," Pretty Boy said abruptly. "Unless it's Mayhem's room, in which case, pick somewhere else. Make safe plans for the next ten to twelve hours. I want time with Mayhem."

He was already standing with me in his arms and I blinked at him. I opened my mouth, but he stared at me with those deep, whiskey brown eyes, and every objection melted away. I didn't want to tell the others to leave. We needed the time as five of us, but Pretty Boy needed me too.

And I needed him.

"Adam—"

"I'll watch Ezra," he said in the driest of tones.

"I am not a child," Ezra said with a scowl that was a little bit of a pout.

"Keep telling yourself that," Bodhi informed him. "Have fun," he continued, gaze tracking to me as Pretty Boy headed for the stairs. "Lunch tomorrow?"

"Sounds like a plan," Pretty Boy tossed over his shoulder. I blew a kiss toward the boys feeling all at once incredibly on display and at the same time, adored. It was hard to argue with the latter, so I'd live with the former.

He didn't slow all the way up the stairs. Even more impressive, he wasn't remotely winded as we hit the top of the stairs.

Once we were in the room, though, it hit me that the bed was disheveled. While we hadn't filled this room with sex, we'd certainly lounged in the bed most of the day.

Inside, Milo shut the door and leaned against it before his gaze collided with mine.

"Are we still okay?" Today had been a lot for me. I couldn't imagine for him. As it was, my body was one long sensual ache, but being in his arms and this close already had my cunt clenching in anticipation. Was I expecting too much?

"Mayhem," he said in a tone that was half-sigh, half-rebuke. "We are *fine*. How are *you?*"

"Sore. Worried. Happy. Furious. Delighted." My emotions were all over the place. "I prefer to have a plan and to be working ahead. I feel like we're a half-dozen steps behind. Part of me is frustrated by that, but then I look at the four of you—and the intensely selfish part of me is so damn happy you're here."

"Have I ever mentioned how much I love your use of the English language?" The way his lips shaped the words sent a lovely thrill through me.

"Have I mentioned how much I love you?" The tender look in his eyes softened even further if that was possible. The press of his lips to mine was a gentle touch, a brush, a caress. There was no demand in the contact, only sweet, gentle possession that was a gift all its own.

I sighed as he carried me over to the bed. When he dropped me, a bubble of laughter escaped. My phone buzzed and his eyes narrowed.

"Hand over the contraband."

"Just let me see who it is." I pulled the phone out of my pocket and bit my lower lip at the name on the screen. Then I held it up to him.

Pretty Boy let out a grunt and took the phone from me. One swipe of his thumb across the screen and he answered it. "I'm sorry, Miss Benedict cannot come to the phone right now, Ivy. I'm about to strip her naked and eat her out until she screams. You have seven boyfriends. Tell one of them to entertain you."

I clapped a hand over my mouth at his droll delivery even as Em let out a screech on the other end of the phone.

"Yeah," Pretty Boy said with a slow smile. "I planned on it. She can call you later. Love you too..." Then he hung up the phone and eyed me.

Still fighting the desire to keep my laughter contained, I nodded. I didn't quite trust myself to speak. So he powered the phone off and set it on the nightstand. He pulled out his own, and it was off too. He put it face down on top of my phone, and I let out a little sigh.

"That's ridiculously romantic," I murmured. Not something I would have ever imagined before. Phones were— devices. Tools. But with the screens face to face like that... I caught his smirk and lifted a foot to poke him.

I didn't get that far as he caught my leg and pulled me to him. "I've missed you, Mayhem," he said. "Missed your laughter. Your glares. Your ferociousness. I've missed *you*."

All my humor fled in the face of that declaration, I half climbed him to wrap my arms around his neck, and he tightened his embrace as I buried my face to his throat. I filled my lungs with his scent.

"I missed you," I whispered. "Having you here is everything."

"Good." He nuzzled a kiss to my forehead, and the roughness of his stubble scraped at my skin. The sting of reality grounded me. "This is where I want to be."

Desire was a languorous creature within me. Need rippled through my system, chasing the heat surfacing just from where he touched me.

"Milo," I said and that pulled his head back. I so rarely used his name. "No matter what happens with King—we'll protect Andrea. I don't want you to have to go back. I know—"

His lips sealed over mine, stealing my breath and the words as he thrust his tongue in to toy with my own. I fisted his hair, savoring every sensuous taste of his kiss and the groan vibrating in his throat. The same one I echoed.

I don't know how long we stayed there. One kiss became two, then three, then it just elongated. Drunk on the feel of him, I tugged at his shirt. Somewhere between the fifth and the dozenth kiss, his clothes were on the floor and mine floated after them.

Twisting, he sat on the bed with me in his lap. The warmth of his hands roaming over my back pulled a long sigh free. Pretty Boy had the most amazing hands. Big, strong, and I loved the way they felt.

There was a callus on his left thumb and another on his right index finger. The roughness added to the sweetness of the contact.

"Fuck," he swore in between kisses when I reached between us to stroke his cock. He stroked his hands to my ass, and when he grazed my anus, I let out a little grunt.

Oh, I was still sore. It wasn't bad, but the bite of pain was still there. A reminder that it was only a few hours earlier that Adam had impaled me on his cock—first in my pussy then again in my ass.

Not something I'd ever considered enjoying before, yet I wanted to do it again—a hint of desperation crept through me at the idea—but maybe not just yet.

Pretty Boy pulled his head back to study me. "Tell me." It wasn't a request, and I swore my face heated at the mere suggestion of describing sex with one of the others.

"I was with Adam and Ezra at the same time..." I had to choose my words carefully. "Adam was—intense, and I've never done anal before."

"Was he careful?" Before I could even answer the question, he had me facedown on the bed and his hands were on my asscheeks—

"Pretty Boy," I snapped, glaring at him over my shoulder. "What—"

"I'm making sure you aren't bleeding and there are no tears," he told me with a ferociousness that silenced my retort. Genuine worry filled his eyes. "You're tough, Mayhem. But a cock in the ass can do damage if you don't know what you're doing."

My irritation flamed out and I pushed back against his hands so he could see. "Adam was careful," I promised him, wanting to soothe him. "I liked it..."

Pretty Boy glanced from my ass back to me. "Yeah?"

"Yeah—it was a little uncomfortable...at first but then... it was—good."

He stroked my ass slowly, massaging the cheeks. "You are definitely red, and if you're still sore, we're going to be careful."

Careful. "Wait—but I am not that..."

He trailed his fingers between my legs and along the seam of my pussy. There was definitely wetness there, and I had to fight the urge to chase his fingers as he skated around my clit before gliding back.

"Your ass is sore, but not this beautiful cunt." A slow smile curved up his lips, and I let out a shudder as he worked a finger into me. "Oh, you're very wet—is that all for me?"

I licked my lips.

"So it's definitely for me, but the others haven't hurt." Lips pursed, he pulled his hand away and then flipped me over onto my back before he went to his knees and hauled me over the bed until my knees were hooked over his shoulders.

"Pretty Boy—"

"Shh," he soothed then licked me from entrance to clit and back again. He came back to my clit and swirled his tongue around it, and I swore my heart pulsed right there as if rushing to meet him.

A soft cry slipped my lips, and he gave a grunt of satisfaction.

"I'm going to eat you until you scream, and I want you to scream my name," he said, giving me the slyest of grins before he winked. "It's okay to want them. But I plan to make sure the only one you're thinking about is me."

Shock and delight curved through me at the sensuous threat. "Do I get to play with your cock too?"

"Maybe," he teased. "If you're a very good girl. But I am going to fill this cunt to the brim, and you're going to feel me for days."

Another delicious shudder went through me as he buried his face against my pussy. He didn't let up at all as he pushed and pushed. The pressure built up so fast I wasn't sure I could handle it. Even when I began to writhe to ease him off, he didn't stop.

"Pretty Boy," I pleaded, but I could barely punch out the syllables, and the last one came out as a cry. Then he scraped his teeth across my clit, and I swore I detonated. A hot rush left me, and my scream broke in the middle as I thrashed.

He was lapping at me with his tongue, and I floated on the overload. It was a heavenly place, somewhere between exultation and pure pleasure. The heavy ropes of need began to tighten again as he increased his suction on my clit.

This time, he used his tongue, his teeth, and his fingers,

and I didn't fight the screams as I soaked his face. He looked so damn pleased with himself as he grinned up at me.

"You ready for more, Mayhem?"

I was ready for everything, I didn't care how boneless I felt. "Do I get to touch you this time?"

He grinned and then shifted upward and thrust that beautifully thick, long cock into me. The world narrowed its focus to where we were joined.

"Your mouth next," he promised and when he fell forward, I caught him, and licked myself from his lips. I was going to be split in half and I was here for it.

I couldn't wait for whatever was next.

And what came after that—him or me—I wanted it all.

I wanted *him*.

I wanted them.

CHAPTER
TWENTY-THREE

MILO

The softness of her breath was the only sound in the darkened room. Lights from the city offered a soft illumination. The floor to ceiling windows being uncovered at night took some getting used to, but you couldn't see inside, even when the lights were on.

Lainey sprawled over me, cheek pressed against my chest and the sheets draping us. I was hot, but I wasn't moving her for anything. Hot and turning over all the data in my head. As much as I could have fucked her all night, I wanted her to sleep.

The presence of other lovers meant making sure she wasn't too sore or too bruised. So many new pieces to find a spot for in the puzzle. It all kept me awake, examining each one for the intricacies of what slot it needed to fill.

Adam Reed had always been a fact of Lainey's life. He was in Ivy's because of her. He'd protected my sister, or attempted to. He protected Lainey from my father. No,

Adam was inextricably in her life, and he'd finally made his move.

I had to wonder if he understood how much she cared because she made room for him immediately. Those feelings for Adam had always been there. I'd seen them the first time he arrived at the Clubhouse and they'd seen each other.

While we might be from two totally different worlds, I got Adam Reed. I understood him. Hell, I respected him. Bodhi—a wild card. Fine. Him, I trusted. Weirdly, Freddie was probably the least trusting of all the Vandals.

He trusted Bodhi. So I would.

That left Ezra fucking Graham...

The softness of fingers tickled against my chest as Lainey walked them up to my face. She tapped two against my lips. Without even cracking an eyelid, she murmured, "I can hear you thinking."

Catching her hand, I pressed a kiss to her palm. "Go back to sleep, Mayhem."

"You need to sleep too." Her protest pushed back against the troubling thoughts, chasing them away. "If you can't sleep..." She finally lifted her head. The tumble of hair around her face and the sleepy eyes made her a picture. "Then I'll be awake with you."

So I wouldn't be alone. She didn't say that, but the implication lingered beneath the words, and I gathered her closer. "Just sorting things out in my head, Mayhem."

"Can I help?"

"You help me every damn day," I promised her. It was true. Having her in my life was—a breath of fresh air and a solid foundation all in one. Mayhem might have brought chaos with her, but it was chaos I needed. Chaos that tore out some of the chains still binding my soul. "I love you," I whispered, and her smile widened.

"I love you too," she answered before brushing her lips to my jaw. "Sleep, Pretty Boy. You're safe with me, and I won't let anything hurt you. Not again."

From anyone else, I might have laughed at that declaration. I tightened my grip around her, and she curled fully into me. This delicate, seemingly fragile woman was anything but...

Indomitable.

Stubborn.

Pr—

"Pretty Boy," she murmured and then she was nuzzling my throat. "Do I need to give you something else to think about?"

"Are you threatening me with a good time?" Fuck, if I wasn't grinning. Then she was squirming down my body, and my dick, which had already been half-hard, stiffened right up. "Mayhem..." Only the word came out on a moan as she swallowed my cock and proceeded to shred my ability to think.

She had one hand wrapped around me as she bobbed her head and sucked on the tip like it was her favorite lollipop. The kittenish licks with her tongue were enough to drive me fucking mad, then she would work me deeper into her throat.

Every stroke took me further. Every soft pop sent a tickle right to my balls. When she made the softest of slurping sensations, I tensed because I was already right on the cusp.

She didn't give me even a moment of mercy, and I had a scant few seconds to whisper, "Mayhem..." I fisted the sheets as the orgasm dragged my balls up tight and I came in a hard rush.

The thud of my heart seemed so loud it practically echoed in my ears. The heat she released in me flooded my system and robbed it of every ounce of tension. She drained it all away, swallowing it with my release.

Fuck.

When she eased back up to curl against me, I kissed her long and slow. I didn't care that it was my cum on her lips or her tongue. That was just hot, but this kiss wasn't about seduction or desire.

It was gratitude and affection. My eyelids were heavier. When I tucked her closer, she rubbed a slow circle against my chest. The soft shushing noise registered even as I was dropping off.

I was going to wake her up with a few orgasms in the morning. That was a promise.

THE NEXT TIME I opened my eyes, it was gray and drizzly outside. Lighter, like the sun was doing its best to come out but couldn't push past the heavier cloud cover. More importantly, the bed was empty. I sat up and scanned the room. It took a beat, but the sound of the shower registered.

Shoving the sheets back, I padded into the bathroom and found Mayhem standing under the spray, eyes closed. The water cascaded over her like a curtain of rain.

"Close the door," she said. "It's chilly."

"Sorry," I murmured, then nudged it shut. The heated floors in here made it toasty. I took a minute to brush my teeth. The fact my toothbrush sat right there in the holder turned me inside out.

She was waiting for me when I walked into the shower. Her smile was everything.

"Do you have to be somewhere early?" Just because we'd all converged on her the day before didn't mean she didn't have her own responsibilities.

"No," she told me. "I have some files to review, but I'm all yours."

"Just what I wanted to hear..." Then I was kissing her. As much as I wanted to take my time, I swore I was hard as a stone and as eager as a teenager. Mayhem short-circuited everything about me.

Lifting her, I kept our mouths fused together as I teased along her slit. She was soaking for me, thank fuck. She angled my cock and slid down, enveloping me in her warmth with almost no preparation.

I dragged my head up to find her meeting my gaze with a heated one of her own. "Fuck me," she ordered. "Hard and fast...I've been thinking about you since I woke up."

"Yes, ma'am." That was an order I was more than happy to follow. I worked my hips as she clung to me. There were deep, soul-searching kisses in between harder, biting ones. She dug her nails into my back, and I clenched her ass with one hand and tried to play with her nipple with the other.

It was fierce, furious, and the clamp of her cunt around my cock was what I was looking for. Then she bit down on my shoulder, and I swore I came from the scrape of her teeth. We rocked there, and I tilted my head back to the spray as I caught my breath.

"That's a good way to wake up," I grunted, and her soft laughter wreathed me. "It was a great way to go to sleep too."

Gradually, she eased down. It was almost too cold for my dick as I slipped free of her. Cum trickled down her leg until she stepped under the water with me. I eased back so she could wash her hair, then she retreated to soap while I lathered up my jaw.

When she took the razor from me, I ducked my head so she could shave me. Her eyes were focused, and she bit her lower lip in concentration as she worked to scrape off the stubble from my cheeks, my upper lip, my jaw, then I tilted my head up so she could get my throat.

There was something so natural about baring my throat to her. The memory of her reddened cheeks and puffy lips made me smile. "I probably should have done this first."

"Then I wouldn't get to do it, and I like feeling you on my face." The possessive note stroked through me. When she stroked her fingers over my jaw then my cheeks, I raised my brows.

"You can do that anytime you want," I promised.

Her swift smile was its own reward. "I like taking care of you."

That feeling was definitely mutual. Eventually though, we rinsed off and had to get out of the shower. Dressing seemed a lot like giving in when I just wanted to take her back to bed.

Still, I resisted the impulse—for now. Months away from her was not an experience I was in any hurry to replicate. Fine, it had been a little over two months.

Didn't matter.

I hated it.

"Is Marlene going to be here?" I should probably apologize to her.

"Not until the weekend. She's visiting her daughter. So it's just us and what we can forage from everything she left." The playful smile Lainey tossed me said it wouldn't be foraging at all.

Still... the minute we went out there, we were back in it, and the guys might still be here. I hadn't honestly cared the night before.

"I'll come back up and change the bedsheets after food."

To my surprise, and delight, we had no company waiting for us. Mayhem's swift frown as she powered up her phone gave me pause. I waited as her phone began to vibrate with messages.

"Adam took Ezra back to his place. Bodhi had work to do but said he'd be back by lunch."

Relief rippled across her face, and I studied her a beat. "Send them a message. You'll feel better if you hear from them."

The light in her eyes made me want to kick myself. She was still guarding her reactions for me. She didn't want *me* to be upset.

"Mayhem..." I crossed back to her and cupped her chin. "We're really okay. Not leaving you. You're not leaving me. They are a part of this. A part of you. I have some issues with Graham—not going to lie. But we'll work it out. Together. All of us."

"I adore you," she whispered.

"And I am a damn lucky man for it." I brushed a kiss to her lips. "Now, message them while I get the coffee made and food foraged. Then we can compare notes."

It was the right note. I could almost see the wheels turning as I brought up business. Another flash of a smile and she turned away with her phone, thumbs flying.

I'd left mine upstairs, but I'd grab it when I went to change the sheets. Breakfast was easy-to-heat muffins and some scrambled eggs. Those I made myself, much to her delight. I was careful with Marlene's pots and pans; I didn't want to get stabbed.

The guys had all answered her, even Ezra, so she seemed much more settled by the time we carried the coffee into the library. "I'm just going to grab my phone and change the sheets."

"You don't have to," she began, but I shook my head.

"I don't mind. It's just another way of looking after you. And you wanted to go through your email while not feeling like you were ignoring me."

That earned me a wrinkled nose before she stuck her tongue out at me. Score one for me.

"I'll be right back."

"Hmm..." The hum made me glance at her when I reached the library door.

"Looking at my ass, Mayhem?"

"It's a very nice ass, Pretty Boy."

"I'm rather fond of yours."

Her grin turned almost smug. "I know."

Chuckling, I took the steps two at a time. Straightening the room didn't take any time. I got clean linens on the bed and dropped the rest into the laundry chute. It got collected at some point.

I also powered up my phone and checked the messages, giving Mayhem a little more time. The doorbell rang, however, and I was at the top of the stairs when I heard her press the security button for the intercom.

"Yes?"

"Miss Benedict," King said, and my spine went cold. "I come bearing gifts and issues that we need to discuss."

Son.

Of.

A.

Bitch.

CHAPTER

TWENTY-FOUR

LAINEY

Adam's messages indicated he would keep an eye on Ezra. Still, they went back to his apartment to let me and Pretty Boy have some time to ourselves. But it was the message that came a little while after the first pair, that came from Adam late into the night that kept rolling around in my head.

I don't know how this will work, but we will make it work. E, however, needs watching. He is all set to throw himself on the fire for us.

For one, I appreciated the confidence and the faith. For two, I adored him for making sure he let me know. And three? He wasn't trying to protect me so much he cut me out or smothered me. Ezra needed us both. I suspected, before this was over, he would need all of us. Maybe I should hire him a bodyguard of his own.

That—that idea might have merit.

I was still turning it over when the doorbell rang. Few people were let up the elevators without a call from the desk. It was probably a regular delivery; still, better to be safe. Adam could just as easily be "testing" my responses. With that amusing thought, I crossed to the intercom and pressed the button.

"Yes?"

"Miss Benedict," Julius King, the very last person I expected to be at *my* door said. "I come bearing gifts and issues that we need to discuss."

Gifts?

"I'm afraid you have me at an advantage, sir," I replied, keeping my tone cool. "Gifts?"

"Something to smooth the waters," he replied, his voice all smooth amusement and coaxing. "In my experience, it's always better to add a little something sweet to business discussions in order to make them more palatable."

"If this is a business discussion, you should have made an appointment with my office." We had a staff who handled these things. "Appearing at my home is not de rigueur, I'm sure you understand."

"Business comes in all shapes and sizes. The nature of your relationships with multiple men is not likely something you want to discuss at the office."

I snorted and caught sight of Pretty Boy at the base of the stairs. I shook my head at him and pressed a finger to my lips. His expression was forbidding, but King was here fishing for *something,* and I wanted to know what that was.

"My relationships, personal or otherwise, are not your concern, Mr. King." I kept my tone stern, inflexible. No room for debate. "If that is all, I trust you to see yourself down in the elevator."

The silence on the far side was quite telling. If he intended to show up and intimidate me, he had made an error.

"Of course," he said after the pause went on almost too long. "I come as a friend only, and I do have a gift for you— one I think you will very much appreciate."

"You can always leave things with my doorman. That is why we have them, after all." It was a little high-handed, but then as Grandfather always said, the tools were there to be used whether you planned on it or not.

A soft chuckle greeted the comment. "I can see why my son is so enamored."

Yes, we were not having *that* discussion. Particularly with Pretty Boy looking like pure thunder. "If that is all," I said. "I have things to do..."

"Miss Benedict. That is not all, as you are aware. There are commitments. Promises. Oaths. It's about time you and I discussed them directly—with regard to the Royals, among other things."

"Directness is not poison," I said, not giving an inch.

"No, but I have often found that one must dance the social dance for business and pleasure. Skipping steps can be a recipe for disaster. I am not a man who is a fan of disaster when it can be averted with a little care."

I did not roll my eyes.

"Maybe you should learn to moderate your expectations and be more direct. I'll start for you—what do you want?" Confrontations should always take place on controlled ground. At the moment, I controlled the landscape here. He stood out there alone and seemingly at ease and patient.

He was on one side of the door and wanted to be on this side. Why? I wasn't one hundred percent certain. I was, however, curious. How much would he give to achieve his goal? We'd see.

Pretty Boy had folded his arms and continued to split

his attention between me and the door. He was deeply unhappy with King's presence. I wasn't all that thrilled myself. Still—I raised my brows. It could be useful.

I swore the "no" just radiated off of him, and I tilted my head. Everything could be an opportunity; we just needed to take advantage.

He shook his head, and I lifted a hand. Then motioned him to the library. If I let King in, then Pretty Boy could listen in the library.

Was I serious? I could practically hear the click of his teeth from here as he snapped his jaw shut.

One hand on my hip, I met him glare for glare. I was not *helpless,* and he would be *right* there. Besides, we'd long established King did not do his own dirty work. He forced his employees—and *teenagers* to do that for him.

Despicable asshole.

"I'd like to speak to you," King said. While his voice seemed cool and even, his delivery was not. "Face to face, and alone. I think you and I could be useful to each other."

Lips pursed, I weighed the pros and the cons, then glanced at Pretty Boy again. He hated everything about this. Chin dipped, he went thoughtful then held up five fingers.

Agreed.

"Five minutes, Mr. King," I told him as Pretty Boy strode across the hall to the library and disappeared inside of it. Once he was inside, I unlocked the front door. "Five minutes only," I continued, meeting his gaze unflinchingly. "I have a great deal to do, and you do not have an appointment."

"Understood." He stood there, his coat folded over his arm and not a package in sight. "May I come in?"

I gave him a long look before I took a single step back

with guarded politeness. "You may," I told him. "But don't sit down, and I won't be serving drinks."

Both choices flew in the face of polite protocol. I didn't care. I was being direct. I also checked my watch and set a five-minute timer.

King pursed his lips. It was a flicker of motion before his expression smoothed over. He didn't care for my tactics. Too bad.

"As you wish." He pivoted to face me. I closed the door, but I didn't move away from it or narrow the distance between us.

"Your time started when you came in," I reminded him. "What do you want, Mr. King?"

"As I said earlier, I definitely see the attraction."

If he was seeking a response, he was about to be disappointed. Controlling my reactions, including my expressions, was one of the first and longest lessons my grandfather had drilled me on.

"Tough," he continued after a moment. He made a brief show of glancing around before focusing on me again. "To the point then."

I didn't say a word, just stared at him. It was unsettling to those who needed an audience. Playing to a blank wall was much more challenging.

"Very well, as you are aware, Milo chose to take Andrea Reed's place."

Since we were both there at the time, it required no comment.

"I assume the sacrifice was made for you, noble as it was." Just the barest hint of sarcasm scratched those words. He was growing more uncomfortable by the moment. "I told you then that I honor my agreements, even when those who make the agreements with me do not honor theirs."

I blinked. Once. Then resumed our staring contest. My watch vibrated at the three minute mark. He was going to run out of time.

So sad for him.

"In light of that, I want to make you an offer—"

The shift in wording wasn't lost on me.

"I said I would not tap you for membership. That was my agreement with Reed. I won't tap your sister, either. That was my agreement with Milo."

He paused again, as if he needed to measure his next words against my response. Unfortunately, I wasn't giving him anything to work with. I didn't intend to, either.

"What I am here to do is propose an alliance, of sorts, between you and me. Business, of course, I wouldn't want to step on my son's toes. Or Graham's. Or Reed's. Or whomever else you are keeping on a string..."

"You are down to one minute," I told him. "So far, I've not heard anything worth opening that door for."

The corners of his lips turned upward. "You are tough. Far tougher than I think anyone gives you credit for—tough. Intelligent. Savvy. You know this world, and you know all the players." He took a step closer. "I would imagine you know them better than the boys do, and that's something I should have taken into account."

I gave him a beat.

"If we work together, we could create a formidable alliance. I might even be persuaded to cut Graham loose... You have your assets at Benedict, and I have mine in several locations—it wouldn't take much to pool them and then take players off the board that you don't want there."

"I'm not entirely certain why you believe any of that would be a gift for me..."

"Oh, that's not the gift." He shifted and opened his

jacket, then extracted an envelope that he extended to me. "That's the gift. Read it. Consider my offer. Call me. We'll make a real appointment. We could do great things together... And while you are on track to become one of the most powerful women in the country, I can get you there much faster."

I took the envelope. It was deep, dark golden yellow and fat. Legal paperwork? Something else? The contents felt like more paper.

He adjusted his jacket as my watch alarm rang.

"Miss Benedict," he said as I opened the door.

"Mr. King."

He nodded, swept the room with another look before giving me a brief stare, then he strolled out. I didn't rush to close the door, but I wasn't patient about it either. Pushing it closed and locking it, I switched the monitor to let me see via external camera again to watch him.

His back was to the apartment as he waited for the elevator. Heat brushed against my back, and I recognized Milo even as he wrapped an arm around my middle. His attention seemed riveted to the screen as much as mine was.

"He knows I'm here," he said against my ear.

"Maybe." I wasn't convinced. Considering the fact he'd come here fishing for "something."

"He offered you Ezra's freedom."

Yes, I'd heard that part. Still didn't mean anything. Then the elevator opened, and he stepped inside and out of sight. When he was gone, I turned off the camera and leaned back into Milo.

"What's in the envelope?"

I lifted it and turned it over. There was no writing on it at all. "Bait would be my guess."

His expression hardened. "Are you going to open it?"

"Yes. Because I want to know what he thinks he has to motivate me."

"I don't want him near you." The growl in his voice shouldn't be so sensuous or caring, but I soaked it up.

"We may have to put up with it, if it gets us what we want." While he didn't disagree with my sentiment, he definitely grumbled on our way back to the library.

The coffee was still at least hot, and after I swallowed a drink, I slit the envelope open.

TWENTY-FIVE

ADAM

"I can't believe you called Cavendish." Ezra's complaints echoed in my ears as I headed to lunch with my father and uncle. "I'm not a *child*." The only thing he hadn't done was stomp his foot.

"All evidence to the contrary," I'd said, then glanced at Cavendish. "I will hopefully not be longer than a couple of hours."

"Take your time," he'd replied with a wave as he settled onto the sofa. "Graham and I can bond."

"Just don't kill him," I said.

"I can promise that," Cavendish replied, and when Ezra glared at me, I patted his cheek.

"Be a good boy."

"Fuck you," he snarled, and I probably shouldn't have laughed at him, but I did. Leaving Lainey with Milo had been a choice. As had bringing Ezra home with me. Short of locking him in the panic room—I had thought of it—the only guarantee of keeping him from flying back to his father or on some other damn fool reckless move, was to leave someone watching him.

Milo was with Lainey, hence Cavendish was my next option. Also the one I preferred. At some point, we were going to have to sit down with Milo and explain Dominic Walsh, the charges, everything. He knew part of the story, but not all of it. This was not a bomb I wanted hanging over Lainey's head.

As for this lunch, I'd rather have blown it off entirely. The one benefit, it was here in Manhattan, rather than on Long Island. However, the orders had been very clear in my father's messages.

Very. Very. Clear. No matter where it was, he wanted me there. No excuses.

Which reminded me. "Call Fletcher."

"Calling Fletcher, mobile." The car's voice activated replied.

"Roadkill Cafe," Fletcher drawled as he answered. "You kill it, we grill it."

"Do you now?" I said, amused enough at the comment. It was different, and he sounded *good*.

"Well, well, well... if it isn't the scion of the family."

I snorted. "The job may be vacant soon, if you're interested."

He snorted. "Not for all the money in all the bank accounts. I have something good here—someone good. Not budging me even with fire."

"Well, do you still do favors for errant cousins?"

"I do them for my favorite cousin, but she's a lot prettier than you are."

It was my turn to snort. "What have you been doing for Lainey?"

"No idea what you're talking about. Very rude of you to

ask." The rebuke landed. Still... "Now, did my second favorite cousin want a favor?"

"You know you can be a bit of a dick." Yes, I was peeved.

"I can be a much bigger dick," he offered. "Try again."

This was why I loved Fletcher and occasionally wanted to throttle him. "I actually need a two-part favor."

"Give you an inch and you'll steal the whole damn stadium." His absolute sigh of despair was amusing. "What can I do for you? Just remember, you get the family discount 'cause you're actually family I like."

I appreciated that. I was two blocks out, so I filled him in on what I needed.

"Her name is Waldemar?"

"Yeah, Margareta Waldemar. I'm looking for connections to Julius King. And anything else you can dig up."

"*And* anything else?" He actually sounded insulted. "I'll get the brand, size, and color of her favorite panties."

I grimaced. "Really don't need that."

"Fine, but I bet I can find it anyway." He sniffed. "What's the second part of the favor?"

"Dad's up to something. I don't know what. It could be another affair. I'm pretty sure he started one as soon as he married Melissa."

"Knowing Harper, probably before," Fletcher commented and I didn't disagree. "You don't think whatever this is, is personal?"

"No, it feels—different. It feels off. There's a lot going on right now. But take a sweep through the company for me. I'd rather be aware of whatever traps he's setting before they spring."

"Will do, might take me a couple of days. We're on a job at the moment. Is it urgent?"

"Not yet," I told him as I pulled into the underground

garage of the building housing the restaurant we were dining in. "Thanks, Fletcher."

"I'd say anytime, but we both know you don't like asking for favors."

No, I did not.

Then he was off the phone and I was gearing up for dealing with whomever would be at lunch. Father told me to bring Lainey to lunch, and since she was about as eager to have food with her mother as I was, maybe less, I "forgot" to invite her.

Besides, if I was having lunch with Lainey, I would prefer that *she* be the meal. I checked my phone one more time before heading up to the rooftop restaurant. The hostess recognized me as the elevator doors opened.

The soft, flirty smile was something I had indulged from time to time. It made her more likely to drop information in my ear. Today, that was a firm no. Lainey had forgiven me, or at least, she'd allowed me a place in her life.

"Just the table," I told the hostess with as much kindness as I could muster. No point in leading her on.

"Of course." Her smile dimmed a fraction, but when I offered her a hundred it increased.

What I wasn't going to flirt for, I had no problems paying. As she led me through the dining room, I spotted a number of familiar faces. Mostly business associates, a couple of politicians, an actor—that was different.

Our table wasn't in the main dining room. How not surprising. Instead, the hostess took me directly to one of the private rooms and opened the door. The table with my father, Melissa, and Hamilton was the only one in the room, and it was near the center. So not only did we have the whole room to ourselves, we were set up far away from prying eyes and ears.

"Thank you," I told her and waved her back out before I headed to the table. Had this been a lunch my mother had been present at, I would have paused to kiss her cheek. Since this was Melissa, I offered her a nod as I circled the table.

Since neither Harper nor Hamilton stood up, I didn't bother with thinly-veiled politeness where they were concerned. I just took my seat, poured myself a glass of water, then met my father's glare across the table.

"You were told to bring Lainey." Well, at least we weren't going to play pretend today.

"I didn't see her this morning. I assume she had other plans." None of that was a lie. I took a sip of the water. "If that was the only reason for this command performance..."

"It was not the *only* reason," my father snapped even as Melissa sighed.

"I can go call her," she said. "We're not that far from my father's apartment here in the city. I think she's still using that one as her primary residence in Manhattan."

"It's fine," Dad said with a sharp shake of his head to Melissa. "We wanted her to be in a good mood when she showed up."

That statement landed. Melissa flinched then reached for her wine glass with a trembling hand. Go Dad, always the cutting asshole.

"Fine, I'm here... what did you want?"

"Order food first," Hamilton interjected. "Then we will have a meal and conversation like civilized people."

I met and held his gaze, not bothering to disguise an ounce of my disdain. "Civilized people can have disagreements and conversations without food. It's the beggars and the hangers-on that seem to require something in order to participate."

His jaw tightened, and a muscle jumped in his cheek. "You little bastard…"

"My parentage is quite secure, thank you. I know my parents were married when I was born." While I hadn't directed it at her, Melissa still reacted to the comment. Nothing to be done for it.

Anyone who wanted to call Lainey or Andrea a bastard would eat my fist. Hamilton could be first in line. Speaking of whom, he went to get to his feet when Dad slapped a hand to the table.

"Sit down," he ordered Hamilton then glanced at Melissa with impatience. "If you're going to cry, take it to the ladies and repair your cosmetics. You know better."

A soft gasp escaped her. Whether it was for the harshness in his tone or the absolute disregard in his manner, I had no idea.

"Please," she said quietly. Almost too quietly. "Excuse me."

Then she was hurrying out of the room with her purse in hand and not glancing back.

"Fantastic, now I'll be stopping at the jewelers today." Dad glared at me. "Why could you not simply bring Elaine as I requested?"

"Would you like the truth or do you need me to cater to your abusive ego?" Honestly, I had no patience for him today. I'd left Ezra with someone he didn't really trust because I couldn't trust Ezra to not do something stupid.

I had any number of problems, and frankly my father's desires and wishes didn't fall into a category I gave a damn about.

"How about I make you an offer for your shares and the ones you're controlling for Fletcher?" The counteroffer was a bold move, seemingly going straight for his target rather than coming at it from a circuitous route.

Hamilton looked shocked. The surprise wasn't feigned, nor was it a ploy. He barely caught himself then had to take a long drink to cover. So, no, this was a distraction not the real goal.

Interesting.

He'd probably take me up on the offer if I agreed though.

"At a valuation of ten times the current market price," I suggested and all the blood drained out of Dad's face. In fact, a vein began to throb in his forehead.

"That's ridiculous."

"So is owning more than seventy five percent of the company. Currently, what I own is enough to stop either of you from doing anything ridiculous. Hamilton gambled away his shares, and I picked up the majority of them."

A point I rather enjoyed.

That earned me another baleful look.

"Fletcher wants nothing to do with any of you; therefore, I have his proxies from now until eternity."

Or until he wanted them back.

"Andrea's not old enough to access her block, but you and Melissa can clearly work things out. Still doesn't matter. Without Jason on your side, you're at a stalemate. You don't have Jason."

"What makes you think I don't?" Oh, I'd insulted him *and* pricked his pride.

Too. Fucking. Bad.

"Because he doesn't like to be in the same room with either of you if he can help it. You and Hamilton are half the reason Fletcher left and never came back. Jason's a bit of a waste at times, but he loved his son."

He would never forgive them for Fletcher's loss. Even if Jason was just as guilty in his own ways. It didn't matter, it meant Jason was at odds with them and more likely to follow my votes because I had Fletcher's proxy.

A waitress appeared with fresh drinks, but I waved off the alcohol. I'd stick with the water. Dad ordered for everyone, including Melissa, who hadn't returned.

Chances were, she wasn't coming back. At least not while I was here.

No loss.

Once the waitress left, I looked at my father again. "Was that all?"

"Lainey's twenty-first birthday is coming up. Very soon."

I was aware. Still, I allowed nothing of my reaction to cross my face.

"Melissa wants to throw her a huge party."

No she didn't.

"At the house."

Right.

"You will make sure she is there."

I turned the command over in my head, then drained the water glass before I stood. "No."

"Excuse me?"

"It's her birthday. If she wants to see her mother, she knows how to use a phone. So does Melissa for that matter. I will not just drag her to some party to be shown off like some prize you've just obtained so all of your business associates and the other families can try to kiss your ring to get at her."

His expression flattened.

"You aren't her father. You're barely Andrea's. Lainey

will have the birthday she wants to have. Since that was everything—good afternoon."

I didn't wait for either of them to respond before I headed out. Now I knew why they'd wanted Lainey here. To guilt her into agreeing. More, they had plans for that party or they wouldn't be doing such a direct approach.

Whatever it was, I had zero intentions of letting any of it happen on any day, much less her birthday.

CHAPTER
TWENTY-SIX

LAINEY

My phone buzzed as Wood pulled up to the restaurant. While I wasn't all that keen on having Karagiani with me, I'd allowed it because Adam was dealing with a family matter—or at least that was what he said—and Ezra. Bodhi called to tell me he would be gone for twenty-four hours. By my count, that meant he would be back before dawn. Pretty Boy had gone to see Em. She'd called again, and whatever they discussed had bothered him enough that I gave him the shove to go.

If I didn't have dinner plans with my grandfather, I would have gone to see Em, too. I missed her. With everything that had been happening, I could go for a long sit-down conversation with her. Though, she was likely to be annoyed with me for having kept so much from her.

She was allowed to scold me. I had done the same to her, after all. She would understand—eventually. Though, she wasn't the only best friend I hadn't spoken to recently.

Tally and I kept missing each other, literally. She'd left a couple of vague messages that were empty of any real information. The last one irked because she'd also been irritated with me and *my* schedule.

If tonight's dinner had been with anyone else—*anyone*—I would have canceled to stay home. I'd been nursing a headache all afternoon. Research seemed to be playing a shell game with all of us. Each time we turned up what seemed like a lead or a clue, it evaporated into dust.

Smoke and mirrors.

Julius King was a product of smoke and mirrors.

Then there was the envelope he dropped off as his "gift." The paperwork included some "interesting" additions. Pretty Boy worried, whether it was true or not, what King hoped to gain by giving it to me.

I didn't worry. I knew exactly what he wanted. An ally. He'd actually meant what he said. He wanted me to work *with* him. Opening doors to him that were currently barred. He wanted acceptance and respect from a community that offered very little of that to those not born into it.

He wanted *power*.

Ultimately, it was what *everyone* wanted. Wanted to acquire it, consolidate it, and hold onto it. No family willingly gave up what was theirs. Even when their wealth diminished and new players entered the game—the power of a name and a bloodline was currency that couldn't be replaced.

Grandfather had come into the city for meetings, so dinner was at his favorite restaurant. An indulgence, and one I could hardly fault him for no matter what my mood was—particularly after I fled the city right after the Fire and Ice party and I hadn't really gotten to spend much time with him.

With freezing rain and snow in the forecast, Wood had driven with absolute care. The last time I'd been in a car with Wood and Karagiani both, there'd been an accident. As we pulled up to the restaurant, I said, "Wood if you want to go for the night, I can call for a different—"

"No, thank you," he said over his shoulder. "I'm just fine to drive. I will be more than happy to come back and get you and Karagiani then take you home. Don't you worry. I have a good book and a thermos of coffee."

I chuckled. "I'm not going to persuade you, am I?"

"No." This time he said it firmly, if kindly.

"Thank you."

"Of course."

Then we were pulling up to the velvet-canopied entrance. A doorman was already moving to open my door. Karagiani slipped out of the passenger seat to circle the car.

"I'll see you soon," Wood said and I nodded.

"If the weather gets worse..."

"I'll be here."

I shook my head. Impossible. They were all impossible. He shouldn't even be back at work, but he insisted he was fine and he had a doctor's note to prove it. Rather than argue and keep him longer, I stepped out and nodded to the doorman who held an umbrella up to keep the weather off.

Karagiani scanned the area, and then we were on our way to the door. Without a word, he followed me inside. The maître d' smiled at my approach.

"Mademoiselle Benedict." He had both arms wide and barely touched my biceps as he leaned in to give me a kiss to each cheek. Granted, it was just to the air next to my cheek, but it was a familiar greeting from a fond acquaintance. He was nearly my grandfather's age, and I'd known the man all my life.

"Good evening, Rudolpho," I said with a smile as he helped me out of my coat then snapped his fingers to a young man to take it to the coatroom. "Is my grandfather already here?"

"Yes, Monsieur Benedict is here and in a fine mood. It will be finer still when he sees you." He flicked a look toward Karagiani. "Joining or...?"

"A separate table for Mr. Karagiani please. He doesn't need to be next to us." I'd prefer privacy with my grandfather regardless.

"Of course, we'll take care of him." Bodyguards were hardly new to the staff, and they understood without asking too many questions. With that, he escorted me to my grandfather's table, which was in a corner on a riser and next to the windows that looked out over a private garden done up in LED lights. It was elegant without being ostentatious.

"There's my girl," Grandfather said as I climbed the steps. He was already on his feet, and I got a real hug, followed by a kiss to the cheek. Then he gave me a very firm look, sweeping me from head to toe.

"Do I pass inspection?"

I'd chosen a simple wraparound dress in dark green. The long sleeves helped to keep away any chill. The fact it fell below the knee meant I could wear lower heels or boots. With the weather, I'd gone with low-heeled leather boots more for comfort and security. Normally, I'd have worn heels but I didn't fancy busting my ass on the stairs.

"You always look beautiful," he said with his kind and blunt charm. "But you seem—"

I raised my eyebrows at the rather heavy sigh escaping him. "Grandfather?"

"You just seem so grown up, my little girl. An adult."

He shook his head, then pulled out a chair for me. I studied him for a moment before I sat down and set my purse down on the chair closest to me. Near enough for me to reach without it standing out from being on the table.

"Well, I am getting older," I reminded him. "Practically ancient."

That earned a genuine laugh from him as he retook his seat. "I've ordered wine and a cheese board for the appetizer. Lamb all right for you this evening, or would you prefer something lighter?"

"The lamb is fine." The assurance seemed to be all he needed as he motioned to the waiter a few feet away. The man who had been simply giving us a moment before he approached poured me a glass of the grenache—a Spanish label from the brief look I had of it.

"Bring the cheeseboard and put in the orders for the lamb," Grandfather informed him. "Then privacy."

"Of course, sir." The waiter left the bottle and made sure to fill my water as well before he departed, giving us the requested privacy.

Grandfather lifted his glass and gave me a small salute, and I mirrored the action. After we'd both sipped, I focused on him. "What's wrong?"

"It's not—wrong, exactly." Hedging was not in his vocabulary. It never had been. So, I just waited him out and met him stare for stare.

This man had raised me to meet all challenges head-on. He taught me to observe the patterns of behavior around me and to learn to predict them. Above all those other lessons, he instructed me on how and when to follow my gut instincts. Particularly if my gut disagreed with my observations.

"I am very proud of you," he said, retaking the reins slowly. "You know that, right?"

"I do," I said. "You have never withheld praise or your opinions on my choices—whether you agreed with them or not."

There had been times when those disagreements led to arguments and debates. Yet, never once had I questioned his respect or his caring, even when we frustrated each other.

"Good," he said. "Sometimes...well, all the time, I miss your grandmother. She always knew what to say and how to gentle even the harshest of criticisms with a soft word."

My heart squeezed for him. His love for her was something I'd always told myself I wanted. Now I had something like it—I couldn't imagine losing someone to their own mind as we'd lost her. Those rare days when she was with us again, they were worth every moment of missing her. Because we still had some hope.

"She could stop you in a tirade with one word." His name.

"Leopold," he said, a half-smile on his face. "Enough."

"But you were already done when she said your name."

He nodded, then looked at his wine again.

"Grandfather," I said gently and he glanced at me. "Just tell me. What's wrong?"

"Your birthday."

My twenty-first. It was soon. I'd lost track of the days, but it was. Suddenly, King's visit gained a little more context. "It's soon." I gave a little shrug. "Please don't tell me we have to have a party."

I just didn't think I could do another so soon. The season was coming. There were charities and at least two more fundraisers to attend come late March.

"You have never been fond of the parties." It was more an observation than a question, so I let it go. The waiter returned with the cheese board, and once he'd served it, he checked our drinks then excused himself. The interaction took bare moments.

"I believe you were the one who told me that parties were work. We could have fun, within reason. Business often came before pleasure, and too many failed to see the pleasure as the obstacle for themselves and the avenue for others." Alcohol gave way to loose lips and tongues. The shadowy corners invited assignations. Not to mention public spectacles were a thing.

All of which I was intimately acquainted with. Adam stealing kisses at the masquerade before Bodhi wandered back into our lives. Pretty Boy punching Ezra. The confrontation between all of them over the fact I was seeing at least two of them at the time and having sex.

Yes, scandal was the meat of so many parties. The price of admission as it were.

"Sometimes I regret that I had to disabuse you of so much of the fun when you were growing up."

I shrugged, not because it wasn't important or I didn't believe him but because... "Grandfather, I wouldn't trade how you raised me for anything. I had a wonderful childhood. I had access to a fantastic education. A school where I met both of my best friends. I have enjoyed my life and everything you've given me. Not to mention the fact that I don't just believe in what I see with my eyes. But I look deeper, I look at the content of the character and not just the show being put on."

Pride showed in his eyes, and he took another drink of wine before he began to fill his plate with the cheese, soft crackers, and fruit. I mirrored his actions, aware that something ate away at him.

"You know that you come into a portion of your inheritance on your birthday."

Again, it wasn't a question. I was very well aware of it. Part of the reason I had been doing so much work at the company over the last few months. Because while I'd always had access, I would actually have a say after my birthday.

"I'm ready," I told him. "Granted, I don't know that I'm prepared for everything. But I am prepared to learn and to keep learning so that I can do my job as well as make you proud."

His smile was swift. "You make me proud every day."

As quickly as it arrived, it vanished again. I'd never seen my grandfather—agitated before. I'd seen him angry. I'd seen him absolutely furious. I'd also seen him coldly dismissive. This nervousness wasn't him, and it made me uneasy.

"My darling girl, as much as I dread this conversation, we need to discuss the possibility of arranging a marriage for you and doing it swiftly."

I blinked.

Then gave myself a little shake when I realized he wasn't joking. "What?"

He leaned forward, food forgotten. "You are going to be an immensely wealthy young lady. I made mistakes with your mother. Mistakes that cost her—cost you. I do not want you to be the prime rib for every hunter to be looking to take their shot. You need to be married, and swiftly. It will cut off the predators. We would arrange a very aggressive prenuptial agreement. I think your friend Hardigan would be a good match. He would definitely serve as a strong deterrent."

I stared at him.

"If that's not something you want to consider, then we find you someone else. Someone who understands their place, and this will free you up. It takes care of one avenue of attack and gives you the greatest amount of control."

Of everything he could have brought up at this dinner, *marriage* was not even on my radar. "Grandfather," I said, picking up the wine. "I don't need to be married to avoid complications. This is hardly the fourteenth century when I can be kidnapped and wed against my will then lose all my assets because women can't inherit or hold property."

I drained the wine with a great deal less control than I preferred to show.

"Of course it isn't, but there have been... there have been rumblings. Rumors. More than one investigation, and I know at least one person requested to see your grand-mother's trust agreements."

"No one can request those who isn't..."

Mother.

"Exactly," he said. "She knows very well that I have cut her off from any access. She made that choice when she became that man's mistress above and beyond anything else. If he wanted her so much and loved her so much, then he would have treated her like a lady and not a whore."

I didn't move.

Adam's father and my mother...

"Without her inheritance, without access to it... he didn't want her. Not like that." Ruthless. Pragmatic. Heart-breaking. "She never listened to reason. Not from your grandmother. Not from me." He pursed his lips. "Then she had you. As much as a punishment for him as she did it to prove something to me. But I called her bluff..."

"Then you took me, paid her a handsome allowance, and she signed off on letting you practically adopt me." I knew this story. Not because they'd told me—he had eventually, because he wanted me to know the truth and to see the paperwork. No, because I'd heard one of my mother's arguments with my grandmother. "This is why you have avoided Andrea."

He actually looked ashamed for a moment. "Anything that child has access to—that man will. That family. I know what he wants. He will never get it from either of us."

My stomach turned.

"I hate asking this of you, darling girl. It's why I am suggesting Hardigan. You need a strong husband. One they cannot leverage against you. You need that ally even more. Because I may not always be here..."

I frowned. What the hell did that mean? Not that I got a chance to ask because suddenly Ezra was at the table. A plastered Ezra, whose expression was equal parts furiousness and arrogant.

"If she needs to get married, then she can marry *me*."

Oh for the love of...

CHAPTER
TWENTY-SEVEN

EZRA

Adam pissed me the fuck off the first night he said we were leaving Lainey's to go back to his place. It wasn't a discussion. It was just a decision. Fine. While I wanted to object, his expression said it wasn't open to debate. I didn't want to leave Lainey's; as hardass as he'd been *here*, he'd also been his most accessible.

At his apartment, it would just be the two of us and a conversation I had avoided for more than a decade. A conversation I wasn't even aware that I wanted to have with him until the stubborn asshole disappeared on me and my heart broke. The idea of surrendering even more power to him than I already had went against everything in me. Lainey *loved* me. She *accepted* me.

While Adam seemed like he wanted to do the same, I wasn't sure we were there. I supposed the lack of outright rejection was enough, right?

Fuck, I hoped so.

But no sooner did we get back to his apartment than his

phone was blowing up with messages and calls. Calls he had to take. Calls he took in another room, behind a closed door he could watch me through but I couldn't listen.

The absolute lack of trust sliced through me.

Since he wanted to watch, I stalked off to take a shower. After, I stole a pair of his pajama bottoms then sauntered back downstairs and poured myself a drink. If he wanted to treat me like some errant little fuckboy, I'd act like one.

I was tempted to sit here and jack myself off while he watched, particularly when his glare intensified over the second glass of whiskey I fixed for myself. Instead, I just moved the decanter over to the sofa and sprawled out so he could get a good look.

It wasn't fair that the more irritated he became, the hotter he was too. There was something about the whiplash of command in his voice. It turned me the fuck on. For a moment there, when I stared into his eyes while we were both buried balls deep in Lainey—I felt it. He *saw* me. We were in that moment together.

It didn't last. How could it?

I was insane to think this could work. He indulged me for Lainey's sake. He fucking worshipped her. So did I...but I wanted him to see me *all* the time, not just in moments. It didn't take long to finish the whiskey, and when it hit me that I was on my feet, I frowned.

"What are we doing?" Oh was that me slurring?

"I'm putting you to bed."

That meant I was sleeping alone.

Fuck. I needed more alcohol. He all but shoved me in the bathroom and I made a show of emptying my bladder and brushing my teeth. I half fell on his bed. It smelled like him, and that just made my heart cramp.

But oblivion was waiting, and the alcohol had numbed

enough. Before I could tumble all the way, he made me sit up. "What the fuck do you want?"

"Take the aspirin," he ordered and pushed a glass of water into my hand. I glared at both, but he glared at me. `

"I fucking hate you some days." The words slipped the leash and darted out.

"Yeah, I get that a lot." But he didn't clarify the comment, just took the glass after I drained it, and then I curled onto my side. I closed my eyes and tried to blot out the world.

The next morning, there was more water and aspirin waiting for me. But no Adam. The other side of the bed was a little mussed, and the pillow had a depression in it. But he hadn't slept in the bed.

Why the fuck was I here?

I downed the aspirin and the water, then threw myself through another shower. It was warm and humid in there. He'd already showered and I'd missed it. Aggravation joined my hangover to pound behind my eyes as I stalked down the stairs. Coffee was waiting for me. But Adam was already dressed and in a suit.

Of all the people in the world to be here—Phillip fucking Cavendish sat on the sofa, thumbing through his phone.

He got me a *babysitter*.

Worse, they were *discussing* me.

When I stomped into the kitchen, it didn't take long for Adam to follow. I poured coffee, then flipped through the cabinets. There was always something in here. Rum. Whiskey. Bourbon.

"I have to go to this lunch..."

I spared him a look. "I thought we were having lunch with Hardigan."

No I didn't, but it sounded better than why was he leaving me with Cavendish?

"I'll be back as soon as I can." When I slammed another cabinet, Adam added, "I also locked up the liquor and tossed out the rest of the whiskey. You need to sober up."

"Go to hell." I wanted to retract it almost as soon as I said it. But Adam just gave me a level look before he turned on his heel and left.

Yeah, why respond to the child.

The only decent thing about Cavendish? He didn't try to talk to me.

Thank. Fuck.

The better thing, he didn't come in the kitchen while I was drinking coffee, nor did he notice when I found the cooking wine and the spare key the staff kept for Adam's liquor cabinet.

By the time I put in a delivery order with my phone, I'd almost found a decent mood.

The next twenty-four hours pretty much went like the last. Only this time, Adam threw my phone out along with the alcohol. His rage was fun. I could almost pretend he cared when the heat of it licked through the alcoholic fog.

It took time, but he finally went to sleep, and when I woke up to see him passed out in the chair in the bedroom, I'd had enough. I got my shit, and I left.

I knew his codes. I knew how to get downstairs. I found my phone before I left. He might have "tossed it," but he hadn't actually gotten rid of it entirely.

The screen was cracked.

Dick.

Downstairs, I had the doorman get me a cab, and I headed out to the closest bar. I needed hair of the dog and then to figure some shit out. I was still there when Karagiani let me know that Lainey was on the move.

Why the fuck was she out without Hardigan or Cavendish? Adam was at the apartment. One of us should be *with* her. My days were blurring together, but I hadn't seen her in long enough that I *needed* to see her, so I got Karagiani to give me his location. He wasn't thrilled, but threatening him with firing got him to tell me.

The cab took forever, but it gave time for the peppermints to work on my breath. I knew the restaurant. Had connections. It got me inside and I found her having dinner with her grandfather.

Karagiani wasn't that far away, but I ignored him as I headed straight for her. I was almost to the table when the conversation registered.

"I hate asking this of you, darling girl. It's why I am suggesting Hardigan. You need a strong husband. One they cannot leverage against you. You need that ally even more. Because I may not always be here..."

Strong husband.

Lainey needed a strong husband? He wanted her to marry Hardigan? Was he *insane*? Hardigan wasn't a bad guy, but his father was fucking King. Hardigan had friends, yes. But he wasn't connected. Hell no.

If her grandfather wanted her to have a husband, then I'd step fucking up. I had connections and I had a name... I could protect her.

"If she needs to get married, then she can marry *me*." I threw the words down like I was tossing a gauntlet, and I had my hand on the back of her chair. Lainey shot me a look that suggested I better remove my grip, but I needed it to stay standing. The room was swaying a little harder than I expected.

"Mr. Graham," Leopold Benedict spit out my name like it was distasteful as he rose to his feet. "I am having a private conversation and meal with my granddaughter. One you were *not* invited to attend. You may excuse yourself now."

"If we're discussing her future, then I should absolutely have been invited." Particularly if we were discussing *Hardigan* as the option for her. "I've known her most of her life." If not all of it. "There isn't anything I wouldn't do for her."

"Including suggesting she marry you when you're already *engaged*." Absolute dislike slid over every single syllable. His scowl landed like a physical blow. "How dare you intimate that she is an afterthought when you're already making plans with another woman? She is not—"

"Grandfather," Lainey interrupted, standing as well. Even with our voices low, she radiated caution. The sweet scent of her perfume wrapped around me like one of those cartoon scents, and I wanted to lean into it and float away.

"Darling girl," he said, the rebuke clear even as he softened his tone. "This *boy* is not the one for you. He can't hold his liquor. He works in service to dark men for dark purposes. He cannot even *stand* at the moment. Cut him loose before he drags you down."

"Ezra is my friend."

Friend?

Friend?

Rejection slammed through me. "I am more than your damn friend," I snapped, and she suddenly pivoted and the hard glare in her dark eyes shut me up. I'd never seen Lainey wreathed in pure violence before. That was always *Adam*. But holy shit, she was like a dark goddess, armed and ready for war.

"Be quiet, Ezra," she commanded and I wanted to go to my knees. "Please. We need to sort this out and not have a scene."

I mimed zipping my lips. It was a little sloppy because I staggered a little, but she braced me with one hand. Her eyes softened and relief flooded me. Yes, she was angry but she still loved me.

Didn't matter if I deserved it or not. I switched my foggy attention to her grandfather and the disapproval radiating off of him.

"Darling girl, this is not a smart decision."

"Sometimes," she said, sliding an arm around me, and I took the invitation to settle my arm on her shoulders. Oh, that helped a lot. I wasn't quite listing anymore. "Sometimes, you have to make the right decision even if it's one that may not bring the result others want."

He shook his head, but even the old curmudgeon couldn't hold a scowl in the face of her determination. "He's going to hurt you."

He—he meant me.

"He *has* hurt you."

"I know," she said. "Doesn't mean I can't care about him. Right now, he clearly needs me or he wouldn't be in this shape. Marriage shouldn't be about business or securing assets. I know that's—important. I'm not dismissing your concerns. But I won't use any of them that way, not Milo or Phillip or Adam—"

Her grandfather's expression turned so fierce at Adam's name, I girded myself.

"—or Ezra. They're my friends. They're much more...I care about them. This is not a discussion you want to have with me right now. But I did hear you, I promise, and we can finish talking about this later."

He sighed, his disappointment a weight I couldn't mistake. When I would have opened my mouth, Lainey stepped on my foot. The pain sparked through the fog, and I shut my mouth, teeth clicking together.

"Trust me?" she continued, not sparing me a single look even as she kept me standing. Did she want me to trust her or...

"Of course, I trust you. It's all of them I don't." His grumble was something I appreciated. I didn't trust anyone with her either. Still, he sighed and moved around the table to press a kiss to her cheek.

Their meal was hardly finished. Maybe we should stay? I wanted Lainey to eat, but I didn't want to be here. Too exposed for her. If my father found out she was out here...

"I'll call you tomorrow," she was saying, and then we were moving. Wait, did I say goodbye? When I would have turned around, she steered me toward the doors. Karagiani fell into step with us. We were leaving?

Then we were outside in the brittle cold and it landed like a slap. Maybe we needed—oh look, a car. Lainey wasn't gentle when she shoved me inside before she climbed in. Karagiani grunted but said nothing.

I opened my mouth but she snapped a look at me so fierce, I tucked my chin down. She also had her phone out. Oh fuck—

"I have him," she was saying. "He showed up at the restaurant—don't *start*, Adam. I was out to dinner with my grandfather. You knew I was going, and I had Karagiani with me. Why was Ezra out wandering drunk and alone?"

I didn't hear what he said, but I slouched in the seat and glared out of the windows. Was she taking me back to my jailer? Clearly, I wasn't allowed to make these decisions anymore.

"No, we're going back to my apartment. I'll sober him up and then figure this out—"

Oh. That sounded better.

"I know," she said, her whole manner softening again and she glanced at me. I tried to smile, but my lips were kind of numb. "I love you too—no, don't rush over. Let me have some time with him then we'll figure this out."

Of course she loved him. But she told me she loved me first. So he could *suck it.*

"Get some rest," she said. "You sound tired."

I turned my attention back to the dark streets, the icy conditions and the—was it snowing again? Huh.

All too soon we were back at her building. "No," she was saying to Karagiani. "I'll take him up. You two go home. I'm in the for the night."

"I should go up with you," Karagiani argued, but she shook her head.

Should he come up? I didn't really want him there. "I got her," I said, and the words didn't quite slur this time. That was an improvement. "Do what you're told."

"Good night, Wood. Karagiani. Thank you both." She was out of the car, and I had to climb over to get out. The doorman gave me a look as he offered me a hand, but I managed without falling on my face.

Raking a hand through my hair, I tried to straighten, but exhaustion slammed into me in waves. I either needed another drink or to sleep for a few hours. But first, get Lainey inside. The walk across the lobby took forever.

Then we were in the elevator. The quiet closed in around us with the doors shutting. The soft hum of the motor as we ascended filled the claustrophobic space. But then so did her perfume.

"Kotyonok..."

"I'm not mad," she said and relief coursed through me. "I'm not thrilled with you at the moment, but I'm not mad. However, we're not talking while you're drunk and already in a mood."

"Sorry," I mumbled.

"I know," she said with the softest of sighs. "It's going to be fine."

I believed her. I was two steps out of the elevator and half-turning to hold out a hand when movement had me spinning. Or maybe it was the walls that were spinning as a fist plowed into my stomach. Two sharp blows and I doubled over, vomiting.

Men were everywhere, and they had Lainey.

TWENTY-EIGHT

LAINEY

E zra leaned heavily on me. He'd grown quieter and quieter the closer we got to the apartment. I hadn't missed the sullen suspicion when I spoke to Adam. The frustration in Adam's voice had also been difficult to hear. Adam was furious that Ezra had slipped out while he was asleep. I could hardly fault him for that; on the other hand, locking him in his room was not the way to go.

And Grandfather...

I was still turning over *that* conversation in my head along with his clear disapproval for my relationship with Ezra. I would have to deal with that at some point and temper his expectations. But of all the discussion points he could have brought up tonight, this was not one I could have imagined at all.

Ezra straightened, raking a hand through his hair. "Kotyonok..."

Regret kissed every syllable. On some level, relief

filtered through me. He could be so abrasive when he'd been drinking. He could also be so damn sweet. It sounded like sweet had won out, and that would make the evening easier.

I hoped.

"I'm not mad," I promised him, but I wouldn't lie. "I'm not thrilled with you at the moment, but I'm not mad. However, we're not talking while you're drunk and already in a mood."

"Sorry," he mumbled, an air of chagrin about him. While not embarrassed, he didn't seem particularly thrilled to be this vulnerable. Not like I could blame him. I hated showing that to the world too.

"I know." I half-sighed the words. "It's going to be fine."

The elevator doors opened and he paced forward a couple of steps before he held out his hand to me. It was—

A man in a black face mask rushed forward, and Ezra went down. I barely had time to respond as two more followed and tried to slam me back against the wall of the elevator. They seemed huge. My purse dropped and took my phone with it as I went for the hands locking around my throat.

I got my fingers wrapped around one thumb and wrenched it backward even as I slammed my foot into the crotch of the big guy trying to strangle me. It took two hard kicks but he let out a pained sound and his grip lightened. I dropped to my feet and then twisted under his arm, still holding his thumb.

The sound of retching filled the hallway along with the sickly sour scents of alcohol and stomach acid. Ezra was on his hands and knees, struggling to get back up. There was a guy standing over him getting ready to hit him. I snagged my purse, yanking the strap to me. The collapsible baton was inside. It was small, the handle fitting in my palm.

I snapped it out, and it locked into place. I struck Ezra's assailant in the arm.

Once.

Twice.

On the third, bone cracked and the man let out a yowl.

A hand fisted my hair and jerked me backwards as another rushed toward me. Pain sparked along my scalp, and tears burned in my eyes. I fell backwards into the guy trying to grip my hair, turning gravity and momentum against him.

In a straight fight, I wasn't winning. They were so much fucking bigger. So I had to cripple and disable as much as I could. There were cameras in the hall and the building had security—

There was a cloth in the man's hand and I smelled something astringent and stinging.

Oh fuck no...

I lashed forward with my feet and slammed my head backward. No cooperation from me. Then all of a sudden the man gripping me from behind vanished and I staggered backwards. There was another man in the hall, and he was between me and the others. He had my captor in his grip, and there was a brutal sound of bone breaking, and the guy went down.

Bodhi.

He dropped the one guy then faced the others. "Well let's go," he said. "You can attack my girl, then you can come for me."

I swallowed and glanced past him to where Ezra was on the floor. He wasn't moving. Fear spiked through me. Bodhi wasn't waiting for a response from the others. He closed the fight on the other three. He was all swift blows and vicious kicks. Blood sprayed from one man's nose as Bodhi took him down with an elbow to his face.

Another rushed Bodhi from behind so I twisted, slamming the baton across the man's knee. He went down, and I caught him with the baton to the chin, before cracking him across the face. Another one collapsed, and I turned to find Bodhi holding the last one standing in a chokehold.

He scanned the hallway. "Just the five?"

"I don't know," I admitted, and it came out more of a croak than I expected. The guy who'd tried to strangle me hadn't been gentle.

Bodhi's eyes narrowed, and the man he was holding collapsed. "Inside," he ordered in a kind of detached yet firm voice that encouraged me not to argue. Weirdly, I didn't even mind the command of it. I still had my hand wrapped tightly around the baton and somehow, I hadn't lost my purse.

"Ezra..." My voice cracked again. Dammit.

"I'll get him."

Yet, no sooner was I at the door and unlocking it than I caught movement from the corner of my eye. One of the downed men pushed upward. He had a gun in his hand. "Bo—"

I didn't even finish his whole name. Bodhi turned, caught the gun, somehow—literally disarmed the guy, then used the handle of the gun to pistol whip the man once, twice, and finally a third time before he collapsed. After that, Bodhi went from downed man to downed man, making sure they were actually down.

"Inside," he repeated, catching my gaze, and I nodded once, getting the door open and disarming the alarm. My gaze landed on the time and surprise ripped through me.

Not even ten full minutes had passed since we arrived at the building. "Lainey B..."

I pivoted at his voice. Wait, what was I... Oh, he had Ezra.

"It's going to be fine," Bodhi told me. "All the way in, I'll drop him on the sofa, then deal with this."

"You're leaving?" The words slipped out even as I tried to shake off the malaise gripping me. I stepped aside so he could carry Ezra in. Ezra was a mess. Blood and bile were on his face. His shirt was soaked. There was an ugly bruise forming across his brow.

Anger sparked to life, and I closed the baton and shoved it back into my purse before following. Bodhi set Ezra on the sofa, head turned in case he was sick again. I needed to grab a bucket. Adrenaline spiked through the fog and helped chase it away.

I caught Bodhi's gaze as he straightened. "You have this?"

"I do," I promised him. "You're coming back after—" I motioned to the hall.

"Yes. Lock the door, keep it locked. I'll take care of this and get a clean-up crew." He paused to give me a long look. "Are you hurt anywhere?"

"My throat," I admitted. "Probably some bruises."

He circled the sofa to catch my hand, and he raised the right one. There was blood speckling my fingers.

"Not mine."

Stroking his thumb over my wrist, he nodded slowly. "Clean up, but I want a full accounting of any injuries."

I raised my brows. "Planning to kiss them and make them better?"

He didn't take his gaze from mine for a single second, and he didn't smile. If anything, he seemed to be imprinting himself right onto my soul. "If you like," he told me with such utter seriousness that I almost regretted the quip. "Look after Graham. I will be right outside. No one is touching you again."

Then he brushed his lips against mine. It was a blink-and-miss-it moment. The contact lit me up as he leaned away.

"Not time for our first—"

I didn't get to finish the sentiment because he wrapped a hand around my nape and then his mouth crashed down on mine. The kiss was fire, it burned through the tendrils of shock until all I could see, taste, and breathe was Bodhi. My heart slammed into my ribs as the ice thickening in my blood melted. The ache in my bones vanished along with the sting across my scalp.

The massage of his hand against my nape loosened the taut muscles and then he stroked his tongue against mine. Stealth, not force, brought us closer, and I pushed up on my toes, straining into the kiss that seemed intent on swallowing me whole. He ended it before I was ready, and I swore a whimper escaped my throat.

But he stroked his thumb along the column of my neck. The gentle touch reminded me of the bruises that were likely to form there. The briefest suggestion of pain couldn't dislodge the relief and desire twining together that his kiss provoked.

"...kiss," I finished belatedly, and the strain in my voice had nothing to do with the earlier strangulation and everything to do with the man standing right there.

"Long past," he murmured. "I'll be back for more. Take care of Graham. Take care of you." Another brief kiss and then he was gone, striding across the room in a fluid motion that almost decried the dark purpose that seemed to fill his posture. Anger sparked and crackled along the edges.

His presence lingered even after the door closed. I stared after him for a moment, then glanced back at Ezra. Aware that Bodhi was right outside the door let me focus on checking him over. The bruise on his forehead was ugly. He opened his eyes when I was cleaning his face. I'd also brought out a small tub in case he got sick again.

"Hey," he said, then worry flooded his eyes and he tried to sit up. I had to half-sit on him to keep him down. "The men..."

"I'm fine," I told him. "You're fine, and a little bruised."

"They didn't hurt you?" The abject fear in his eyes gutted me.

"I'm fine," I repeated and when he dragged me closer to hug, I returned the embrace fiercely. "I'm really okay. We had backup..."

"Backup?" Confusion clouded his eyes, and he winced as he tried to look past me. "Fuck, my head hurts."

"You took a nasty blow..." One I was worried about.

"I have a hard head, Kotyonok, don't worry." Yes, he absolutely did. So hard, in fact, that he was insisting on getting up a few moments later, but I got him upstairs and into the shower. "What about the..."

I redirected him into the shower. Despite the blow and the vomiting, he was still drunk, and it showed in how he moved.

"Bodhi is taking care of it."

He frowned. "Bodhi..."

"Yes, Bodhi. He saved us both. Now. Shower." I was still dressed, but I got him out of his soiled clothes and into the shower. Then I stayed with him to keep an eye on him.

"I'm sorry," he murmured.

"It wasn't your fault," I reminded him.

"If I had..."

"Ezra." I didn't mean to snap, but he needed to not go down this route. "It's not your fault. It's not mine. It's not Adam's or Milo's or Bodhi's. Whoever was behind those men, we'll figure it out and we'll deal with it. You're safe, that's the important part."

"My father threatened you," he whispered, and I could read the torture in his eyes.

"Well, that's a mistake he's made. Trust me—please." I wanted to say trust us, but right now, if he could just trust me, it would do.

He nodded after a long moment. Once he was out and dry, I got him into pajamas then nudged him to the bed.

"What about you?"

"I need to clean up and then I need to talk to Bodhi."

He scowled again.

"Don't start," I told him, then perched on the side of the bed. I'd put him in my bed for a reason. "Don't start. Don't argue. Don't decide to bolt in the middle of the night. If you decide you're going to drink again—get me. You shouldn't be drinking alone."

His whole expression crumpled. "I fucked up, Kotyonok. I fucked up bad."

"No you didn't—and even if you did," I said with a sigh, "we'll fix it, yeah? All of us."

"He hates me." His eyes were already closing as I brushed the damp hair from his forehead. He had more than a few bruises, another reason I'd wanted a good look at him. But no one had stabbed or shot him. That was a mark in the win column.

I didn't want to ask, but he stared up at me.

"Adam hates me."

"No," I told him. "He doesn't."

"He won't talk to me. Just ignored me and then I left...I mean I can't be a fuckboy and an asshole both."

I didn't laugh at him. "You can also be Ezra, one of the sweetest, kindest people I know—when you aren't lashing out."

He made a little sound of protest.

Leaning forward, I pressed my lips to his forehead. "Sleep. Don't run away. We'll talk in the morning. Unless you want me to get a doctor for you..."

"No I'm fine," he said, then made another face. "Promise you won't go out?"

"I'll be here. I promise." Not a difficult promise to make. I sat with him until he finally went to sleep then dragged myself up. Exhaustion wore at me, but there was too much to be done. I found a change of clothes and more, then left him to sleep while I went to use the shower in the guest room.

I'd just slipped under the spray when the door opened and Bodhi stood there. He swept his gaze over me, and I read the request in his eyes, so I just pushed the shower door open.

CHAPTER
TWENTY-NINE

BODHI

I'd never rushed an information gathering trip before. Not like this. I didn't want to be out of town for longer than necessary. Instead of finding a place to stay for the night, I'd merely taken the meeting, paid for the information, then boarded another flight back to New York.

If Julius King had a third child, and I had no reason to believe that information was false, that child was also not listed on any birth records indicating Julius King or Jeff Hardigan were the father within the northeast corridor for the past twenty years. I'd left instructions to widen the net.

Still, considering Hardigan's reaction to the news and Lainey's deeper concerns, I wanted more information on this alleged third child. I didn't think it had anything to do with *my* missing sibling. That said, I couldn't discount it either. Therefore, until every rock had been kicked over and examined, anything was possible.

Collin had his instructions, and I was putting more money into the hunt. That meant more hunters. Once we had the U.S. blanketed, I'd arrange for Canada, Mexico, and then Europe. We'd continually widen the radius until I knew who was involved. Collin worried about the expenses and how to disseminate such a large influx of data.

He could handle it.

As soon as I landed, I got a car and had it take me to Lainey's. She had dinner with her grandfather that evening, and she was alone. While she didn't care for the bodyguard, she'd added that she had requested he accompany her. Reading between the lines, she did it because it was both practical and offered comfort to those of us *not* with her.

It wasn't terrifically late when I arrived, but I wanted to be there so she could get rid of the bodyguard as soon as she got back. The code and card she'd given me for the elevator let me go straight to her floor. The last thing I expected to walk into was waiting for me.

A group of five—no there had been seven but only five were left standing—men in ski masks and dark suits were assaulting my girl. Graham was down, but Lainey B was a fighter and she was *fighting*.

Anger rarely served anyone. Even when I was irritated, I didn't let anger sway me. Anger blinded a person, provoked blind responses that defied reason. I preferred to avoid such complications.

But seeing that man drag her backwards pissed me off.

He died before I'd fully pulled him away. It took significant force and torque to break a neck.

It was almost child's play in my current mood. I wanted to inflict maximum pain. I really only needed one of them alive to question. But I needed it to be the right one. If it turned out to be the dead man—oh well.

I didn't worry about the level of damage I inflicted. My hands ached and my knuckles were busted open on one hand, but there was a savage sense of satisfaction that they were down and she wasn't. A sound behind me had me twisting with my last captive in arm. I had him in a choke-hold, and Lainey B took out one of the men who'd tried to get back to his feet.

Tried because she didn't let him.

Knee.

Jaw.

Face.

And down he went.

She was a goddess with that baton. She met my gaze, and the fire in her eyes matched the inferno that had been burning deep in the dark of my pitiless soul. It had burned in silence, almost ice cold in its intensity. Yet, one glance from her and the heat scorched me.

Then I saw the red marks on her throat, and she croaked as she tried to speak. I barely registered the content, only the sure knowledge one of these bastards had strangled her.

It cost me everything to put her inside with Graham then deal with the mess. I had contacts and associates. The Network offered a series of cleaners in every city. There were also wranglers who would take these assholes into custody until I had time to deal with them.

The cost was higher than normal, but the situation was also beyond the normal. Three things stuck with me as I waited for the cleanup crew to arrive—

The cameras in the hall were all off.

Even Lainey B's.

There were seven men in total. Armed. No ID. They were also carrying drugs—in the form of automatic injectors and standard chloroform. I found one rag on the floor. They'd come prepared to take prisoners.

Graham?

Lainey B?

Both?

The third, and most damning in my opinion, was the fact this all happened in the hall between the elevator and her apartment. No one else was present. Three penthouses on this level? And no one heard anything?

Convenient.

Once the crew arrived, I left them to it and accepted the card with the info that would give me directions to where the wranglers stored my guests. Apparently another one died while I waited.

Not that I cared.

By the time they were done, it would be bare out here and all evidence removed.

Inside, I checked her security system. The cameras for the hall were in manual mode. That could have happened from here or somewhere else, based on the system.

Time to change that.

Once I armed the security and made sure the door was locked, I went in search of Lainey B and found her in the second bedroom's en suite. She was standing in the shower with water cascading over her. I stripped off my clothes, aware of the speckles of blood on them and on my hands. I was also drinking in the sight of her. There were marks on her back that would likely become bruises.

More on her throat that grew visible as she tilted her head under the water. As stiff and erect as my cock was, it could wait while I made sure to map every single injury on her. I planned to make sure the surviving attackers understood just how bad for their health this choice had been.

Then she faced me, her eyes locking on mine before she pushed the door open. The kiss we'd shared downstairs was our first, real kiss, and it left me hungry for more. It was why I'd avoided kissing her at all other opportunities. Once I kissed her—I wasn't going to want to stop.

I didn't want to stop.

Ever.

In the shower with her, I pulled the door closed so the hot steamy air didn't escape. As it was, I closed the distance between us until I had her pressed right up against the warm tile and she had to tilt her head back to look up at me.

"How badly are you hurt?" I'd seen the red marks on her back. There were more on her arm. They were in the shape of fingers there. The same with her throat. As it was, I trailed my fingers over the soft skin there, careful of the deep flush the marks carried that told me all I needed to know about blood rushing to the area.

"I'm okay," she murmured, and the roughness of her voice had me lifting my gaze to meet hers again. My awareness of her seemed to reach a fever pitch. The way the water slid over her skin. The tautness of her nipples as they pebbled and peaked. The sudden appearance of goosebumps spreading over her skin.

The softness of her mouth as she kept her head tilted back. The hint of her teeth as she scraped them over her lower lip. The dip to her eyelashes. The way her wet hair slicked against her skin. Each and every breath she took. The contrast between the slope of her hips and the slightness of her figure compared to the ferocity of the woman in the hall.

"I'm really okay—" she continued, and the words penetrated the laser focus of my mind, which seemed to be one thousand percent hers. All hers. Lainey B—she was all grown up. The little girl I'd admired had grown into a woman I... "I am okay," she said again until my gaze locked on hers. "I promise. I'm going to be sore, but I was more worried about Ezra and how to protect him with so many of them."

"He's fine?" I just needed to be sure so I could dismiss worrying about him for the next few hours.

"He is," she said, granting me the permission I'd been seeking. "He'll probably be more miserable tomorrow. Thank you so much for showing up."

"I just wish I'd been earlier," I told her. Early enough to have triggered the trap before she did. Early enough to have gotten rid of them before they laid one finger on her. I pressed a kiss to her eyebrow, then her eyelid. Then I left a trail of kisses to her jaw, then her throat. I spread gentle kisses along the marks, laving each one with my tongue. Testing them, reassuring myself she was fine.

When I feathered my fingers over her ribs, she sucked in a deep breath. I went still. "Pain?"

"No," she promised, her voice dipping even rougher, and I smiled against her skin. I loved the way she felt against my lips. A shudder went through her as I kissed to her collarbone. She really was so much slighter than me. I hadn't truly paid attention to it before. But this delicate frame housed so much strength.

"Have I mentioned how incredible I found your use of that baton?" I should tell her. I gripped her hips and lifted her so I could keep kissing a path to her chest, and I closed my lips around her nipple. She sank her fingers into my hair, and I hummed as I sucked the nipple tighter to my teeth. I wanted to bite, lick, and leave a trail of my own marks across her skin.

At the same time, I wanted there to be no pain, no harm. I needed to feed her pleasure upon pleasure until the endorphins erased all the pain left by their attackers. Distantly, I kept a list of what they'd done. I'd have her check Graham later. If I was getting a pound of flesh for her, I could afford to take some for him too.

"I trained—" She let out a gasp as I mouthed a good portion of her breast and not just her nipple before I moved to the other neglected nipple. "Trained with it...easier to carry than a gun sometimes."

Oh, she knew how to use a gun. "Smart," I murmured, nibbling a path around that nipple, then teasing it with my tongue. She tightened her grip in my hair, but she didn't pull. "Do I need condoms?"

I bought some.

"No," she said, with a shudder that I felt all the way down to my toes. My cock pulsed at the low, throaty quality of her voice. "I'm—I have an implant for pregnancy and I'm healthy—I promise. I know Ezra is a mess but..."

I leaned my head back and found her eyes heavy-lidded and her pupils blown. "You trust him." That was all I needed to know.

"Yes, mess and all." She swiped her tongue over her lips, and then she was kissing me. I honestly didn't know who made the first move, but the feel of her wrapping around me was perfect. My cock nestled right against her hot and slick cunt. I rocked my hips just to tease us both as I plundered her lips.

This woman was everything I never realized I needed. She fit me. Not a missing piece. Not a broken piece. But the piece that belonged. The complement. She fit *me*. Complications and all.

"Phillip," she whispered, her voice a gasp as her breath came in little sharp pants, and the sound of my name on her lips pulled my balls up tight.

I struck the water to turn it off, then carried her soaking wet out of the shower to the bed. We could change it later. I set her down and followed her, chasing her kiss as she opened to me. She was hot and wet everywhere we touched. Her teeth were sharp against my lower lip.

"Anything I need to know about what you don't like?" I asked as I began kissing my way down her body. I hadn't reached her cunt in the shower, and as much as my cock was eager to sink into her, I had other plans.

"Um..." Her sentence died and I caught the soundless lift of her whole body as her back arched when I sucked her clit to my teeth. Okay, she liked her clit played with. This was excellent information.

I had more gathering to do, and I eased a finger into her channel. The clamp of her inner muscles even as her abdomen went taut offered me more insight. Yes, she liked to be eaten out.

Good thing I was hungry.

CHAPTER

THIRTY

LAINEY

The devastating way he watched me as he laved at my pussy held me captive far more than the shape of his hands on my hips. The sharp focus in his eyes had my lips parting. I dug my fingers into the bed covers. We were both dripping wet, and the whole bed would need to be changed—then he locked his lips over my clit. The sting of the stubble on his cheeks added a bite of pain to my thighs even as he scraped his teeth over that bundle of nerves.

My thoughts shattered on a whim, and no amount of control kept the cry bottled in my throat. I didn't want to scream and risk startling Ezra. At the same time, I wanted to move closer and escape the tongue lashing Bodhi delivered with such accurate precision. He dragged me upward by my hips as he pushed to his knees and buried his face even more firmly against my slit.

Fists pounding on the bed, I curled my legs and toes. The orgasm pulsing through me would not be denied, and the first flood of dampness that escaped made him huff with a deep, dark chuckle that absolutely undid the last bare measures of my control. I tried to twist to bury my face against the bed to scream but he had me bent in half with my shoulders pinned while he devoured me.

Lifting his face, he grinned down at me. I sucked in one noisy breath after another. His face gleamed. The lights in the bathroom illuminated where my release painted his cheeks and lips.

When he dragged his tongue over his lower lip, my tummy clenched and so did my pussy. "You squirt," he murmured.

Was that surprise or wonder in his voice? Maybe both? Heat scorched my face even as my pulse pounded. My breath came in short, almost gasping pants. Not even the fight in the hall had left me this winded.

"I liked that," he said. "I've never had a woman do that for me before. I didn't think you could get more perfect. Prove me wrong again." Without giving me a moment to gather myself, he licked me from entrance to clit then back again. The massage of his tongue and lips interspersed with the nibbles of his teeth had me thrashing as the coils of tension drew taut.

It was too much. Even as I tried to buck, I wasn't even sure if I was trying to escape or press closer to him. The climb took so much longer. Sweat soaked my skin. The heat rolling off of him chased away even the thought of a chill. When he finally settled on my clit with so much pressure the pain twined with pleasure, I came again. The burst of liquid escaping me should be humiliating.

Yet, there was no way to experience shame when he gazed at me as though he could pleasure me with his eyes alone. Shivers raced over my flesh, pebbling the skin and he lowered my hips carefully. The stretch and pull of every muscle was a distant echo as I trembled.

Then I was in his lap, cradled against him as he brushed kisses over my face. I could smell my own release. As he made his way to my lips, I tasted myself too. He murmured a litany of indistinguishable sounds that soothed and incited in equal measure. Cradling his face, I opened my mouth to his kiss. I wanted to drink in all of him, deepen every contact and savor every connection.

Wrecked didn't begin to describe how I felt. His blown pupils were visible each time I opened my eyes to find him studying me. Watching. Drinking me in. I could drown in the darkness in his eyes, but there was no faltering or falling. There was fire in the darkness and heat. It wrapped around me in a cocoon so tight I couldn't escape even if I wanted.

Fleeing wasn't even remotely on my list of desires.

Stroking my nails down his cheek, I savored the crisp sound of his stubble against my skin. It was bristly, the texture scratchy. Had he ever had a beard? I couldn't imagine it. With the lock of hair falling over his forehead, he had a rakishness about him that promised to seduce me all over again.

He reacted like a cat to my petting and broke the kiss only to tilt his head back so I could scratch and stroke under his chin. Tension corded his muscles, leaving his biceps prominent as though flexed and the line of his shoulders straight and firm. Even his abdominals seemed to flex with every breath he took.

As he ran his hands over my back, the gentle strokes eased some of my own shaking, and it registered, he'd been trying to pet me down from under the avalanche of pleasure. "Philip," I whispered and his lashes parted to let me see his eyes again. "Bodhi."

"I almost like how you say my name," he whispered.

"Trouble." The tease slipped out, and he chuckled. "The best kind of trouble."

"If you say so, Buttercup." That ridiculous nickname wrapped me up in another kind of embrace. A private one. We'd always housed secrets between us, delicate misdirects and gentle, unspoken truths. He held himself on a leash similar to the one I'd clung to before he frayed it to bare strings then sliced through them.

"I do," I promised him. "You're the kind of trouble I always want."

"You will never go without," he added his oath to mine. "I told you—I've never been one for relationships. It's too late for you now. You have me. You're never going to lose me."

There was something so deeply comforting in that declaration. Even though an inherent darkness licked all along it, I didn't care about the suggestion of violence it offered. If anything, it was that savagery that I craved. I'd fought for and with Adam and Ezra for so long, a part of me was desperate to be claimed.

Claimed as Pretty Boy had claimed me.

Needed as Ezra had proven over and over again he needed me.

Wanted as Adam had. Wanted and desired past the points of reason and all the way to madness.

Phillip. Bodhi. Trouble.

He was all of these things, and the sleepy ropes of tension began to wind tighter and tighter.

"You're mine," I told him, adjusting my position in his lap so I could straddle him. He balanced me easily, lifting me as if I were lighter than a feather. The feel of his cock was right there at my entrance, his crown nudging inside as though even more eager than the two of us. "Mine," I repeated, because as much as I wanted and needed his pledge, I needed him to understand my commitment.

"All yours," he agreed with a kind of ferocity that should have frightened me. The wildness was on display. The glimpse of something so pure and primitive, it threatened to shatter me all over again. The fatness of his cock stretched me as he pushed up with his hips and down with his hands.

Stretching around him had my mouth opening as all the air whooshed out of my lungs. The wetness of his lips beckoned to me. He was so beautiful and raw and absolutely unfettered.

That barely restrained primal side of him seemed to snap the rest of it in me. I gripped his face and kissed him as I flexed around his cock, trying to accommodate his girth. He lifted my hips then dragged me down to slam all the way inside of me. He didn't quite hit my cervix, yet I swore I could feel the stretch of him so deep, it left me desperate.

"You have no idea how fucking exquisite you are," he said, each word delivered with punctuation to mirror the thrusts of his cock filling me. I rotated and rolled my hips, as eager to feel him as he was me. Every motion rubbed my nipples against his chest. I slid a hand into his hair, fisting it as I dragged him in for another kiss.

The words had an edge to them, something unexpected and dark that unfurled in my tummy. I wanted more of him, shameless to demand more of the heat cascading through me.

"Bodhi," I whispered in between the kisses. "Harder."

He surged upward as we left the bed entirely. The wall

was at my back. The coldness of it leaving me hissing even as he cupped my head to keep it from banging against the hard surface.

The change in angle and position drove him even deeper. The stretch pulled all around my pussy. There was a bite to the pleasure. A hint of pain.

"Fuck yes," I exclaimed as he nipped and kissed his way down my throat. Every drive of his body into mine deepened the haze across my vision. He licked and sucked at my pulse point. The harsher scrape of his teeth detonated deep in my core, and I screamed.

The sound ripped out of me as he continued to fuck deeper into me until there was no doubt he'd imprinted himself on my body, my mind, *and* my soul.

The orgasms he wrenched out of me with every move were downright painful. But I wanted that sensual pain even more. The pain of him filling me to the brim.

Lips at my ear, he pumped harder and deeper into my core, half-shoving me up the wall, and the only thing keeping me in place was the cage of his arms. He dwarfed me as I dug my nails into his back, and his skin seemed to burn everywhere we touched.

The harshness of his pants echoed my own, and somewhere along the way we lost the thread of seduction. This was both lovemaking and pure, carnal sex. The primitive nature of it was as enticing as it was overpowering. The haze of pleasure coated everything as he pushed me toward another, impossible orgasm. I wanted to thrash, but I couldn't do anything but cling to him.

When my vision whited out entirely, only the distant feel of his stuttering hips followed by a wicked heat blooming inside of me seemed to penetrate. I shuddered and shook, riding the myriad of sensations.

Resurfacing took time, and there was an echo of pain and soreness all over my body. We were on the bed again, some part of my mind acknowledged. He lay against the pillows, wearing me like some blanket. His half-hardened cock was still inside of me. Dampness soaked our thighs. There was a smell of sex in the air, a musk that I would forever associate with him now.

Awareness of his hand trailing from my shoulders to my ass then back again began to penetrate gradually. I wanted more, and I didn't think I could ever move again. Time lost all meaning as we floated there. It wasn't until the sound of the door opening registered and Bodhi shifting, a flash of a blade in his hand, that I managed to break the blanket of pleasure to find Ezra staring at us.

Cooling sweat had left me chilled in some places while everywhere I touched Bodhi blazed hot. Worry coated my stomach with acid as Ezra glared at Bodhi and then Bodhi lowered the blade. I had no idea where that had come from.

"I think Graham needs us to go sleep in the other room," Bodhi suggested in an easy voice as though the world hadn't just shattered around me entirely. For his part, Ezra frowned and I had to swim harder to emerge long enough to—

"Yeah," he said slowly. "I'd like that."

Unlike us, Ezra was still in pajamas.

"Get her a washcloth," Bodhi told him while I still fumbled for words. Then—the most unexpected thing happened, they worked together to clean me and wipe up the evidence of cum from my thighs. My pussy ached inside and out, but it was the most delicious sensation. When I was on my feet, I still floated, and they got me into my own room. Bodhi sent Ezra over to the far side of the bed and tucked me in next to him.

Then he vanished. I was still coming to terms with that when he returned and helped me sit up to drink some water. Oh, that tasted amazing. "We didn't finish our shower."

The belated words set off a giggle in me so unexpected I cracked up all over again. They both stared at me, then even Ezra began to chuckle as Bodhi smiled. "In the morning," he told me. "You need to sleep now."

The fact that Bodhi slid into the bed with us and wrapped around me from behind so I could face Ezra bound me up in the most pleasurable knots. We were only missing Pretty Boy and Adam, but this was good.

"I'm sorry, Kotyonok," Ezra whispered, and I lifted his fingers to my lips.

One kiss to them and I managed to mumble, "We'll fix it. We'll fix all of it." As much as I wanted to continue to comfort him, sleep dragged me down, and the soft rumble of their voices as they continued to talk kept me there.

CHAPTER
THIRTY-ONE

MILO

Ivy and the guys met me in Fayetteville, North Carolina. It was halfway between Manhattan and Orlando, Florida. The fact she was in Orlando for a show took me back. When I left that morning, Mayhem made me take a gift with me for Ivy. Then she promised she would be careful until I could get back to her. I didn't miss the wistfulness in her eyes. She wanted to be there with us.

Fuck if I didn't want her here too.

Still, I barely pulled into a spot at the hotel when I caught sight of Ivy on the move. After I put the car into park, I shoved out of the car and braced for her as she launched. Her hug was everything. Behind her, ranging out came four of the seven boyfriends. Vaughn, Freddie, and Rome were on the road with her.

Mickey being there though? Yeah. Doc wanted to talk to me about all of this. Thankfully, he'd gone to see Ivy and not me.

"Hey," I said, lifting my chin to them as I returned Ivy's hug. Freddie grinned and so did Vaughn. Rome only nodded, but his gaze had gone searching as he scanned the road behind me.

No problem. Ivy was out in the open, and we didn't take risks with her. That worked for me. Finally, she pulled back so I could set her down but she whacked my shoulder with a closed fist.

"Ow," I said drily. Not that it hurt. The look she gave me told me she wasn't remotely impressed. Her eyes were full of questions, but before she could start, I tucked her under my arm and then offered a hand to Mickey, who was the first one to us. "Save the yelling for when we're inside, yeah?"

Better than having her tell me off in the parking lot. At least it was warmer down here than it was in Manhattan.

"Don't worry, Little Bit," Mickey said to Ivy as he gave my hand a firm, albeit brief shake. "We told you we'd pin him down if we had to."

I didn't roll my eyes. She needed to yell, and I'd let her get it out of her system here as far from King as I could put both of us for the moment. I'd rather she were on the west coast somewhere, but Orlando was a hike.

"Tell you what, let's order some pizzas and I'll fill you in on what I can, then if you still want to yell at me after, you can."

Ivy gave me a narrow-eyed look, and I could practically read the protest.

"Oh, and before I forget." I let her go long enough to reach into the car for the small gift bag and card that Mayhem had given me. Then I handed them to Ivy. She crinkled her nose.

"I cannot be bribed," she argued.

"Good," I said with a grin as I locked the car. "'Cause it's not from me. I promised Mayhem I'd hand you that when I got here."

"C'mon, Starling," Rome said. "Better to be inside again."

Some of her objections melted away as she hugged the present to herself. Then she let Rome pull her ahead of us, and I fell into step with Mickey and Vaughn while Freddie moved ahead. A protective circle remained around Ivy, and I appreciated it more than they knew.

"How bad is it?" Mickey asked.

"It could be worse," I told him. "To be honest, it could be a lot worse. This situation is about two parts weird, one part frustrating, and one part downright fucking aggravating."

He nodded.

Neither of them asked me why we hadn't just killed him. There were a lot of reasons why, not the least of which was finding out what other secrets he was hiding. The latest one that Bodhi and Mayhem found left me with far more questions than answers.

They were in a second floor room. The hotel wasn't a five star, but it was definitely comfortable, and the open access to the parking lot made sense. Easier to evacuate if we needed. They'd also gotten two rooms side by side with a connecting door. A third room was on the far side if I stayed the night.

Good, I preferred an empty room between me and any shenanigans. I texted Mayhem that I was here but didn't wait for a response. By now, she was out to dinner with her grandfather. I'd left mid-morning, and it was already well into evening.

"Same pizza order?" Freddie asked from where he stood by the phone when I followed Doc and Vaughn inside.

"Yep."

"Good to know living large hasn't changed your tastes," Freddie said with a grin. "You do remember we don't eat pizza with a knife and a fork."

I spared him a middle finger and Vaughn snorted as he dropped onto the bed to sprawl next to where Ivy was opening her present.

"Oh, I love this," she said as she held up the platinum necklace with a diamond centered compass hanging from it. It was beautiful.

Mickey handed me a beer he'd pulled out of the fridge before handing out others to Vaughn and Ivy. She wrinkled her nose at it.

"You don't perform for three more days," Mickey told her patiently. "One beer isn't breaking your routine too much."

"That's true. The pizza is gonna be way more in the way of splurging."

"Uh huh," he said in the driest of possible tones, and she laughed at him. The easy smile pulled a similar one out of him, and I took a drink of the beer as I absorbed the details of the four of them with her. The awareness they had of her every move and how they shifted for each other, as well as looked after each other... I liked it.

Rome hopped up to sit on the desk the room offered, while Mickey took the desk chair, and Freddie dropped to lay across the bed on Ivy's other side when he finished ordering the pizza. That left the second queen in the room for me to perch on. You'd think the room was crowded with all of us in here, but it just reminded me of the three who weren't present.

Fuck it, the four. Mayhem should be here too.

"I miss her," Ivy said as she finished reading the card, then glanced at me with a sheen of tears in her eyes. "She also said I need to forgive you because there's so much you both don't know yet, and it's hard to brief when there are so many questions."

I lifted my beer to take a drink, paused a beat to stare at my kid sister, then shook my head before I took a swallow. Of course, Mayhem had taken a step to ease the path for me. She knew this wasn't easy for either of us.

"I don't deserve that woman," I muttered and Ivy laughed.

"No, but she is the best and she adores you so, you have to keep her safe."

Yes, yes I did. "Not a problem for me," I promised. "So... let me start at the beginning and I'll bring you five up to speed. I can't tell you everything." It was important they understood that. "Because not all of it is mine to share."

There was a lot of shit going down. "But I'll tell you everything I can."

Ivy clipped on the necklace that Mayhem had sent her before she focused on me. "I want to know everything. Then I want to help."

Yeah, I could have predicted the last part. Leaning forward, I said, "You may not be able to do much *yet*, Ivy. But when, and *if*, I need your help, you will be the first one I call." Right after I talked to the guys, and the fact Vaughn actually looked amused when Ivy let out a little growl of protest told me I hadn't covered that fact up.

Not that I'd been trying.

"Fine," she said, then crossed one leg over the other. "Hit us with it."

It took almost two hours and most of the pizzas and

two beers to bring them up to speed with the past few months. Ivy's reaction to me mentioning Ezra and his actions, particularly the engagement, were interesting. Despite her frown and narrowed eyes, she didn't ask a single question until I told her the very last of it.

"I don't have a way to confirm what Bodhi and Mayhem discovered about the sperm donor having a third child." That part bothered me more than I cared to admit. I hated the idea we might have a sibling out there in the world who needed us and we had no way to find them or even identify them. At the same time... "It could be bullshit."

"Or we could have another brother or sister out there," Ivy said with a slow sigh. "I'm assuming Bodhi is still looking?"

"He said as much, though what it has to do with everything, I don't know. I was tempted to confront King with it directly. But his obsession with you makes me think he'd bring up this sibling."

"If he thought it would benefit him," Mickey said, offering up his insight for the first time since I'd begun the tale.

Of everyone here, Mickey was the only other person who knew our father. At least from when King had been my father. Mickey's relationship with Julius King began when he'd been Jeff Hardigan and Mickey had been a reckless teenager.

"Little Bit, I know you think challenging him might get you answers—but Milo's already walking away from him." The last he said with a firm look at me. "I'd prefer if you didn't go baiting the bull yet. I agree with Milo, we don't know why he's so damn insistent on a relationship with you."

"Except he's respected the boundaries I put up." Was she asking us or telling us?

"Has he?" Vaughn asked. "Or is he simply aware that to get at you, he would have to come through the rest of us and we're ready for him?"

"If I'm honest, Ivy," I said, choosing my next words carefully. "I don't know if he isn't just using you as leverage to punish me for not choosing him when I was a kid."

She made a face. "He's such an asshole."

"Yes he is," Rome said. "You're done with him?" The question he directed at me seemed weighted, and I lifted my shoulders.

"Currently, we need to protect Mayhem's younger sister. But I'm not living with the son of a bitch anymore, and I'm not staying away from Mayhem. Whatever he's doing—he's as crooked as he ever was. He just dresses in nicer clothes." Which was what it seemed when you boiled it all down. Honestly, what did I bring to the table for him?

Access to Ivy? Never going to happen.

Access to Mayhem? Over my dead body.

It was late when Mickey and I stepped out to take a walk. It was as much to scan the area and make sure we had the lay of the land as it was to get some privacy.

"Vaughn looks better," I said after we made it to the far end of the building. The parking lot was quiet. The cars parked there were either loaded for road trips or rentals. They were empty though, so their people were inside.

"He's getting there. Little Bit is good for him, and she gets it. I think she gets it almost more than we do, and she doesn't let him hide away inside himself. When he broods, she broods with him."

I chuckled. "I know it's not funny but..."

"No," Mickey deadpanned, "it's actually very funny. It makes him laugh when she practices her brooding face."

I grinned. As easy as the smiles came, they faded again.

"Tell me what's going on with you," Mickey said. "For real—your girl is with other guys?"

"It's not all that different from you guys and Ivy."

"Except we know each other. We've known each other for years, and the boys were all brothers..."

"You're still a brother," I reminded him. "The old fart, but still a brother."

He smirked. "Jackass."

"Sometimes." I blew out a breath. "Believe it or not, I'm more okay with it than I thought I would be. I'm not fond of how out of control Ezra seems to be or how he hurts her. I get that he means to protect her. I get that he'd die for her —that's enough to keep me from killing him."

"She loves him." It wasn't a question, and I nodded. That was the other part. Mayhem loved him. She loved him, Adam, and apparently Bodhi. Of the three—

"You know that's the part that's even stranger: I didn't think I could do what you guys are."

"But loving her is everything, even if you have to share, because it makes her happy."

"Pretty much. I get along well with Adam. We're more alike than I think either of us cares to admit. Bodhi's a wild card but—he reminds me of Rome and Freddie and even Liam at times. His loyalty is worth the crazy."

His devotion to Mayhem was clear too.

"Kid," Mickey said as he slowed. "Don't keep playing this game with Jeff. If he wants to punish you—well he's a sick fuck to blame a seven-year-old for being more of a man than he could ever muster. If he wants to control you—then he's just a dick. You don't need to put yourself through hell with him to prove anything."

"You know it's funny... I'm almost glad he's given me an excuse to take him down. He's been using kids for as long as I can remember—you, Adam, Ezra...now he wants to target a twelve-year-old girl? Because at his heart, he's a wannabe mob boss with delusions of grandeur? How many other lives has he destroyed?"

I faced Mickey.

"That's not on you," Mickey reminded me.

"Not the ones before maybe..."

"None of them," Mickey stressed. "*None* of them are on you. Even if you'd chosen to go with him or let him browbeat you into going, he would still be the piece of shit that he is—the only difference is you would have been another of his victims, kept around to do his dirty work."

That was one way to look at it. "Thing is, Mickey, maybe you're right. Maybe none of them are my fault. But what happens next? That is on me. I need to take him down. I need to make sure there are no other lives that he destroys. To do that, I need to know everything he is doing."

"Then we'll have your back. Though the temptation to just put two in his head is there."

I got that. "If I thought that would end it on the spot? I'd do it."

"But you think he has a contingency..."

"I always did. Love it or hate it, he and I are alike in some ways. I'm just a better human being."

"You're a lot more than that." Mickey clapped me on the shoulder. "But like I said, we got you. When you're ready to move, we'll move with you."

Yes they would. Vandal had always had my back. The

Vandals I'd built based on what he taught me, they had my back too.

A couple of hours later, I sent a message to all the players—Adam, Bodhi, and Ezra. It was time the four of us sat down and talked.

For real.

I crashed in the extra room for a few hours. I was heading back to Manhattan first thing in the morning.

THIRTY-TWO

LAINEY

The meeting with the attorneys was scheduled for later in the day. I couldn't believe we were already in February. The last few days had seemed like months packed into the space of a week. Pretty Boy was due back later that afternoon. I woke up curled up between Bodhi and Ezra. While Bodhi was awake, Ezra was not. When the latter finally did wake up, he was hungover as hell.

Marlene was also back and yeah...she'd long since cleaned up the guest room and bathroom. The downstairs was well on its way to being repaired. There was breakfast, coffee, and a bit of hair of the dog for Ezra to help with his head. Though I let her know to lock up the rest despite the baleful eye Ezra turned in my direction. It wasn't until we were alone that he focused on Bodhi.

"What happened to the assholes in the hall?"

That—I hadn't even considered asking him that question. As it was, I'd just accepted what he'd said about taking care of it. Considering Marlene hummed with amusement and not terror, I had to presume there hadn't been evidence of a bloody battle out there.

Most of my bruises were hidden, including the ones around my throat. The dark turtleneck added a bit of a drama, and I'd used a gold necklace to accentuate the color of my top. Then if eyes were drawn to my throat for any reason, they'd get caught up on the necklace.

"They're dealt with for now," Bodhi answered with a kind of calm I could envy. There was something—almost effortless about him today. It utterly belied the intensity of the night before except when his gaze touched on mine. Then I was there again, the whole of his focus latched onto me, and heat bloomed in my center. "We'll have them for questioning when we're ready. Another day or two and they will be convinced there is no surviving. That will make them beg."

"You're planning on letting them go after?" The absolute skepticism in Ezra's voice made me hide a smile behind a napkin. Marlene stepped out from the kitchen and the conversation shifted. She brought out fresh platters of bacon, eggs, and then another carafe of coffee. The guys were decimating the food.

"I plan to do a lot of things," Bodhi told him without missing a beat. "What about you?"

The tonal change wasn't lost on Ezra, and he scowled. "I didn't object to you staying—"

"Ezra," I said, not letting him race headlong down this road. It wasn't incumbent on Ezra to make that decision.

He transferred his stricken gaze to me. Anger sparked in his eyes, but I didn't look away, nor did I let him bully his way out of this. Instead I sipped my coffee and met him stare for stare.

A sigh escaped him as Marlene excused herself. She was heading upstairs to straighten. At least the worst of the sheets had been in the guest room. Finally, Ezra ducked his head. "Look, I know you didn't invite me to that dinner last night. But Karagiani said you were out, and I wanted to see you."

"Okay," I told him, accepting that at face value. "Did you need that much liquid courage to find me?" I knew the answer.

The question I had, though, was did he?

He flicked a glance at Bodhi then back to me. "Can we talk somewhere private?"

"We could, but I trust Bodhi and I would like very much if you would learn to trust him too." Last night had been a big step. "He didn't object to sleeping with you there, did he?"

Ezra made a face, and I swore he was nearly pouting. "You're treating me like a child."

"Really? I didn't think so," I murmured as I set my coffee down then folded my hands to study him. "I thought I was having a discussion with you. Not throwing down ultimatums or having a temper tantrum because I wasn't getting my way."

Both of which he'd done in the last twenty-four hours.

"You're hurting," I pressed onward. "I don't like that. Those men last night hurt you again."

He ducked his chin further, and it really did feel like he was trying to avoid the scold.

"Whether you remember it or not, Bodhi also saved us."

"He saved you," Ezra mumbled.

"He saved *us*," I repeated. "I was losing that fight. There were too many, and I couldn't get to you. If not for him, we might have been waking up somewhere far more uncomfortable." If we'd woken at all.

Ezra scrubbed a hand over his face then flicked a look over to Bodhi, who had let me handle this. "We don't like each other."

Bodhi shrugged. "You don't like me. I don't feel strongly about you one way or the other—except Lainey B loves you, which means you need to be safe for her."

Surprise flickered across Ezra, and I quashed the sense of hurt that his persistent doubt in my feelings elicited. The kind of mistrust he had in others came from a lifetime of abuse. I got it.

On so many levels I got it.

Didn't mean it didn't hurt.

Letting out a long sigh, he nodded. "Thanks for being there. For her. For me."

"Happy to help," Bodhi said with such ease, it was impossible to disbelieve him. "Very happy in this case. Tonight, we'll discuss everything with Reed and Hardigan. Put together a plan."

Everyone would be here.

The rest of breakfast passed with a kind of indefinable tension. When Ezra disappeared upstairs to shower, I stared after him.

"You can't fix him, Buttercup." Bodhi's quiet words pulled my attention to him. I didn't deny the charge.

"I want to fix the situation more than just fix him. He's—"

"He doesn't trust anyone. He's hiding with all of his pain in the bottom of the bottle. Pursuing it like it will solve things. It's also how he attempts to push away the ones he loves, so that he can be justified in destroying himself."

I made a face. "He's an alcoholic."

"Maybe." Bodhi shrugged. "I don't know how much of it is a compulsion he can't resist and how much of it is a pursuit to avoid dealing with his present. There's—a lot going on there."

Despair unfolded within me. "He ran away from Adam."

"I noticed." No judgment existed in Bodhi's tone. "He's as in love with Reed as he is with you. But he feels safer with you, even if his presence endangers you."

"I can take care of myself," I reminded him.

"I saw. Doesn't mean I won't break the bones in every hand that is ever raised against you." The ease with violence should probably disturb me, yet there was an incredible air of civility to his mannerisms. "The same goes for the ones you love."

A smile touched my lips, and I chuckled. "A couple of years ago, I was so angry with the pair who kept everyone away from me. Now I have almost everything I ever wanted. Yet—we're under attack from so many sides." And Grandfather wanted me to get married. Oh, that gave me a headache.

He reached over to wrap his hand around my nape, not pulling me closer or pushing me away. A light massage. "Well fix it, Lainey B. Whatever needs to be fixed, we'll fix. What we can't just fix, we'll support and help him get what he needs to fix himself."

"We'll find your sibling," I promised him. "Because I haven't forgotten your quest either. This isn't going to be one hundred percent about me."

"It can be," he told me with an amused smile. "But thank you."

When I leaned toward him, he dropped a light kiss on my lips, and then I settled my head against his shoulder. I didn't want to drop everything on him. Still, I rested there for now. The rest of the day loomed ahead. Including meetings with attorneys, a call to Tally—since we were still missing each other—and I wanted to arrange a meal with Andrea.

"Your birthday is soon," Bodhi said quietly.

"I don't want a party." Frankly, I'd had had my fill of them.

"Noted." No comments or reminders that parties were excellent opportunities. "What do you want?"

"All of you." I could probably ask for more charitable causes or think of others, but today I was feeling just a bit selfish. I wanted the four of them, and I wanted *us* to find happiness.

THE MEETING with the attorneys was ridiculously long. Bodhi had wanted to take me, but I needed someone to keep an eye on Ezra. I wasn't positive he wouldn't run—again. Since he was desperately avoiding Adam for some reason, I had a feeling we were going to have to corner him, keep him sober, and *then* talk.

While Bodhi hadn't liked it, I left with Karagiani at my side and Wood driving. I attempted to reach Tally from the car, and all I got was her voicemail. I left a message for her there and again at the Marlowe household. I'd been very preoccupied the last few weeks, I needed to correct that.

A message from Em arrived just before we got to the attorney's office, and I had to laugh.

The necklace is perfect. He looks good. Thanks for making him come see me. When do I get to see you?

Soon.

It was an easy promise to make.

I'm glad he went. He needs to remember he has family and that we will protect him too.

The possessiveness unfurling within me was not something I was used to putting on display. Em would always be my best friend. Pretty Boy would always be her brother. But he was mine too. Just like Pretty Boy and I would always protect Em, Em and I would always protect Pretty Boy.

Yes, he does. Mickey may still come to Manhattan. No one wants me going up there, but if I can help—tell me.

I will. Then I added, *If Doc comes, give me a heads up. I want to be able to make sure he and Pretty Boy have backup.*

Done.

I could almost picture her fierce nod. Then we were at the attorneys' office, so I let her know I would talk to her soon. One of the best parts of messaging with Em now—we didn't have to hide it. We weren't sneaking secrets in controlled apps.

The next four hours left me with a headache and a lot to review. The sheer volume of financial data would probably have intimidated me even three years earlier. But I'd spent the bulk of time since I turned eighteen at Grandfather's side as he tutored me in business management and finances. While I could have gone to college, he'd given me a much more thorough education.

A degree was still tempting, but it could also wait. While I'd always known the amount I would inherit was large, today was the first time I'd gotten a good look at just how extensive it was. The money also came with a great deal of responsibility not only for the family legacy, but for the investments, the companies, and the numerous employees and their families.

Nothing about it was simple. It was going to take me months to learn all of it. But Grandfather's concern about a possible husband made a little more sense. If only to have someone to help me carry the burden. That said, I wasn't marrying anyone to be my shield. Marrying for love might be a ridiculously romantic notion, but I was allowed to have them.

I wanted a relationship like he had with my grandmother. The ferocious loyalty and devotion. I was building something similar, brick by brick, with four different men. Strong, stubborn, and intelligent men who might not always get along and yet seemed determined to make it work—for me.

While I could be the one who opened the door, they needed to build friendships and trust that could sustain them too. Then there was Ezra and Adam...they could be more if Ezra would get out of his own way. Adam seemed to at least entertain the idea.

If anything, that thought just made my head pound more. Once I was back in the car, I sipped the coffee that Wood had picked up for me, and there was also a croissant sandwich that Marlene had insisted he bring me.

I didn't laugh, but I did smile.

Then my phone rang, and I didn't recognize the number. I debated answering it or sending it to voicemail, but curiosity pricked me. "Hello?" I kept my voice neutral.

"Miss Benedict," a warm, familiar feminine voice with a touch of an Eastern European accent greeted me. "I hope this isn't a bad time."

Well... now this was interesting. "No, Mrs. Waldemar. It's not. What can I do for you?"

THIRTY-THREE

ADAM

"How many were there?" The fact I even had to ask made my head pound. No one had seen fit to inform me of the assault and kidnapping attempt until I arrived this afternoon *after* Lainey was already out at her attorneys' office. I searched Ezra immediately, looking for any injuries. My stomach bottomed out over the idea of Lainey having to fend for herself while Ezra was too drunk to assist.

"Seven total," Cavendish answered. "Four survivors."

Ezra jerked around to look at him. So, he hadn't known that part.

"Where are they?" were the first real words Hardigan had spoken since he arrived back at the apartment. He'd also been the last to arrive, and he looked even less pleased about this than I was.

"Secure, until we're ready to interrogate them. I wanted

to soften them up. They had no ID. No fingerprints. None of them were capable of talking by the time we were done. Two of them had injuries that needed to be treated to keep them alive. The other two are probably nursing concussions." Cavendish took a seat in the living room and leaned back like he owned the place.

While I'd never cared for having him around, it was not the first time he'd come to our aid or protected Lainey.

"So we don't know if they were working for my father or not?" Ezra seemed rough. Instead of alcohol, though, he was drinking black coffee. It was strong enough it made my hair stand on end from the smell of it. Marlene had prepared two different carafes for us before she excused herself.

Lainey's housekeeper had given all of us a sweeping look before she informed us that dinner would be served promptly at seven. If we planned to stay, we all needed to clean up. I rather doubted that Lainey was standing on ceremony, but I understood being put on notice.

Once she left us alone, Cavendish took the lead and described the attack. The more I turned it over in my head, the more it seemed likely Graham Senior was behind it. He'd threatened Lainey. He'd apparently threatened me as well, but I wasn't the one who'd been attacked.

As much as I wanted to snap at Ezra for leaving the apartment and apparently tracking Lainey down, I bit my tongue. The past few days and lack of sleep hadn't left me in the best state of mind. The fact I'd been fielding calls from my father, from Hamilton, and now *Jason* of all people, didn't bode well. As much as I loathed Uncle Hamilton, I could tolerate Jason.

His involvement meant my father was exerting some

control over him. If necessary, I'd get Fletcher involved, but I didn't want to ask him to deal with his father. He had a good life far away from us, better to keep it that way.

I filled a glass with water, and while I'd prefer a whiskey, it was better to keep alcohol off the menu for now. No point in giving Ezra ideas. "I want to be there for the questioning."

"I think all of us should be," Milo said, and I met his gaze. He hadn't taken a seat since he walked in. In fact, his initial arrival had been marked by a guarded, searching stare before he demanded to know what happened.

Bodhi had answered him bluntly, and Ezra had shrunk into himself. I'd give Hardigan credit though, as much as he might want to punch Ezra in the face, he hadn't.

"Lainey B as well," Bodhi said. "She has the right to interrogate them if she wants."

Well, as long as we were all on the same page.

"I don't know how to fix this," Ezra said. "I thought—agreeing to what he wanted would have shut them down."

"It may have," Milo said before I could. "We don't know for certain this was your father. It could have been mine."

Fucking King. And dammit.. "It could have been mine." They weren't aware of the latest moves, and it might be time to bring everyone up to speed.

"Explain," Cavendish said, focusing on me. The demand was clear, but it wasn't a command so much as a need. One that resonated with me. We *needed* to know where all the threats were coming from, and right now they seemed to be coming from all sides.

"He and Melissa want to throw her a birthday party."

"She doesn't want one," Cavendish said. Weirdly, it didn't surprise me that he knew this. Stranger still, it didn't bother me that she'd confided in him. As unpredictable and wild as he could be, I didn't doubt for an instant he wouldn't slaughter anything and everything coming at her.

That worked for me.

That worked for me really, really well.

"Not surprising." She didn't care for big events that focused on her, and the last major party had been a shock to her system. But we all left that alone—for now. "The party, of course, has nothing to do with her and everything to do with her inheritance. My father was stressing far too much over this. He has no access to Benedict money. Melissa was disinherited, and the old man has never claimed Andrea. Probably because of my father."

Another thing to hate the bastard for.

"Wait—all of you are wealthy or from very wealthy families," Milo stated. It wasn't a question, so we didn't respond. Instead we all focused on him. "Why do your fathers care so much about her money? Or don't care so much? Graham's father wants her nowhere near him. Your father wants—what? To negotiate her inheritance?" Then he flicked a look at Cavendish.

"My father doesn't confide his interests in me because I don't care and he knows that. But he is no threat to Lainey B. If he becomes one, I'll deal with it. For now, he's confined to his own interests including whatever deal he seems to be developing with King."

My headache seemed to intensify.

"My father wants access to the Benedict money—it doesn't surprise me." The admission cost me nothing. "Yes, we have plenty. One can always have more. If you aren't making money or developing money..."

"You're wasting it," Ezra finished for me. "Power is not free, nor is it an asset to be squandered."

"Someone," Cavendish summed it up, "will always have more power, more access, and more to burn than you. To take them down, you have to be ready to take it all down."

"Opportunities are only affordable when you make use of them." I'd been hearing that my whole life.

"Or," Ezra continued, "when you claim them. Risk is necessary to success. If you can't be bothered to take a chance..."

"Then chance will come for you and rob you of any future potential." At that, Cavendish snorted. "You can tell these were all men raised in the same time period."

"Relatively speaking though none of them are allies. Odd when you consider..." Then I just stopped as some puzzle pieces slotted into place.

"They were all Royals," Milo said, his guarded expression having turned thoughtful. "Weren't they?"

"Never really thought about it," Ezra admitted, but anger darkened his eyes. "We were all tapped—you know except for Cavendish..."

"I was tapped," the man in question said, and I wasn't the only one who did a double take. "I wasn't interested. I sent his bully boys back in bags. They left me alone. When they came for Collin, I did the same thing."

Collin Cavendish—his cousin. I cut a look to Ezra and recognized the same surprise there. We'd never been sent to tap any of them. "Was that after King took over?"

For his part, Cavendish—Bodhi. I needed to use his name. If he was going to be around, then I could use it. "He was always in charge as far as we knew," I admitted. At this point, that was what? Fifteen years? Easily.

"None of you have any idea when he took over?" Milo studied each of us, but it was me that he lingered on finally.

"No," I said. "I'd never even heard of them before I was

tapped. Ezra followed me. Our deal kept Lainey out of it. Then later, we tapped Liam."

"Because he was targeting me." There was no arrogance in that statement, and I found myself studying Milo Hardigan a little closer.

"Yes," I said with a slow nod. "To be honest, I had no idea who you were to him. Why he was interested in Braxton Harbor, or why you would even be on his radar. You were a nobody. No offense."

"None taken," Milo said slowly as he set his empty cup down. "I was a nobody."

"I always thought it had more to do with O'Connell," Ezra admitted. "He wanted control over the O'Connell fortune. While he was adopted, Liam was the only heir unless you count his twin." He shot me a look.

"We didn't know about the twin then," I said and nodded. "We found out not long after, but we didn't know about him during school. Liam protected his weak points."

"Rome's never been a weakness," Milo corrected. "No matter what he told himself. Threatening Liam's twin will only get you on his bad side."

I snorted. "We figured that out and *we*," I continued to make sure they understood, "never threatened his twin."

"But King did." It wasn't a question.

"He did more than that," Ezra said. "He wanted you taken down—and when Liam dragged his heels about it, he sent me in."

I braced for it. The fact he wanted to drop this bomb on Milo right now probably wasn't the smartest idea. Then again, was there a good time to tell someone you'd helped set them up so they would be sent to jail?

"He sent you in for what?" Milo asked. The flat tonality

was hard to read. Even more, the way he narrowed his eyes and focused on Ezra betrayed very little of his mood.

"To do what Liam wasn't willing to do." Straightening more, Ezra met Milo's gaze head-on. Pride filtered through me. Ezra didn't have to do this right now. In fact, it probably wasn't the smartest thing to do when we were all on the same page. As close to being on the same page as we could be. "Turned you into the cops. Killed the guys who went after your girl. Made it look like you did it... set it all up."

No mincing words. He just laid it out there.

Milo's expression didn't change.

"It was just a job. Didn't know you. Didn't care. Hardly the first 'problem' we'd removed. Thought I was doing Liam a favor." No he hadn't, even his own self-disgust seemed to indicate that it was definitely not what he was thinking. "The thing was... if they had attacked her, then... they deserved it. What did I care? They were trash. Taking out the trash was something to do. Didn't know then that they'd been as set up as we all were."

He swallowed, but he didn't flinch away from Milo's hard stare or Bodhi's bland one. They were both waiting for the other shoe to drop. The fact Bodhi flicked a look at me said he'd already figured out that I knew what Ezra was talking about, and I just shrugged.

Yes, I did.

The big problem I saw was telling Milo didn't change anything. It couldn't give him those years back...

"When I did figure out what it all meant," Ezra said slowly, "I asked my cousin for help. He wasn't a full-fledged lawyer yet, he was still in law school. But he knew what to say and how to say it... he told you how to get that deal."

"Walsh," Milo said abruptly. "You sent that lawyer." It wasn't a question.

"The assignment—when I took it—was about eliminating a threat, not destroying someone. When I realized what I'd done and how it would impact you—I couldn't live with it. Not and look myself in the eye. I didn't give a damn about who you were—like I said, you were a nobody. But my actions destroyed your life."

"So you got me a deal. One that I had to accept or they would go after the Vandals."

Ezra winced. "I told him to say that because I didn't think you'd do it, but Liam was stupid about the Vandals and you might be too... if you were off the board, even for a little while, maybe King would get bored and look somewhere else."

Based on what we knew then...not an unfair assessment.

"You knew it was me when you came to Braxton Harbor later... after Mayhem and I..."

After Lainey disappeared to go help Emersyn. When Ezra had seen him again. "Yeah," Ezra admitted. "You were Emersyn's brother and apparently hooking up with our girl. I knew who you were just like I knew what I did. I want to tell you I'm sorry, but I'm not. You didn't deserve what King was doing, and I did what I could to mitigate it."

"But you chose Lainey," Milo said, and the fist in my gut unclenched.

"Yeah," Ezra said.

"I would have too," Milo told him. Ezra slumped at the acknowledgment. That was a better response than we could have hoped for.

"So, now that you two have kissed and made up," Bodhi said. "We need a plan."

"I have one," Ezra said, and I rubbed a hand over my face.

"Yeah," Milo said. "We need a better plan than that."

Yes, we fucking did.

THIRTY-FOUR

LAINEY

Three days. We got three days after the attempted kidnapping to just—be. Well, not really, be. Plans were made. Bodhi had prisoners, and once upon a time that very notion would have bothered me. But these particular *prisoners* had gone after Ezra. We didn't know which of us, if not both, had been the target. That said, I was not fond of letting anyone go who might do us harm.

In the meanwhile, there was the call from Margareta Waldemar and the invitation she'd issued. Neither Adam nor Pretty Boy had been fans of me accepting it. But I told them what I'd told her, "I can't commit to anything right now. I can call you next week and let you know what my schedule is then."

After my birthday. After the paperwork for the trusts had been executed. The sheer volume of it all had given me a headache. Grandfather had always told me that the Benedict inheritance wasn't just about money, it was also about legacy. Based on what the attorneys briefed me on, we had holdings in places and countries all over the world.

Diversification had been Grandfather's game and his father's before him. We were beholden to no one market. If anything, if a rising tide raised all ships—even when one market faltered, we would be fine because another market could lift us up. The numbers were enough to make my head swim. It was the intricacy of it all that impressed me more than anything.

Grandfather had set up a structure within the various corporate entities that would bolster each other. Benedict was global and it flourished in nearly all conditions. The scope of it all was breathtaking. Now I understood even more why he'd been so focused on my tackling more and more of the business the past three years.

Why I'd also been introduced to both front room negotiations and back room deals. I also had a solid idea of why art played such a huge part in our financial investments, to keep our capital mobile if not liquid. That was just what we'd been able to cover the first afternoon.

"Hey," Pretty Boy said as he brought fresh coffee into the library. It was early. Well before dawn, but sleep had been elusive. The fact we were going to question our "guests" today had been weighing on me. "Where's your head at?"

After setting the tumblers of coffee down, he picked me up, digital tablet and all, and set me in his lap. "Research," I said. "Well, that's where it should be at, but—I can't focus. I feel like I'm missing something. From the paperwork that King left to the attorneys and their disclosures, to Grandfather's prescription..."

The last earned me a fierce look. "Don't get me wrong, I

respect your grandfather, but you don't need to marry a single person if you don't want to."

I touched his cheek. "He's worried that I'm going to be doing all of this on my own. The more I look at it all, the more overwhelming it all seems. I can see why he wants me to have backup."

"You have backup. I know Adam offered to look at anything you needed and I'm sure Bodhi can too—"

"I have you, too," I reminded him. "Your exceptionally clever mind, with your eye for details and the intricate nature of legalities."

"Yes," he told me with a faint smile. "You do. Though, I have to admit, I've only ever seen one other company that comes close to what you've described, and it wasn't even a fifth of that." At my raised eyebrows, he said, "It was a company owned by someone in the skin trade. He bought and sold people, buried it all behind the smoke and mirrors of real estate."

Disgust curled through me.

"Exactly," he said, tapping my nose. "It's actually one of the first things Adam and I worked on together, though I think we only had one discussion. So yes, I am absolutely yours if you need anything."

A sigh escaped me, and I curled into him. "King knows some of the business holdings. That was why he brought all that paperwork. He knows some of them, he's fishing for the others. But he thinks identifying my father will give him some kind of leg up in my life."

"You don't really care about that, though, do you?"

"No," I said with a shrug. "Not particularly. He could literally be anyone. My mother wanted to punish Adam's father. At least, I think she did. Maybe she let herself get carried away. I know three things about that situation—

she told no one who got her pregnant with me. Not me. Not my grandfather. Not Harper. No one. It was one of the sore subjects between them and one of the few subjects I ever truly saw her and Harper argue about."

Those arguments had never been pretty. I doubted I was supposed to see it, but Harper was convinced she'd betrayed him to someone else. She'd told him he could learn to live with the disappointment, as she had.

"The second thing I know is that when she announced she was pregnant, it resulted in another horrible falling out between her and her mother—my grandmother. Grandfather was so furious with her, he threatened to cut her off entirely unless she signed over custody. Then he would provide her with an allowance only. When she dared to tell him she could just walk away with me—he said she could try, but if she was penniless she couldn't afford the attorneys or the court fees as he sued for custody. Then he would have me and she would have nothing at all."

"Your grandfather told you that?" Pretty Boy stared at me, a raw kind of fury in his eyes.

"Actually no, he did explain it after I had an argument with Melissa and she painted him in very vivid and negative broad strokes. My grandparents adopted me, but they never pretended to be my parents, and they did allow me to see my mother. I think, if she'd ever been able to tear herself away from Harper, they might have stood a chance at reconciling."

Now? It would never happen. She'd made her own mother miserable and Grandfather would never forgive her or Harper.

I sighed, rubbing a circle against Pretty Boy's chest before I reached for one of the cups of coffee.

"What's the third thing, Mayhem?"

"Whoever he is? He could just as easily have fought for me if he'd cared to find out. Grandfather didn't pay him off —and that doesn't mean he wouldn't have, but I trust my grandfather. He'd have told me if he had. The fact he doesn't know who he is any more than I do or Harper does —it's always weighed on him. Kind of like—what happens if he shows up in my life again, particularly after I come into my inheritance?" No, my grandfather would have dealt with the problem.

"I'm sorry," Milo murmured before pressing a kiss to my forehead. "Absent parents leave a hole, even when you know they suck."

It was my turn to study him. "How are you doing with all of this?"

He'd not returned to King since coming home, and frankly, I was glad for it. Adam and I had both increased security around Andrea. Currently, she was staying at school or with friends, and she checked in regularly as did our additional security.

"I'm fine," he told me, and at my raised eyebrows, he pressed a kiss to my nose before he reached for his own coffee. "I'm really fine, Mayhem. I hated living there. Even with what drips and drabs I managed to learn about his business, I hated being there and I hated being away from you. Do I trust him? Not a chance. Do I think he wants something? Yes. But after the crap that went down the other night? You're not getting me out of here again, and if he wants to try and blackmail us into it—he won't enjoy the reaction."

Pride fisted in my chest. Pretty Boy being home had elevated everything. Even my rapidly approaching birth-day. Adam, Ezra, and Bodhi were all staying here too, though in shifts. Ezra was in the guest room, though I'd woken twice to him climbing into bed with me and Pretty Boy. I knew Ezra didn't want to be alone and Milo didn't seem to complain. Though the fact I couldn't get Ezra and Adam to sit down and talk was another source of frustration.

"I love having you here, and I will fight him if he tries to come for you again." I would have fought him before, awareness of which I saw in Milo's eyes as his expression softened. The fact the guys were all talking and getting along had also not been lost on me. "I do have a question though," I admitted.

"What?" He rubbed my leg, and I took a sip of the coffee as I split my attention between him and the tablet.

"Do I need to be worried about what you four are plotting?" Because in the past three days, I'd also walked in on a few conversations composed of different groupings and some of the conversations shifted when I came in. Some, not all.

He chuckled. "No, I don't think so—as Bodhi keeps saying, we need to talk as men do from time to time."

I leaned away and studied him. "Excuse me?"

Soft laughter escaped him as he squeezed my side. "Apparently, it's a thing."

"I know it's a thing," I muttered. "My grandfather started it."

Then he laughed for real as I shook my head.

"Talk as men do. Don't make me have to smack all of you."

"I'll do my best," he murmured, then pressed another kiss to my forehead. "Trust me. It's not terrible. I'm getting to know them and their issues, and they are getting to know me. The one thing we all have in common is you. Of the three of them, I understand Adam probably best. Bodhi

—he reminds me of others I've known, and I'm working on dealing with Ezra."

I winced. "Dealing with?"

"Again, nothing for you to worry about. Getting along is something the four of us have to learn. Ezra also needs to stop making arbitrary decisions that affect you—that said, I know he'd die for you. In fact, it's the one thing the four of us definitely have in common. We'd all die for you, and that makes figuring out the rest of the bullshit easier."

Sipping the coffee, I turned that over in my head. "You know—this isn't how I imagined any of this? All of us? And... I know I'm being selfish."

"I don't care," he told me with such ease it baffled me. "I mean it, I don't care. Be selfish. You're not losing me. I'm not losing you. They can stay or they can go—I think Bodhi is definitely in for the long haul. Which I appreciate. Adam is struggling."

"So is Ezra."

Clearly they'd noticed it.

"Well, until he and Adam figure their shit out, they might continue to struggle." Pretty Boy brushed the hair back behind my ear. "I'm tempted to trap them in a room and push the issue. They don't seem to talk when I'm not there, at least not that I've noticed, but I'm worried..."

"If you're there, they'll only focus on you?" Well, at least I understood how much he got it now. He really understood the whole of us.

"You're really observant," I murmured.

"Been around for a while," he teased, then gave me another light kiss. "Now, finish whatever this reading is that's kept you up most of the night. We'll let Adam and Ezra sort their own shit out. We can be there for them both."

"If I decide to lock them in a room?" I was kind of curious.

"Bodhi and I will make sure they can't get out until they figure it out."

I grinned. "I love you."

"I know." He winked.

"They don't know who hired them," Bodhi said, real disgust in his voice. Adam stood to the side, shirt sleeves rolled up and arms folded as he studied the men in their various holding cells. Bodhi and Pretty Boy had been on them for hours, and they hadn't been gentle.

The only request the guys had made was for me to stay out of sight. They hadn't wanted Ezra in there either. Not yet. As much as I wanted to prove otherwise, I discovered I really didn't have the stomach for torture.

Fighting? Yes.

Defending? Absolutely.

Torture? No.

"Agreed," Pretty Boy said from where he washed his hands. The water was turning pink, and I sighed as I paced over to the observation window. "If they knew, they'd tell us. We know they were to grab everyone who was there—so it wasn't just Ezra or Lainey."

"So it could be one or the other or both of us who were the targets. But they were to take anyone who was with me? Or with him?" What if it had been Marlene who'd come in then?

"Sorry, Buttercup," Bodhi told me with a kind of genuine ferocity that insisted you believe him. "I wanted a better answer for you. They were paid through a private contractor, no names. Not even where they were to take you or him."

Adam raked a hand through his hair. "Just a number to call when the targets were acquired for more details. Which means they literally have nothing to tell us."

"Except the number." I glanced around at the three of them. "They had that."

"It's already disconnected. It was probably a VOIP, but I'll call Fletcher." Adam rubbed the back of his neck. It didn't sound like it would work out anyway. A knock at the door had Bodhi turning and one of our "hosts," the wranglers he'd told us about, stepped in and passed an envelope to Bodhi before he nodded and left again.

Annoyance scraped through me and I glanced around the room we'd been using. The only one of us not here...

"Why isn't Ezra back yet?"

"Because he left," Bodhi said, a muscle ticking in his jaw as he passed me the note that the wrangler had given him.

I stared at the words on the page and Adam swore.

Lainey,

We know who sent them, and we know why. I checked my messages. My father is not going to stop. I can do this. I can protect you. Trust me.

Ezra

Five minutes. He'd gone to the restroom for five minutes and now...

"I'm going to kill him," Adam muttered as he headed for the door.

Dammit.

CHAPTER
THIRTY-FIVE

EZRA

"I'm sorry," Oksana murmured as I flipped through the paperwork the attorneys had lined up for us. Among the various contracts were a prenuptial agreement, a pre-marriage contract—apparently different things—and another one that included real estate. "Mother and I—we had a disagreement."

Oksana's accent seemed even stronger, and she'd fled to me as soon as I arrived. My father's glare greeted me with nearly as much force. But I didn't focus on him. Instead, I shook Mr. Dovzhenko's hand. His wife had reddened eyes, a great deal like Oksana's own. They were both miserable. Mr. Dovzhenko, on the other hand, looked ready to snap my neck. Anger crackled around him as he gripped my hand with enough force that my bones protested.

I didn't back down. Father's message had been abundantly clear. As had Oksana's terror.

"The paperwork is fine," my father snapped as I checked each page. "Just sign it."

"No," I told him without glancing up.

"Excuse me?" He demanded, and I lifted my head to meet his gaze as he stalked over. My mother stood frozen behind him, a glass of wine in hand.

"You heard me," I said, locking eyes with my father. "I'm here. I'm doing as you've required. But I'm not a signing a fucking thing until I've reviewed every single comma. If you don't like it—you can marry her."

The words landed like blows. Oksana dug her nails into my arm. I was sorry for her fear. Scaring her wasn't high on my list. That said, being bullied into this marriage had never been the outcome I wanted. To say I trusted no one in this room would be putting it mildly.

"You do not trust your father," Dovzhenko said, a speculative gleam in his eyes, and I snorted.

"I don't trust you either," I informed him. "So don't look too pleased." I was done with being the whipping boy for them. For my father. For anyone. The past few days had given me a very clear taste of what I wanted.

It also told me what I was willing to do to protect what I loved. Adam may never forgive me, and I could live with that. He would be there for our girl, and she would look after him. The other two—well, they'd protect her and him. That was enough, particularly if I removed this particular knife from our throat.

We had too many enemies, and for some reason they were beginning to surround us—surround *her*. The more I thought about it, the more I realized the pressure increased the closer we came to her birthday.

Her birthday, the day she would receive the first full measure of her inheritance. With wealth came power, and our girl was gonna be more powerful than all of them. She had to make it to that birthday then the one after it and every other single birthday. My father wanted this deal with Dovzhenko so badly, he could have it.

The terms were going to be mine. Not his.

The real estate had been put in Dovzhenko's name. "This doesn't work for me," I said, striking out his name. "Put Oksana's in or mine, but what is ours will be ours or it can be hers." I really didn't give a damn. "What it won't be —is either of yours." I met Dovzhenko's gaze steadily.

All friendliness bled out of his eyes as he met me stare for stare.

"You don't get to dictate this," my father interjected. "You will do as you're—"

"Why are you defying us?" Dovzhenko asked, cutting my father off.

"Because you want me to marry your daughter for some reason. So does he. You two are definitely negotiating some mutually beneficial business deal. He gets something. You get something. And the two of you actually think you get to continue to dictate to us?" I continued to ignore my father.

"More spirit than I expected." Dovzhenko looked thoughtful.

"This is not the agreement." My father was suddenly in my face and he seized my shirt. Oksana let out a little squeal of sound as she tried to retreat, but there really wasn't anywhere to go.

"Too bad." I dropped the pen and the paperwork. "I'm not signing shit that I don't agree with. Which means we aren't getting married. You're going to let down your side of the bargain and honestly—I don't care. Disinherit me if you want."

"Wallace..." Mother was suddenly there.

"Dinah, be quiet." The growl in his voice had me narrowing my eyes. For one split second, he raised his hand and she flinched. I belted him. I wasn't Adam or Liam or even Bodhi and Milo. But I could damn well throw a punch.

I wasn't entirely sure who was more stunned, my mother or my father. She put her hands over her mouth, and he staggered. Blood decorated his mouth, and my hand ached from where my fist connected.

Dovzhenko said nothing, his eyes speculative. Fine, I'd rather just fight my own father.

"Let's be clear on this subject. I am not the one who wants this marriage. Period." I caught Oksana's tearful eyes. "She's terrified of you assholes." Now I swept Dovzhenko into the comments before I focused on my father again. "She has been given no more choice in this than I have."

"I told you what would happen if you didn't obey me."

"Yes," I said. "You did. But obeying you to marry her doesn't mean shackling myself to your whims for the rest of my life. You want grandkids and whatever deal you're getting from him. Neither of those require my indentured servitude. Hell, they barely involve me at all."

"You do not want to marry my daughter?" Dovzhenko eyed me.

"No," I told him. "Take a good look at her, she doesn't want to marry me either."

"That's not true, Papa," Oksana said hurriedly. "I know I have shamed you, and Ezra is a good man." Russian spilled out of her hurriedly, and I shook my head.

Instead of cutting her off, her father listened to her. Then outrage crossed his face.

"Don't," I said before he could take a step. She'd already

hidden behind me. "Like I told him, we're not indentured servants. Yes, I know all about her lover and the love she had for him. I know she wanted to marry him. I also know what you did to get rid of him. I don't care."

"You do not care that your wife will not be a virgin?" Shock stamped across his face, and I damn near laughed aloud,

"In the great grand scheme of things that I'm worried about? Her experience or lack thereof doesn't even rate in the top one hundred. Frankly, the fact you're so involved is kind of disgusting."

Fresh anger filled his eyes, and I snorted. Whatever, I was pissing everyone off today.

"Look, this isn't the old world, we don't need a woman's chastity to secure a bloodline while men fuck everything that moves. I'd rather she knew what she enjoyed when it came to sex anyway. Hell, you don't even need sex these days to secure a bloodline. One donation, a fertilized egg and implantation and boom. Heir."

My mother gawped at me.

She wasn't alone, Oksana's mother looked even more outraged.

"My point," I continued, rather enjoying this even if it was just for the shock value alone. "You want us to get married. Whatever you two want out of this deal, you've already set it up. It's our turn now. Oksana and I aren't doing this without some measure of security—which means, if the marriage dissolves for whatever reason—she will have the security to do what she wants, when she wants and with whom she wants."

"You just want a way to get out of this," Dad protested. "You want a way to cut bait and run. You think if you manipulate, you can what—marry her for six months then dissolve it so you can pursue your depraved lifestyle again?"

"What do you care?" I asked him. "You'll have what you want by then." I locked my gaze on his and held it even when his eyes slid to the side. "Or is there more to this than you decided to share?"

As much as I'd hated sneaking off on Lainey and Adam today, I'd been right to do this. Right to meet these assholes head-on. I'd never been so sober as I was at the moment. The pounding headache from my hangover had even abated.

Some.

"Well?" I prodded when he didn't answer. Instead of looking at me, Dad turned to Dovzhenko.

The silence in the room stretched out with a kind of brutal finality. Oksana dug her nails into my arm, but I ignored her as I watched the interplay between her father and mine. There was a lot more going on here than just whatever deal they'd cooked up.

"His terms are acceptable to me," Dovzhenko said finally, and I swore my father looked almost disappointed. "A man should protect his wife, whether he asked for her or not. He is refusing to give us dominion over their marriage. Also acceptable. I would prefer the home were in her name, though." The last he said to me.

I shrugged. Since it had been my idea, that was clearly also fine with me.

"Any other terms?" Since her father directed the question at me and not my father, I glanced at the papers.

"I want to finish reading those, and I want contingencies for divorce and separation."

Dislike tightened his expression, and I thought my

father was going to have a stroke, but I continued to ignore him. "I would prefer that divorce is not an option."

"It's always an option. Better to address it and expectations now rather than later, don't you think?" How was this not reasonable?

"Get the attorneys back in here," he ordered then waved me toward the papers. "Read."

It took me the better part of another hour to go through everything, and to make suggestions. I wished Nicky was here to handle some of this, but he wasn't. So for now, I made the best of a bad situation. We had to maintain the marriage for at least one year. If at the end of that first year, we decided to separate, then the secondary clauses would all kick in.

Oksana would be cared for, and whatever arrangement my father wanted, he would have as would Dovzhenko. For her part, Oksana looked so confused, and our mothers looked miserable. Then again, why they thought this sham of a marriage was anything more than a business negotiation, I had no idea.

Finally, once everything was done, we waited for the justice of the peace to be ready to go. I'd added a stipulation that an official "wedding ceremony" would not take place unless we reached the one year mark and wanted to continue with the wedding.

My father didn't care for that, but the legalities would be in place in case a grandchild came along. Not that I planned on that ever happening. I'd get myself snipped first.

They poured a round of wine for us all to toast, and I downed the full glass like it was a shot of vodka. This marriage wasn't ideal, but I'd negotiated the best possible outcome and a year wasn't that long of a sentence. Oksana relaxed, gradually, and the tension seemed to bleed out of everyone.

Then it was our turn. We were being called in, but we didn't even make it out of the waiting room before the doors slammed open.

CHAPTER
THIRTY-SIX

LAINEY

Ezra taking off didn't surprise me. I wish I could say it did. The fact he waited until we were distracted with the questioning and focused on what answers we could get while stonewalling Adam and pushing him away?

That was classic Ezra. Adam's pure irritation betrayed just how invested he was, and I got it. Maybe more than any of them, I got it. Ezra's ability to blow hot and cold had been a fact of my life for as long as I'd known him. The words in his note were stuck on repeat in my head.

I can do this. I can protect you.

Not for the first time, and based on our long relationship, probably not the last, I wanted to punch him. While I was not like the guys, I didn't just resort to physical violence when I was furious—I was starting to see what advantages it had. I'd been on my phone all the way back to the apartment while Bodhi drove. Adam was on his. Pretty

347

Boy rode up front with Bodhi, and I kept my leg pressed firmly to Adam's.

Periodically, the tension in his muscles would seem to stretch so tight it seemed to vibrate. That would be when I leaned into him. At one point, he curled his arm around me and pressed his lips to the top of my head, just holding me there.

"Any luck?" Pretty Boy asked, glancing over his shoulder. The holding facility had been in New Jersey, so the drive back to Manhattan was taking a minute.

"He's not answering," I said. "Which, actually, doesn't surprise me. If he went to see his father, he either went out to Long Island or..."

"Or they are in Queens." The absolute disgust in Adam's voice had me glancing at him. He held up his phone and there was a message from a name I didn't recognize. "Office of the Clerk."

I checked the time. We'd just come through the tunnel. If we could get over to the bridge...

My phone buzzed. Andrea's name popped up on the screen and I frowned.

Swiping left, I almost groaned.

Did I get the date wrong? I'm at your building, but they said you aren't answering.

"Why is she in the city?" Adam's question echoed my own.

"I have no idea. I didn't even know she was coming."

"Your birthday maybe," Pretty Boy suggested.

My damn birthday. I was so over *everyone* bringing it up. "Maybe."

"We'll drop you at the apartment," Adam said, and as much as I wanted to reject it, particularly because I wanted to prove to Ezra what he seemed to need us to prove. That we loved him. I couldn't just leave Andrea cooling her heels at the apartment.

Marlene wasn't there. If she was...

"We'll get him, Mayhem," Pretty Boy said, holding my gaze and then he gave the barest flicker of a look toward Adam then back again. "We'll take care of him."

He was promising to get Ezra, save him from himself and to look after Adam too. I had no idea what I'd done to get so lucky. "Call me when you have him?"

"Yes," Adam said. "Tell Andrea, I want to know how the hell she got back in the city. She's not supposed to leave the school without clearing it with one of us."

I made a face at him.

"Yes," he said with a scowl that melted into something more affectionate. "I know *you* never listened. She's usually better than that."

I elbowed him as I switched my phone to check the exterior cameras on the apartment. Bodhi had installed another one and added it so we had better angles. No one was on the floor waiting. It was all rather innocuous looking considering the actual carnage that had occurred there.

Adam tucked his head against my shoulder as he studied the image with me. "Good. Send her up to lock herself in."

That was my plan. I messaged her the codes to take the elevator up and to let herself in the apartment. Also reminded her to rearm the system once she was in. Her tongue sticking out at me emoji had me shaking my head. I didn't want to smother her as they'd smothered me. Yet at the same time, I understood it so much more now.

"She can't go with us," I murmured, more for myself

than for them. The understanding in Milo's eyes when he glanced back at me said he got it.

"We don't know what we're heading into," Adam reminded me. Which was true and none of us would risk Andrea. As much as I wanted to be there for Ezra—I had to trust the guys to get him. To get him and bring him home.

We were still a good twenty minutes away... "I could just get out up here and take the subway."

"No," Bodhi said even as Adam and Pretty Boy echoed him in the same moment.

"It was only a suggestion." Traffic was heavy. Then again, I didn't expect the guys would let me make my own way. Not with the recent attack. Another reason I didn't want Andrea just waiting for me.

"You have your baton? And your gun?" Bodhi asked as he pulled in front of the apartment building.

"Yes," I promised. Then I gave Adam a quick kiss. "Try to listen to Ezra before you punch him."

"No guarantees," he grumbled. "Remember, I want to know how she got out of the school and back here."

I chuckled. "No guarantees." The laughter helped dislodge some of the worry. I reached up and squeezed Pretty Boy's shoulder then brushed a kiss to his cheek even as I whispered, "Thank you," to him and Bodhi both.

Bodhi gave me a firm look. "Do not leave the apartment without notifying us." It was as much a request as a command.

I raised my brows, but I wasn't going to hold them up with an argument. Not when informing them was not the same as asking permission.

"I will. Good luck, drive safe and fast."

I adjusted my purse so the cross strap fit across my body then I climbed out. They didn't pull away until the doorman let me into the building. Then I was striding across the lobby to the residential elevators. I'd dressed in casual today, since I wasn't sure that "torture" and "interrogation" had a dress code.

The jeans and boots kept me warm as did the long-sleeved shirt and jacket. I had a heavier coat over my arm, but I wasn't outside long enough to need it. The ride up went quickly, but that didn't stop me checking my phone twice more. Once to check the cameras outside the apartment and once to see if Ezra answered.

Impatience crept through me. The guys would find him, and as much as I wanted to be with them—we couldn't leave Andrea here on her own. Adam's grumpiness pulled another smile to my lips. Like him, I wanted to know, but more out of curiosity than some driving desire to shut down the avenue should she need it later.

It seemed to take forever and no time at all to get to my apartment. I had my keys, but I just entered the code to unlock it rather than pull them out. Pushing the door inward, I summoned a smile. Andrea didn't know about all the insanity swirling around us and she didn't need to know.

Not when she could still safely be a kid.

"Before you jump out and yell surprise," I called. "I have to run interference for you with Adam so I have questions—then we can—"

The door slammed closed behind me and a large hand covered my mouth. I was already slamming my elbow backwards. But the tightness wrapped around me increased and the chemicals on the gloved hand made my vision blurry.

The harder I fought, the fuzzier the world went. Sound retreated along with sight, and I was tumbling down into a well. Even as I scrabbled for consciousness it slipped away. The man above me came into focus, briefly.

I knew him...

Then darkness swallowed me whole.

～

Awareness came back in flickering film like waves. Motion. Stop. Motion. Stop.

My head pounded in time with the flickers. Cold invaded, sliding over my skin like ice spreading out on the ground. The motion would stop and the world darkened again.

The next time the images started to flicker, I realized I was blinking my eyes. The movement was so infinitesimal that the brush of my eyelashes seemed impressive. Thus began a pattern of cold, dark, movement. Cold. Dark. Movement.

Eternity spanned out, elongating the briefest flickers. The desert of my mouth had my lips sticking together. I couldn't seem to dislodge my tongue from where it stuck inside my cheek.

Swallowing was impossible.

There wasn't even a suggestion of spit.

The cold rippled over me like water, only I wasn't wet. With agonizing slowness, I managed to turn. Bit by bit, I cobbled together a few facts.

I was lying on a bed—or maybe a sofa. The fabric was rough on my skin. Almost too stiff. The cold was because I was naked. That reality hit me with a jolt of adrenaline and I tried to sit up. My limbs were too loose and not obeying me. I couldn't stay upright. I collapsed again, but the room swam in and out of focus.

Everything had a fuzzy edge to it.

It was also pitch dark.

Pitch dark.

Naked.

Bed.

Andrea—

I'd been in my apartment, then someone grabbed me. Even as the puzzle pieces slotted together, I couldn't hold onto them or consciousness. I did manage to twist when my stomach rebelled. Forcing my breathing to slow, I quelled the urge to vomit.

Barely.

Where was I?

Who had taken me...

The thoughts fell apart as I passed out again.

The next time I emerged, I was shivering. Goosebumps raced over my skin, and I managed to hug myself. The cold was unbearable, but it was waking me up and chasing away the fog of drugs.

I curled my knees to my chest, even as I made myself suck in more and more oxygen. My mouth was still dry, my head hurt like hell, but I was a great deal more awake this time.

Wherever I was, I had no intention of staying. Whoever took me was going to regret this if it was the last thing I did...

~

The Royals will return in Violent Chaos

AFTERWORD

Sooner or later, you knew it had to happen. Lainey has been the one left behind or the one leaving—but we knew where she was. Now, her guys are on a quest to save Ezra from himself (that man, I swear, I love him but I also want to throttle him) and Lainey is off to see her sister.

I love that the guys trust her to look after herself, but ambushes work for a reason. So hang in there. Violent Chaos is coming.

I promise.

xoxo

Heather

P.S. Yes, I'm in my corner with coffee, snacks, and my laptop.

Reader group:
facebook.com/groups/heatherspack
Spoiler group:
facebook.com/groups/teammadatheather

VIOLENT CHAOS

BAY RIDGE ROYALS BOOK 5

I've never seen the point in an emotional connection...

Madness runs in my blood or so my family history would suggest. For more than thirteen years, I've been driven by one quest. One desire. One goal. It's about more than just DNA and legacy, it's about a promise. One I swore I would never give up...

I never could have planned for her. For Lainey B. For how the girl who kept my secret became a woman who is truly my partner. I've been running alone for so long, I didn't think I could be with someone.

She's perfect for me.

She *fits* me.

I don't even mind that she comes with attachments. They're hers, that makes them mine too.

Now, someone has made a mistake. They've targeted what is ours—what is *mine*.

They have no idea the hell I will unleash.

But they are going to find out.

BENEDICT FAMILY

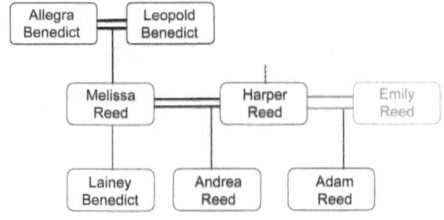

HARDIGAN FAMILY

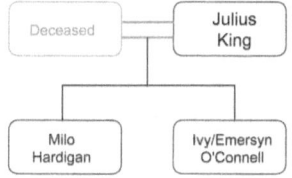

REED FAMILY

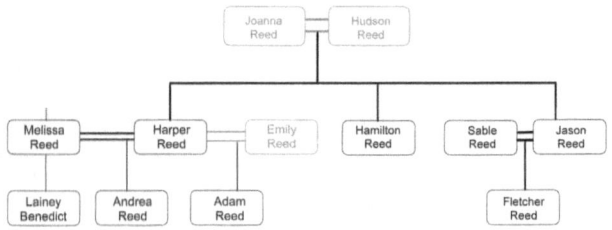

GRAHAM FAMILY

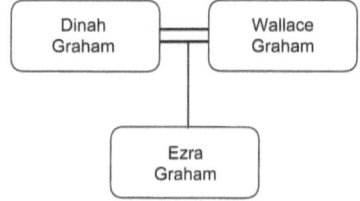

CAVENDISH FAMILY

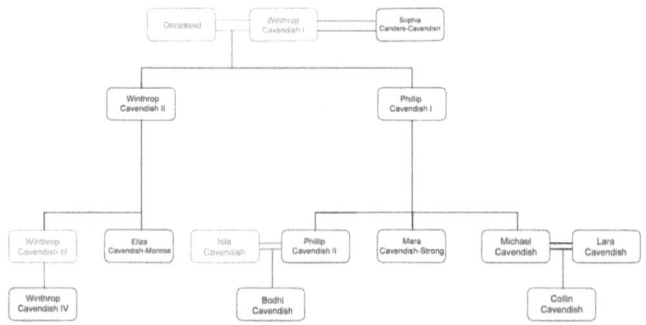

MARLOWE FAMILY

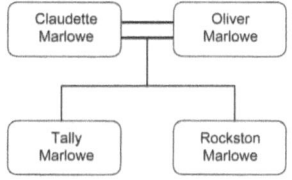

ABOUT HEATHER LONG

I *love* books. Not just a little bit, but a lot. Books were my best friends when I was growing up. Books didn't care if I was new to a town or to a class. They were always there, my trustiest of companions. Until they turned on me and said I had to write them.

I can tell you that my own personal happily ever after included writing books. I've always said that an HEA is a work in progress. It's true in my marriage, my friendships, and in my career. I am constantly nurturing my muse as we dive into new tales, new tropes, new characters and more.

After seventeen years in Texas, we relocated to the Pacific Northwest in search of seasons, new experiences, and new geography. I can't wait to discover what life (and my muse) have in store for me.

Maybe writing was always my destiny and romance my fate. After all, my grandmother wasn't a fan of picture books and used to read me her Harlequin Romance novels.

Follow Heather & Sign up for her newsletter:
www.heatherlong.net
TikTok

Also by Heather Long

82nd Street Vandals

Savage Vandal

Vicious Rebel

Ruthless Traitor

Dirty Devil

Shamelessly Loyal (Novella)

Brutal Fighter

Dangerous Renegade

Merciless Spy

Reckless Thief

Fierce Dancer

Bay Ridge Royals

Shamelessly Loyal (Novella)

Battle Lines

Deceptive Truce

Wicked Surrender

Violent Chaos

Desperate Victory

Blue Ivy Prep

Problem Child

Mad Boys

Party Crashers

Money Shot

Bravo Team Wolf

When Danger Bites

Bitten Under Fire

Cardinal Sins

Kill Song

First Chorus

High Note

Last Word

Chance Monroe

Earth Witches Aren't Easy

Plan Witch from Out of Town

Bad Witch Rising

Fevered Hearts

Marshal of Hel Dorado

Brave are the Lonely

Micah & Mrs. Miller

A Fistful of Dreams

Raising Kane

Wanted: Fevered or Alive

Wild and Fevered

The Quick & The Fevered

A Man Called Wyatt

Heart of the Nebula

Queenmaker

Deal Breaker

Throne Taker

Lone Star Leathernecks

Semper Fi Cowboy

As You Were, Cowboy

Shackled Souls

Succubus Chained

Succubus Unchained

Succubus Blessed

Shackled Souls (Omnibus)

STANDALONES

Kiss of Fate (w/Blake Blessing)

Taste of Karma (w/Blake Blessing)

I'll Be Home... (w/Tate James)

Untouchable

Rules and Roses

Changes and Chocolates

Keys and Kisses

Whispers and Wishes

Hangovers and Holidays

Brazen and Breathless

Trials and Tiaras

Wolves of Willow Bend

Outlaw Wolves

Wolf Unleashed

www.ingramcontent.com/pod-product-compliance
Lightning Source LLC
Chambersburg PA
CBHW030554020726
47494CB00005B/1609